THE UNDEAD UPROAR

A CHARLIE RHODES COZY MYSTERY BOOK FIVE

AMANDA M LEE

WINCHESTERSHAW PUBLICATIONS

ONE

"Lift that end."

"I am lifting."

"Lift it higher."

"With what muscles?" I leaned against the wall, not letting go of my end of the couch, and fixed my boyfriend Jack Hanson with a dark look. "I'm doing the best I can."

Jack, his dark hair pulled back in a short ponytail at the nape of his neck, smirked. He looked serene, patient even. When he spoke, however, I knew that wasn't the case. "Get a move on, Charlie. We need to get your stuff completely transferred before we get a call that there's another case. We're so close."

I huffed and cleared my throat. "It's a good thing you're cute," I muttered, readjusting my grip as I strained to hold up my end of the couch. It didn't look heavy until I tried to carry it up a flight of stairs. "Otherwise I would totally dump you."

Jack merely smiled. He was used to my griping. He didn't appear worried in the least that I meant what I said. That's because I, Charlie Rhodes, was smitten with him. Yeah, I said it. Smitten. I never knew what that word meant until Jack and I started dating.

We met as co-workers. I always believed that saying about not defecating where you eat and never intended to date someone I worked with. From the first day I met him, though, Jack called to me … even as he irritated me. I'm still not sure why.

On paper, he should've been the last person I wanted to spend time with. He was former military, a rule-follower. He liked things regimented and neat. Me? I'm messy. My apartment is messy. My personal life is messy. Heck, my head is messy. Jack doesn't appear to care about any of that. He's pretty easygoing — at least when he's not in charge of my security — and he seems fine with the fact that I live a messy life.

Of course, he doesn't know all the facts. He's missing one vital piece of the puzzle. That's what bugged me as he helped me move from a first-floor apartment that he deemed unsafe to a second-floor apartment that he'd picked out.

Yeah, I still wasn't sure how it happened.

"We're almost there, Charlie," he prodded. His grip on the other end of the couch never faltered. He was strong, although the T-shirt he wore hid his bulging muscles. I'd seen him shirtless before. In fact, I was trying to figure out a way to see him shirtless again once we got the couch to my new apartment. I was thinking that offering to wash his shirt while he waited was the best way to go. It might come across as awkward — especially because we hadn't stripped and spent the night together yet — but I was ready to put in the effort and try. I didn't care how goofy I looked.

"Okay." I heaved out a sigh at his patient expression. He didn't offer a lick of complaint as he waited for me to ready myself. "Let's do it quick. I'm going to count to three and then we're going to run to the new apartment. How does that sound?"

His smile widened. "Sure. Let's do it."

"Here we go." I blew out a big breath, sucked in another, and bobbed my head.

Jack pushed with everything he had and, before I knew it, we were up the stairs and heading straight into my new living room. He didn't stop even when I faltered, pushing until the couch landed in the middle of the open space.

I fell on the couch and looked at the ceiling when he stopped shoving. "Wow. I did it."

He cast me a sidelong look before rolling onto the couch next to me. "Yes. *You* did it."

His tone made me smile. "Okay, maybe you did it."

"We both did it," he corrected, grabbing my hand and flipping it over to examine my palm. Several blisters were appearing and my heart actually stuttered when he pressed a quick kiss to each one. It was a simple and achingly romantic gesture ... and it made me feel giddy.

"Um ... ." I could feel my cheeks burning as he smiled.

"Get over it, Charlie." He pressed one more kiss to the palm of my hand and then released me. "There's no reason to get all worked up. I was simply ... kissing your boo-boo."

"Yes, and I'm not supposed to get worked up about that apparently." I shook my head. "Good grief."

He laughed at my reaction and briefly closed his eyes. We'd been working the entire day. He showed up before the sun to help me move, something I wasn't all that keen about but he insisted was necessary. When I first moved into the building I thought it wouldn't be a big deal to live on the main floor. It was the East Coast, after all. What could possibly happen? Jack started making noise about it before we enjoyed our first date. He didn't think it was safe for a single woman. I was fairly certain I should be offended by his antiquated outlook, but I was so certain the landlord would shoot me down if I asked to move that I did it out of deference to him. To my utter surprise, the landlord initially said no and then came back with a yes. He wasn't even raising my rent, which made zero sense, so now we were moving all my stuff up one floor so I was no longer vulnerable on the main floor.

I never felt vulnerable. I didn't fear that someone would show up at my window or try to enter through my patio door. I knew things Jack didn't. He had no idea I was telekinetic and psychic, that I could fight an enemy on more than one level. He had no idea that he was a member of a group looking for paranormal beings – and that he just happened to be dating one.

I felt like a coward for not telling him. Part of me wanted to spill the beans, but I was afraid. It wasn't that I feared he would tell our boss, Chris Biggs, what I was. That's not how Jack rolled. He would never share my secret. He would, however, look at me differently. Of that I had no doubt.

I didn't want to change the way he looked at me. His gaze often made me go weak in the knees ... as did his smile. He might never smile at me again in that manner if I told him. And yet, I knew it was a necessity. There was no moving forward unless he knew about my past.

When I first joined the Legacy Foundation, I didn't think I wanted any attachments. I volunteered to join the group for very little money because I was curious about myself. My parents disappeared when I was a kid. I had only vague memories of them — and even those were shrouded in doubt because I didn't know if they were true or fragments of dreams — and no matter how hard I tried, I couldn't remember why they'd abandoned me the way they did. I had a lot of questions and almost no answers. That's why I joined the Legacy Foundation.

The plan was to learn what I could and then disappear without anyone being the wiser. I thought there was a possibility I could've hidden among them forever without them figuring out what I was. That idea fell by the wayside when we were looking for the Chupacabra in Texas. I saw it — although almost nobody believed me — and I had to use my magic to save two of my co-workers. One of those individuals was my boss. He was out cold at the time and remembered nothing of my display. The woman, though, was a different story.

Millie Watson, Chris's aunt, was a mix between Lucy Ricardo and Rambo. She was tough as nails and loyal to a fault. She also wasn't an idiot, which is something she repeatedly told me when I tried to deny what she saw. Two killers gave chase that night and I managed to take both of them out. I needed help, though, which is where my magic came in.

Millie promised not to share my secret. I believed her. She was cool that way. She would never blab secrets out of class. Still, the fact that she knew made me vulnerable. There was every chance she might accidentally say something that could be overheard by others. Or, worse. Millie liked to visit bars on every outing. I lived in constant fear that she might one night drink too much and not realize what she was saying.

The fact that Millie knew and Jack didn't wasn't another worry. Jack would have to find out, and not simply because he was also technically my boss and head of security. I cared about him a great deal. He made my heart flutter as if I was a silly school girl and he'd offered to carry my books. We would be stuck in a holding pattern if I didn't tell him, never moving forward because I was holding back. I recognized that. It was another fear I lived with daily. I had to tell him. I couldn't fight the urge much longer.

After that, things might be worse. How would he look at me once he knew I was a freak of nature? Jack tended to land on the side of pragmatism when we worked a case. He always looked for the real-world explanation. When we were looking for Bigfoot, he was convinced it was a human in the woods. When we were looking for the Chupacabra, he was convinced it was a human in the woods. Hmm, now that I think about it, when we were looking for a werewolf, he also thought it was a human in the woods. All those times, the murderer turned out to be a human in the woods. I really had seen the Chupacabra, though. Right before I passed out after falling down the stairs, I saw it. I also saw witches cast spells and a man shift into a wolf. The others in my group weren't that lucky. They didn't know what I knew ... another doubt plaguing me.

I often felt as if I was treading shark-infested waters, no boat in sight. Was there a way out of this? Could I figure out a way to tell Jack and not lose him? The notion of the stalwart security guru walking away right after I made myself vulnerable was the stuff of nightmares.

"What's wrong with you?" Jack murmured as he slipped his arm around my waist and drew me to him, his lips busy on my forehead as he brushed a series of kisses against my furrowed brow.

"Nothing is wrong." I forced myself to be bright and happy. "I'm just thinking about how sore I'll be later from moving that couch."

"I'll give you a massage." There was nothing sexy about the way he said the words and yet we both blushed when meeting the other's steady gaze. We were at that weird part of the relationship where we were spending tons of time together — almost every moment we could when not at work — and yet we hadn't rolled into bed together.

Oh, we'd shared a bed multiple times. We'd even done it while on cases. We'd just never shared everything else. At first, I didn't think much of it because I figured it would happen at the exact right moment. The more things dragged out, though, it became apparent that we were going to have to create the moment. Jack was too much of a gentleman to make a move. That left me, and I was dead clumsy when it came to taking the first step on the romantic front.

"I still don't know how I ended up with a second-floor apartment without having to pay more," I mused, opting to focus on safer conversation. "When I first looked at renting here, second-floor apartments were two-hundred dollars more a month."

"Maybe the landlord likes you."

"Maybe." I didn't believe that for a second. "Or maybe something else is going on."

"Like what?"

I shrugged. "Maybe he heard I work for an important monster-hunting group and he's an elf or something. He might want to get on my good side so I don't start digging into his background."

Jack let loose a snort. "He's got a beer belly big enough to balance a pizza box on. I very much doubt he's an elf."

"You don't know. Just because *Lord of the Rings* told us elves look like Orlando Bloom that doesn't mean that Danny DeVito isn't the real deal."

"Oh, what a picture you draw in my head." He snuffled as he moved his nose to my neck. "You smell good. What is that?"

"Sweat. We just moved a couch up the stairs."

"No. There's something else. You smell like clementines or something."

"Oh. I got a new perfume."

"I like it."

"Yeah?"

"Yeah." He moved his mouth to mine and gave me a soft kiss. We were getting more and more comfortable around one another. That was a good thing. Unfortunately, every outing hit a wall. We made out until our lips were ready to bleed, but neither of us was brave enough to take things one step further. I had no doubt today would end the same way. I had every intention of enjoying it until that happened, though.

"Did we get everything out of the apartment?" I asked on a gasp as we separated for air.

"We did." He kissed me again. "The couch was the last thing. We double-checked because we were looking for an excuse to put off moving the couch."

I vaguely remembered that. "Right."

He pulled back and stared into my eyes, something unsaid flitting through his inquisitive blue orbs. "What are you thinking, Charlie?"

The question caught me off guard even though he often asked it. I thought questions like that were supposed to be asked by women. That's what pop culture and movies taught me anyway. He always seemed to be searching for an answer, as if he wanted to crawl inside my head and look around.

"I'm thinking that ... we should get pizza."

He made a face. "That's not what you were thinking."

He wasn't wrong. That didn't mean I could tell him what I was thinking. It would ruin our day, and I had no intention of doing that. It had been perfect from start to finish.

"I was thinking that you're really pretty." I uttered it on a sigh as I touched his silky hair. "You're so pretty it makes my heart skip a beat sometimes."

He arched an eyebrow, surprised. "That is a very ... weird thing to say."

I laughed. "I can't help it. Have you looked at yourself? You could be an elf. One of the Orlando Bloom ones."

"Ah, well, at least I'm getting thrown in with the higher order of elves." His smile was mischievous. "You could be an elf, too. One of those in the Will Ferrell movie. They're my favorite."

I snickered as I elbowed him. "Why does that feel like an insult?"

"It shouldn't. They really are my favorite." He playfully wrestled with me, laughing when I squirmed. "I want to put you in one of those hats ... and the curved shoes. Oh, I wonder if they make a little outfit we can buy. How awesome would that be?"

"You're such a pervert. I'm not wearing one of those outfits. You'll just have to get used to me naked."

The sexual tension hung heavy over the room and it was far too late to take it back when I realized what I said.

"Oh, um ... ."

"Shh." Jack pursed his lips and leaned closer, his breath hot on my mouth as he stopped his lips from touching mine.

I felt ridiculous. He was close enough to kiss and yet we weren't kissing. We also weren't talking. We were simply staring.

"What are you doing?" I was breathless.

"Shh," he repeated.

"Jack ... ."

"You just can't stay quiet for five minutes, can you?" His lips curved up as he shook his head. "I think it might be physically impossible for you to be quiet for more than five minutes."

"That shows what you know. I'm quiet for hours on end every night when I sleep."

"Yeah, yeah, yeah." He frowned when his phone started dinging in his pocket. "Oh, man." He was rueful when he pulled away from me. "This had better be good. Hanson." He barked out his name when he answered, his fingers automatically going to mine so they could dance as we waited for the conversation to end. The look on Jack's face as he straightened on the couch told me that wasn't going to happen.

"I've got it," Jack said after a few minutes of listening. "No, you don't have to call Charlie. She's with me. We'll meet you at the plane in an hour."

He sighed as he disconnected and looked at me. "I guess that's an end to our day. We have an assignment."

"At least we managed to move everything before the call came in."

"Yeah." He leaned over and gave me another kiss, this one short and sweet. "Pack your bags for a warm climate. It's hot where we're going."

"Oh, yeah?" My mind was already on the trip. "Where is that?"

"New Orleans."

"I've always wanted to go there. How cool. What creature are we chasing? Please tell me it's a vampire."

Jack smirked. "It's not a vampire. But you're close."

"What's close to a vampire?"

"Apparently we're searching for zombies. Chris is convinced the dead are rising from their graves."

I had no idea what to make of that. "Wait .... what?"

TWO

*J*ack and I arrived at the plane together. The Legacy Foundation was run by an extremely wealthy conglomerate — Chris's uncle was the head of the group — and one of the perks was a private plane. As someone who had only flown twice in her life before joining the elite team, in coach at that, the plane was still miraculous to me.

Jack carried our bags to the back of the plane and shoved them in the storage compartment before pointing toward a set of seats at the middle of the aircraft. Millie Watson and Bernard Hill, our technology and equipment guru, were already seated across from us. Millie only smiled when she saw we were together, which made my cheeks burn as I snapped my seatbelt.

"We'll go over everything when we're in the air," Chris announced as he entered the plane. He had a willowy blonde with him. Hannah Silver was a brilliant scientist who could double as a model. When I first saw her I thought the cosmos were playing a joke on me, but she's ridiculously competent and easy to get along with. She's one of those people you want to spend time around even though she often makes you feel inadequate. She and Chris had recently started dating, too, and they were joined at the hip ... and other places. Unlike Jack and me, they'd progressed to the next step and weren't shy about sharing rooms on assignments.

I envied them that.

"No problem," Jack said as he settled in his seat. "I'm kind of curious about how you've leaped to zombies this go-around, so I'm dying to hear all about it."

Chris rolled his eyes. "Don't be a spoilsport right from the start. That's no way to start a trip."

"I'll try to refrain from letting my zombie doubts ruin the trip for everyone," Jack replied dryly.

"I won't. I'm going to make fun of everyone who thinks it could possibly be a zombie for the entire trip," a woman announced as she boarded the plane. Laura Chapman was the last member of our group. She was in her thirties, built like a stripper, and had the attitude of a rabid raccoon locked in a garbage can. Her long auburn hair drifted past her shoulders and her eyes immediately sought — and found — Jack as she scanned the plane. The fact that I was sitting next to him clearly didn't make her happy. "Where am I supposed to sit?"

"I suggest the lavatory," Millie replied, her eyes flashing with mirth. She enjoyed messing with Laura. Heck, most of us did. She was the only person in our group I didn't like. If she left tomorrow, I wouldn't miss her in the least. In fact, things would be easier if she just quit ... or joined another group.

"Maybe I'll sit next to you," Laura shot back as she cut through the plane. She dragged a large suitcase on wheels behind her. She always over-packed. The idea of a go-bag was foreign to her.

"I'm afraid the seat next to me is already taken," Millie said sweetly. "Even if it wasn't, there would be no room for you."

"Whatever." Laura's expression was dour as she left her suitcase in the back and then picked a seat at an angle from Jack and me. That meant she could stare at us during the flight, which only made our situation more untenable.

For some reason — and I had theories as to why — Laura had decided she was hot to trot for Jack and wouldn't stop flirting with him. She was well aware that we were dating. She was also aware that

Jack overtly disliked her. That didn't stop her from giving chase. Apparently her need to win was greater than her common sense. I didn't understand her attitude. At all.

"And how are you, Charlie?" she asked sweetly as she fastened her seatbelt. "Are you having a good day? I certainly hope so. I would hate for you to be uncomfortable and complain for no good reason."

I knew what she was referring to and the charge grated. "I didn't report you to management, Laura. I wish you would stop acting like I did."

"I know it was you." Her eyes were dark. "You're the reason I'm on probation."

"No, you're the reason you're on probation," Jack shot back, his temper coming out to play. "You attacked Charlie in St. Pete. You actually pushed her into shark-infested waters, where she could've been really hurt. You did all of this to yourself."

"I did not push her into the water!" Laura's expression was so dark I thought it might actually eat the little bit of sun peeking through the plane's windows. "Stop saying that. You only believe that because Charlie told you a nonsense story."

"Charlie didn't tell me any story. I was there."

"Oh, whatever." She made a face. "Are we taking off or what?"

Chris was busy discussing something with the pilot so he didn't turn around and address the question. In recent weeks he'd taken to ignoring Laura more than acknowledging her presence. Whether he realized it or not, that only served to make her crazier. I was convinced she was one off-the-cuff statement from turning into the kid from *The Exorcist* and vomiting pea soup on us.

"We'll take off when the pilot is ready," Jack said, leaning back in his seat and staring at the fan above him. "Is it hot and stuffy all of a sudden, or is it just me?"

"It's just you," Laura replied, feigning sweetness. "You can't help yourself from getting warm all over when you see me."

"Are you taking credit for the nauseated feeling as well? That's good. When I throw up, I'll make sure it's all over you."

I patted his arm before reaching up and adjusting the air flow so it was pointed directly at his face. "Close your eyes. It will only take us two hours to get to New Orleans. You can take a nap."

"That sounds good, especially after our afternoon was ruined."

"Oh, really?" Millie grinned as she watched the interaction. "What were you guys doing before the call came in? I hope it was something dirty."

"It was." I nodded. "We were moving my stuff to a second-floor apartment. It was a lot of work and we were both sweaty when we finished."

"I'm pretty sure she was talking about a different sort of dirty," Laura drawled.

I was well aware of that, but I pretended I didn't hear Laura. It was for the best, because she was always looking for a reason to pick a fight with me. "I still don't know how I got the better apartment for no extra money," I admitted.

"Just consider yourself lucky," Millie said.

"I wouldn't get too comfortable," Laura shot back. "Karma is coming after you for reporting me, so that apartment will probably spring a leak by the time you get back."

Jack made a disgusted sound deep in his throat as he shifted. "She didn't report you!"

"Oh, you're just standing up for her because you think she's some tiny bird you need to protect. Admit it."

"I'll admit it." Jack is not the sort of person who can hide his feelings. When he's annoyed, it's written all over his face. He looked as if he was ready to go to war as he opened his eyes and leaned forward. "I'm the one who reported you."

Laura didn't immediately respond, instead blinking several times in rapid succession. "I don't believe you," she said finally. "You're not the type."

"I'm not the type to want a professional atmosphere? I think you're wrong there. That's all I want. What you pulled with Charlie is unacceptable."

"We're not supposed to date people in our group," Laura gritted out. "I was doing my duty when I reported you."

"And that blew up in your face, didn't it? Don't act surprised that the probation order stuck. You've wiggled out of punishment multiple times. Perhaps this is your karma."

"I'm not the one in the wrong."

"Oh, don't go there," Millie admonished. "You're always in the wrong. Besides, Jack isn't the only one who reported you. I did too."

Laura's mouth dropped open. "You? Why?"

"You know why." Millie winked at me before settling in for takeoff. "Now, shut up, Laura. We're not even in the air yet and I already want to push you out a window. For once in your life, do the smart thing and shut your hole. We would all appreciate it."

"I know I would." Jack was back to relaxing. "Take a load off, Charlie. We're going to have to hear zombie stories soon enough. You might as well take a break while you can."

I'd heard worse offers.

CHRIS WAS ENTHUSIASTIC when it came to the paranormal. He was like a child watching a monster movie for the first time. His wonderment always overcame his fear.

Once the plane was in the air and it was safe to walk around without seatbelts, he convened a meeting in the center of the plane and got straight to business.

"Four bodies have gone missing from a single New Orleans cemetery in the last week," he announced gravely as he took his position.

"I don't want to be a spoilsport off the bat, but body theft is a real thing," Jack pointed out. "Bodies are stolen and sold for medical research. Sometimes bodies are stolen for sexual reasons, which I won't get into because it's gross. I'm sure you can imagine what I'm talking about."

"And I'm officially sick to my stomach," I muttered, shaking my head. "Why did you have to go there?"

He slid me an amused look before continuing. "You had better have more than just missing bodies as a reason for ruining what was supposed to be a day off for most of us." He slid his eyes to Laura and his grin widened. "Except Laura, who has to keep picking up filing duty as penance, I mean. The rest of us were enjoying a well-deserved day off."

"Oh, stuff it," Laura grumbled under her breath.

Chris ignored the mini-squabble. "I have more than missing bodies. I checked to make sure this wasn't some sex experiment gone awry. The four bodies range in age from twenty-nine to eighty-four. Two are men. Two are women. No preferential offender — and that's what an individual who steals bodies for sex is — would be okay with that much variation."

"Fair enough." Jack shuddered. "Let's talk about something other than having sex with dead bodies."

"My body isn't dead where sex is concerned," Laura offered.

I had to press my lips together to keep from laughing at Jack's annoyed expression. "Go back to the bodies," I insisted, if only to earn a reprieve from Laura's desperate maneuvering and the inevitability that Jack would blow his stack. "How did the victims die?"

"They're not technically victims," Chris countered. "The twenty-nine-year-old died in a car accident." He double-checked his iPad to make sure he had the details right. "The eighty-four-year-old was in a nursing home. He died of Alzheimer's. Other than that, we have a fifty-five-year-old woman who died of a heart attack and a thirty-four-year-old man who died of a drug overdose."

"Oh." I rubbed my chin as I considered the new information. "Could it be possible that our thief was only interested in one body and stole the other three to cover his or her tracks?"

Chris looked intrigued. "What do you mean?"

"Well, let's just say the intended target was the twenty-nine-year-old and her boyfriend was devastated and decided he wanted to keep her body. He probably knew he would be the prime suspect once the authorities figured out she was gone, so maybe he stole the other bodies as a forensic countermeasure."

"I see someone has been watching *Criminal Minds* for all the buzz-words," Laura lamented.

I pretended I didn't hear her. "I'm not saying that's definitely how it went down, but it's a possibility. I don't see how that points to zombies."

"I agree that zombies wouldn't be my first inclination," Chris said. "But that's not the situation we're dealing with. In fact, that's the opposite of what we're dealing with. Our bodies have been seen since they disappeared."

"I'm pretty sure there's a contradiction in there," Millie offered. "If the bodies have been found, then they haven't disappeared."

"I didn't say the bodies have been found. I said they'd been seen."

His purposeful word choice had me leaning forward. "What are you talking about?"

"The bodies have been seen after the fact around New Orleans ... and they haven't been resting on the ground or even propped up on benches. The bodies were seen walking around."

I was officially dumbfounded. "Get out!"

Jack slid me a quelling look. It was almost as if he could sense my anticipation ratcheting up. "Don't get ahead of yourself," he admonished. "We haven't heard the entire story yet."

"I never get ahead of myself."

"You always get ahead of yourself," Jack complained. "I mean ... I like your enthusiasm and how you're always gung-ho, but you don't have to believe every story that Chris brings to the group. Zombies aren't real."

"Tell that to Daryl on *The Walking Dead*," Millie challenged.

"Daryl isn't real."

"Oh, he's real here." She tapped the side of her head and slid him a sly grin. "He's all kinds of real."

"Oh, geez!" Jack slapped his hand to his forehead and murmured a string of curses that I couldn't quite make out. He was always the naysayer in our group. I was fine with that. And he wasn't wrong about me being excited at the prospect of zombies.

"If the bodies rose from the grave, wouldn't there be an infestation of them in the city by now?" I asked, hoping the question came off as intelligent rather than ridiculous. "That's a busy area, right? I'm guessing the whole town would consist of zombies at that rate."

Chris's expression was dubious. "Flesh-eating zombies are not real."

"Yeah, Charlie," Millie teased. "Flesh-eating zombies are nonsense. But there are different types of zombies."

This was the first I'd heard anything of the sort. "And what kind of zombies are we talking about?"

"The voodoo kind." Chris's smile widened. "New Orleans is the birthplace of voodoo in America. Those are the types of zombies I'm talking about."

I was still confused. "And how are they different?"

"They're not different," Jack replied. "They're both a bunch of nonsense."

"They're very different," Chris corrected. "Flesh-eating zombies generally involve people dying and coming back to life. As we all know, this creates certain logistical problems for the zombies because they would deteriorate at such a rate they would be a threat for only thirty days or so. If you could find a place to hole up for a month, you would be perfectly fine."

I didn't as much as blink. "Good to know."

"Voodoo zombies are massively different," he continued. "They stem from Haitian lore. I believe the first story revolves around a plantation owner who wanted free labor, so he reanimated bodies to work his fields."

I frowned. "That simply sounds like a fancy way of enslaving people."

"I agree. I've done a lot of research on voodoo, although there's surprisingly little out there when it comes to literature. In Haitian lore, zombies are raised from the dead — just like other zombies — but it's done by a sorcerer called a bokor, who then keeps the zombie under his spell and controls him or her because they have no free will."

"That still doesn't solve the decomposition problem," I pointed out.

"No, but this would be done on a much smaller scale," Chris argued. "Four bodies is not an army. There are plenty more bodies out there for a bokor to resurrect if he's looking for cheap labor."

"Okay, I'll bite," Jack interjected. "Where have these bodies that were taken been seen?"

"Around the French Quarter, which is where all of them lived."

"Maybe it's just a case of mistaken identity."

"That's possible, but the bodies were seen by family members," Chris explained. "In one instance, the estranged wife of the thirty-four-year-old who died from the drug overdose said she saw him standing outside by the gate ... and staring at the house. She ran out to him, convinced there was some sort of mistake, but when she reached him she found his eyes were completely white and she veered at the last moment to save herself."

"Save herself from what?" I asked. "You just said this sort of zombie doesn't eat people, which is a total bummer because I think I would be awesome in a zombie apocalypse. I would definitely survive long enough to rebuild society."

Jack's lips quirked. "I'm glad you have a plan for when the world falls apart."

"I've got multiple plans."

"But we're not dealing with an apocalypse," Chris said. "We're dealing with one person enslaving the abandoned bodies of the deceased. It's not the zombies we're looking for as much as the bokor."

"Well, that sounds great," Jack said as he crossed his feet at the ankles and slid me a look. "Charlie probably hasn't tasted authentic Cajun food. I can't wait until she has her first bite of gumbo. Oh, and she'll be hopped up on so much sugar we won't be able to contain her after some beignets."

I had no idea what those were, but I was always keen to try new food. "Bring it on."

"We'll worry about the food later," Chris admonished. "We're going straight to the hotel when we land. We'll talk about a plan after that."

"Awesome." Jack appeared happy to turn away from Chris and focus on me. "How do you feel about crawfish?"

I shrugged. "I don't think I've ever tried them."

"This might be a fun trip after all."

That's what I was hoping for.

THREE

Our hotel was located directly on Bourbon Street. I let out a little gasp the second I walked into the ornate lobby of the Royal Dauphine. Theatrical? Definitely. The hotel was beautiful, though, and I'd never been to a nicer place.

Jack was amused as he dropped our bags on the floor. Chris and Hannah were at the front desk securing rooms — apparently the Legacy Foundation had a corporate account with the hotel and it was easy for them to secure lodging on short notice.

"Impressed?" he asked.

"It's beautiful." I meant it. "I didn't get to travel much when I was younger for obvious reasons. I've always wanted to come here. This city has the most amazing history. Between the voodoo culture, the proximity to bayou country and the above-ground cemeteries, this place has always been on my bucket list."

"Well, hopefully you won't die while you're here," he teased. "If you do, I promise to keep your zombified form with me forever."

I furrowed my brow.

"That came out creepier than I intended," he admitted after a beat. "I didn't mean I would do gross stuff with you or anything, just that I wouldn't leave you behind. I mean ... I'm going to stop talking about that."

"I think that's a good idea," I agreed, lifting my head to gaze at the ceiling. "I can't wait to look around. But ... we probably have to work first, huh?"

"I'm sure we'll be able to do both." He briefly ran his hand down my arm before moving back. "I'm going to take a look at the room situation. Don't wander around without me, okay? This isn't the sort of city where it's safe for you to be all ... Charlie."

I was certain there was an insult buried in there. "Believe it or not, I've been taking care of myself for a really long time. I think I can handle New Orleans."

"I'm sure you can." Jack remained stoic. "But New Orleans does have a high crime rate."

"Most urban areas do."

"Yes, but New Orleans is different. It's a tourist hub and parts of it never really did come back after Hurricane Katrina. You're not to wander around with a purse. Put your identification and some cash in your pocket. There are a lot of pickpockets and muggers around, and you make an enticing target."

"Because I look weak?"

"Because you're adorable and people will assume that makes you an easy mark."

Despite my initial bridling at his remarks, I warmed all over at the "adorable" comment. "Okay. I'll do what you say."

"That would be a nice change of pace."

Once he was gone, Millie meandered over to me. She seemed almost as excited as me, though I had a feeling it was for different reasons. "There's a carousel bar at the Hotel Monteleone," she announced. "It actually moves. I want to go there while we're in town. I love that place."

"You've been here before?" I was jealous. "That's cool."

"This is my favorite city in the world," Millie admitted. "If they didn't have bugs the size of my head in the summer — and enough humidity to steam cruciferous vegetables — I would consider relocating here when I retire."

"And when will that be? I was under the impression you were going to work forever."

"Not forever," she corrected. "I want to earn my keep and not live off the money I got from Myron in the divorce. Don't get me wrong, I'll still spend that money, but I like making my own money."

I could understand that. "I have a lot of things I want to see. Like, for example, St. Louis Cemetery has three locations and two of them are registered historic landmarks."

"That's a lovely knowledge base you've got going on there," she said dryly.

"There's also LaLaurie Mansion. That's where Delphine LaLaurie supposedly tortured and killed her slaves in horrendous fashion. There's debate over how much of the stories are true, but even if only a quarter of them are real that means she was still one of the worst serial killers ever."

"And that sounds like a happy visit." Despite her dour words, Millie smiled. "You look happy, girl."

"I am happy. Am I not supposed to be happy?" I glanced around to see if people were eavesdropping. "I mean ... I know we're here investigating dead bodies that supposedly got up and started walking around, but it's not as if the people in question were murdered."

"I'm not talking about that. I'm talking about Jack."

"Oh." I wished I could control my blushing. I felt the heat creeping up my cheeks. Millie was a good person, but she enjoyed embarrassing me. "Things with Jack are good."

"I can tell. You guys were obviously together before we got the call. Are you finally doing overnight visits?"

The question made me ridiculously uncomfortable. "That's private."

Millie narrowed her eyes. "Oh, geez. You're not, are you? What's wrong? Does he look bad naked or something? Wait, what am I saying? There's no way that guy looks bad naked. I've seen him with his shirt off. Even if he has a tiny twig he has other attributes to make up for it."

I was mortified. "Millie!"

Several heads turned in our direction, including Jack's. He frowned for a moment and then shook his head before resuming his conversation with Chris.

"You need to chill out," Millie admonished. "There's no reason for you to get so worked up. It was a simple question."

"It was an invasive question."

"I'm pretty sure that's the same thing."

"No, it's not."

"Well, I don't care if it's invasive." Millie folded her arms over her chest and looked me up and down. "You're not a virgin, right?"

I wanted to dig a hole and crawl into it. I couldn't believe she had the audacity to ask me that in front of people. Sure, none of those people appeared to be listening, but that didn't make it any better. "Of course not."

"So, what's the issue?"

"There is no issue."

"There has to be. You and Jack have been dating for weeks and you still haven't done the naked tango. That's not normal ... at least in my world."

"It doesn't matter what's normal in your world," I snapped, annoyed. "We're taking things at our own pace."

Millie held up her hands in capitulation, obviously surprised by my tone. "I was teasing you, Charlie. There's no reason to get upset."

"I'm not upset." I rubbed the spot between my eyebrows and looked away from her. "Things are good. Why isn't that enough?"

"It's more than enough." Millie adjusted her tone quickly. "I didn't realize you were so nervous. It's okay. You and Jack will figure things out on your own. I just thought I would give you a little push if it was something minor. Apparently it's more than that."

"And what do you think it is?"

"Your magic."

I pinched the bridge of my nose to ward off what I was sure would be a whopper of a headache if I let it get a foothold. "Don't say that word."

"No one is around." She adopted a soothing voice. "I'm the only one who knows and I promised to take your secret to the grave. I meant it. You don't have to worry about me."

"Which is why we're having this conversation in the middle of a crowded hotel lobby."

"No one is listening," she reassured me. "I get it. From your perspective, you're in a tough spot. You have to tell Jack the truth before things go too far and you're dreading it. It's easier to wait than jump him ... even though he is all kinds of hot."

I wanted to admonish her, but she wasn't wrong. Jack was definitely hot. "I just don't know how to tell him. I'm afraid it will mean the end of us before we even really got started."

"I know." Millie patted my arm. "The thing is, you don't have anything to fear. Jack will be surprised at first and then accept everything you are with the grace I've seen him exude since he joined our group. That's simply who he is."

I wished I could believe as easily as her. "And what if he doesn't?"

"I don't think that's a possibility."

"Anything is possible. I believe you told me that not long before you saw me in action. You can't say that you weren't surprised by what went down that day. You were probably afraid of me, too."

"Not afraid. I was surprised. But after I thought about it, it made sense. You're a good person at your core, Charlie. You can do some extraordinary things. There's nothing wrong with that. Jack will see it the same way."

Hope washed over me in a wave before I managed to tamp it down. "I'm going to tell him. I just don't know how to do it."

"Follow your heart."

"That's not very good advice."

"It's the only advice I have. Jack is a good man. You're a good woman. Fate brought you together for a reason. It'll work out."

"I hope so."

"I *know* so."

. . .

JACK SPENT SO much time at the front desk because he wanted to make sure I got a good room. His room was across the hall — and because it didn't have a view I had a sneaking suspicion it was originally supposed to be my room — but the one he pointed me toward as we reached our floor was absolutely breathtaking.

"Wow!" I didn't know what else to say as I dropped my bag on the floor. "This is a suite. There's a sitting room and everything."

"There is." Jack smiled at my reaction. "It looks nice, huh?"

"Nice?" Was he joking? "This is straight out of a dream."

"You haven't even taken the full tour yet," he said, gesturing toward the huge set of balcony doors on the far side of the room. "Look out there."

He was obviously looking forward to my reaction, so I didn't make him wait. I swept in that direction, fumbled with the lock for what felt like forever, and then practically skipped onto the balcony. Once outside, I pulled up short.

"Is this ... ?"

"Bourbon Street," he acknowledged. "I wanted to make sure you got the good view because you seem to be in love with the city."

That's when I knew for sure. "This was supposed to be your room because you're head of security."

"I'm fine where I'm at."

"Yeah, but ... ."

"No buts." He swooped in and gave me a kiss before I could muster the energy to argue. "You deserve this room. I'm right across the hall. I can come over and enjoy your view when I need a fix."

"Yeah." I stared into his eyes for a long time. "Thank you."

"Don't thank me." He gave me another kiss and then reluctantly pulled back. "We don't have much time. We're all supposed to meet in the lobby in an hour, but I figured we could do a quick turn around the block so you can get a feel for the city before we have to start working."

"That's a great idea."

"Somehow I knew you would say that."

EMELINE LANDRY owned the Royal Dauphine. The hotel had been in her family for decades. She and her husband ran it together for thirty years before he died last year. She was sad talking about him, but she clearly loved sharing her knowledge of New Orleans history with anyone who wanted to listen.

"This area was hit hard during the hurricane, but we got off lucky compared to others," she explained. "We refurbished all the rooms in the aftermath and now I think the hotel is even grander than it was before."

"It's beautiful," I enthused, glancing around. "I absolutely love it. Although ... you haven't seen any zombies walking around, have you?"

Jack shot me a quelling look. "She didn't mean for the question to come off so weird."

"It's not a weird question," I argued. "It's a legitimate question."

"It's a weird question." Jack moved his hand to my back and rubbed it up and down. "We are here for a specific reason, though. Apparently people have been reporting the bodies of their deceased loved ones walking around. Has that made the news down here?"

"It has." Emeline made a face. "It's all over the television and in the newspapers, too. Everyone and their brother have been out looking for signs of their loved ones. It's ridiculous."

"I guess that means you don't believe in zombies?" Jack asked, his lips quirking.

"I know it's probably not nice to say given how many in the community believe in nonsense like that, but I definitely think that someone has been smoking some funky hash."

The woman was blunt, I had to give her that. Still, I was curious about the phenomenon. "What are people saying? I mean ... have the authorities stumbled across any of these bodies?"

"No, and that's what everyone seems to be ignoring. If it were really happening, it seems to me the cops would've assumed at least one of those so-called zombies was a drunk lurching around on Bourbon Street. That's not the case."

"What about the family members who claim to have seen them? Has anyone tried talking to them?"

"That I don't know. I can't remember reading anything like that in the newspaper. I think that's what I would try to do first. I mean, my poor Barry died a year ago — God bless his soul — and I would definitely like to see him again. If he showed up outside the hotel I'm pretty sure I would ask him a few questions."

"And no one has been attacked, right?" Reconciling the zombies Chris was talking about with the ones I'd seen on television wasn't easy.

"Definitely not," Emeline replied. "Trust me. If the dead had risen and started attacking, that is not something the authorities could keep under their hats. That's not how it works here."

I left Jack to continue asking questions and moved to the front door. Even though he warned me about walking around alone, I couldn't stop myself from stepping outside.

The street smelled of ... something ... I couldn't quite identify. Spices of some sort. That's the only word I could think to describe the scent. Sure, I smelled alcohol, too. I guess plenty had been spilled over the years thanks to the notorious revelry on the bustling street. It was the spices that struck me, though.

I inhaled again, deeply, and smiled. Big cities sometimes threw me ... and not in a good way. Because I had a few psychic abilities — including the occasional flash from someone's past if my defenses were down — I tended to avoid huge throngs of people. It wasn't Mardi Gras season, which was good, but the area was still full of people.

Some were artists selling their wares. Others were on vacation, having a good time. Still others looked to be pickpockets, and when I focused on the young face across the way that was watching to see where I would go, he flashed me a sheepish smile before slinking away. The only person who seemed to be completely unaware of his surroundings was a barker standing in the middle of the road holding up a sign. It read "The world will end in fire," and he wore a toga of sorts as he yelled out words I couldn't quite make out to passersby.

As if sensing my eyes on him, he turned. His skin was a dusky shade that signified to me he was probably mixed race. In a city as racially diverse as New Orleans, that seemed normal. His eyes were an electric shade of gray, almost blue but not quite, and they locked with mine across a sea of people.

"The end is coming," he intoned.

"Oh, yeah?" He was a good fifty feet away, but I had no problem hearing him despite the din. "Why do you think that?"

"The dead are rising."

"That's the rumor."

"When the dead rise, the rapture comes."

I focused on his sign. "What does that have to do with fire?"

"You'll see, magic girl." His grin made me uncomfortable and I shifted from one foot to the other. It was possible he called every woman "magic girl." It was also possible he sensed something about me. Often, special gifts are assumed to be lunacy, and I couldn't help but wonder if that's what was happening here.

I didn't get much of chance to dwell on it because Jack appeared at my side, his expression grim.

"What did I say about wandering away?"

I shot him a withering look. "I'm an adult ... and I was just looking around the street. You don't have to worry about me."

"Oh, if only that were true." He smirked at my dour stare. "Don't wander too far from the others in the group, okay? You look like the world's easiest mark."

I thought about the pickpocket. He didn't seem to feel the same way. I could hardly point that out to Jack, though. "I'll do my best to stay out of trouble. That's all I can promise."

"I guess that will have to be enough." His gaze lingered on me and then he turned to the barker, who was staring at us intensely. "What's his deal?"

"He says the world is going to end in fire because the dead are rising."

"Ah." Jack didn't look particularly perturbed. "Every town has its crazies. He's an example of someone you want to avoid."

"I'll keep that in mind."

"Come on." He grabbed my hand and tugged. "We have thirty minutes. We can't go far, but we can go around the block. I'll take you to see more later."

"Sounds like a plan to me."

FOUR

*T*he brief trip around the block wasn't enough. There were
so many things to see ... and hear ... and smell.

"What is that?" I lifted my nose.

Jack chuckled. "You look like a dog trying to find a bone."

I frowned. "That doesn't sound very complimentary."

"I'm sorry. As for that smell, I believe that's gumbo. We'll get some
later. You'll like it."

I wasn't exactly picky when it came to food. "I'm sure I will. When
I was a kid my parents were obsessed with making me a well-rounded
eater. I had to eat things I absolutely hated. I can eat almost anything
now."

He slid me a sidelong look. "Well, I would prefer you stuck to
things you actually like. That's just me, though. If you don't like
gumbo, there's also red beans and rice, etouffee, jambalaya and a host
of other things like po' boy sandwiches and seafood broil. You'll find
something you like."

"I'm sure I will." He was hard to read sometimes. Now was one of
those instances. "I didn't mean to offend you with the comment about
the food."

He lifted an eyebrow. "You didn't offend me. I don't like thinking about you being forced to eat things you don't like or starve. That makes me angry."

"Weren't you in the military?"

"I was."

"I hear the food isn't exactly fine cuisine. Why is it different for you?"

"Because I knew what I was signing up for. You were a traumatized kid. I don't like it. And, before you think of something else smart to say, I'm never going to like it. You can't change my mind on that."

He was almost belligerent, which made me smile. "I guarantee I'll find something I like here. I promise."

His expression softened. "I know." He squeezed my hand and then reluctantly tugged me back toward the hotel. "We need to start back. Chris wants to head to the cemetery right away. We need to get that out of the way. I promise to take you around again later."

"It's okay." I meant it. "I'm anxious to learn about the zombies."

"It's not zombies."

"You don't know that."

"I know zombies aren't real."

He probably figured psychics and telekinesis weren't real either. "Do you believe in anything?"

He obviously wasn't expecting the question because he tilted his head to the side and furrowed his brow. "I don't know. I guess I believe in witches, but only up to a point. I think it's more that people convince themselves they're witches and try to cast spells that might sometimes work but only because it's a self-fulfilling prophecy."

That wasn't what I wanted to hear. "What about psychics?"

He shrugged, noncommittal. "I know people who swear by psychics. I'm not sure I believe in them. That's one of the personas that grifters take on for a reason. I mean ... it's easy to convince someone of something they really want to believe."

"Right." I couldn't help being down.

"And now I've upset you," he muttered, frustration evident. "I don't want you to stop believing, Charlie. If that's what you're worried about, don't. One of the things I like best about you is your enthusiasm."

It was a nice thing to say, but it didn't necessarily make me feel better. "It's okay. I guess we're just never going to see eye-to-eye on that stuff."

"Probably not," he agreed. "That doesn't mean you're not allowed to believe what you want."

"That's not what you said when I thought there was a sixty-foot shark hunting the waters off Florida."

"Yes, but that was different. I mean ... a sixty-foot shark can't hide in this day and age with all the technology we have."

I didn't believe that, but it ultimately didn't matter. We were looking for zombies, not prehistoric sharks. "We should head back. I want to see this cemetery. You never know, we might stumble across a zombie."

"We're not going to stumble across a zombie."

"We might."

"We won't."

I refused to let it go. "We might."

He heaved out a sigh as he met my gaze. "You're lucky you're cute."

I felt pretty lucky ... at least for today.

ST. LOUIS CEMETERY NO. 3 WAS exactly what I'd hoped for. Because New Orleans was located so close to the water and the water table was so high, most graves are above ground. We're talking mausoleums and elaborate sarcophagi. It was like walking into the middle of an artistic rendering.

"This cemetery is two miles from the French Quarter and thirty blocks from the Mississippi," Hannah read from her phone as she followed Chris. "It opened in 1854 and the crypts are considered more elaborate. There are even a few marble tombs.

"It was flooded by Katrina in 2005 but it escaped relatively unscathed, which the other cemeteries couldn't claim," she continued.

"Because of its location, it's less visited than the two other St. Louis cemeteries."

"It's fantastic." I was almost breathless when I stepped forward. Because I wasn't paying close enough attention, I almost tripped over my own feet.

"Hello." Jack grabbed my arm before I could topple to the ground, hauling me up and pinning me to his side. "Do you want to crack open your head? Be careful."

"I think it would be awesome if she cracked open her head," Laura cackled from behind us.

"And I think it would be awesome if we could find a mausoleum to lock you in," Jack shot back.

"Just ignore her," Millie instructed, her eyes landing on Jack. "You're playing right into her hands when you respond that way."

Jack made a face. "She bugs me."

"She bugs all of us. She likes bugging us. Don't give her power."

A quick look at Jack told me he agreed with what Millie said. He didn't want to encourage Laura.

"We should look around," I suggested, hoping to break the tension. "Were the bodies all stolen from the same area?"

Chris shook his head. "Four different locations."

"I suggest we break up into groups and search each location separately," Laura offered. "I'll go with Jack, and Charlie can be on her own."

Jack's expression was withering. "Don't push it."

"The cemetery isn't so big we can't all go together," Chris argued. "I think that's probably the best way to go about things. I want to see each location with my own eyes."

"I'm fine with that." Jack pulled out his phone and engaged his GPS. "I programmed all four burial locations. Let's tackle them in an orderly fashion."

"That's a fantastic idea." Chris beamed at him. "Which way first?"

Jack pointed before taking the lead. He gave me a serious look, which told me exactly what he expected. He wanted me to keep up.

For some reason he was even more worked up than usual, but I couldn't understand why.

"How many times have you been here?" I asked, hoping to change the subject. I much preferred his company when he wasn't completely worked up and attempting to give himself high blood pressure.

"Four or five times," he replied after a beat, his gaze on the GPS. "I visited twice when I was on leave from the military. I've been here two or three times since joining the Legacy Foundation."

"Really?" I was officially intrigued. "Do you guys come here often?"

He smirked. "It's New Orleans, Charlie. When you think of the most haunted place in the world, where is it?"

That was a good question. "Salem."

"Massachusetts?"

"Is there another Salem?"

"Yeah. Oregon."

"Oh." I felt like an idiot. "Then definitely Massachusetts."

"I guess I can see that," he said after a beat. "New Orleans is bigger, though. It has more mystique."

"Bigger isn't always better."

His eyes gleamed with flirtatious intent. "Oh, yeah?"

"Don't be gross," I chided, causing him to chuckle. "Also, the Lizzie Borden Bed and Breakfast is supposed to be haunted. So is some prison in Philadelphia and an ocean liner in California. I can't remember their names, but I've read about them."

"Haven't you ever wondered who actually wants to stay at the Lizzie Borden Bed and Breakfast? I mean ... how does that even come up?"

"I would totally like to stay there. I love the idea of ghosts ... even ones carrying axes."

Jack didn't look convinced. "I have every intention of taking you away once you have some vacation time accrued. We're not going there, though."

I tamped down the sudden agitation rolling through me at the mention of an overnight trip with just Jack and me to anchor the conversation. "Can we go to the Stanley Hotel in Estes Park?"

"That's the hotel where *The Shining* was filmed, right?"

I nodded. "It's supposed to be haunted."

"Don't you want to go somewhere that isn't haunted?"

"Disney World. I always wanted to go there as a kid. But you don't strike me as a Disney World sort of guy."

"That shows what you know. I would love to go to Disney World."

His answer surprised me. "Really?"

"Yup. I also wouldn't mind seeing *The Shining* hotel. See, I can compromise. That means you'll have to visit places I want to see, too."

"I can live with that. Where do you want to visit?"

"The Alamo."

"I believe that's supposed to be haunted, too."

"Gettysburg."

I made a face. "Are all the places you want to visit old battle-grounds?"

He shrugged. "Maybe."

"We're going to need to compromise."

"Sure. We'll spend half the week at the Alamo and the other half at the Stanley Hotel."

"I can live with that."

This time the smile he let loose was legitimate. "So can I."

Laura cleared her throat behind us and wedged herself between us. She'd obviously been listening. Because I was in no mood to deal with her, I willingly moved to my left when Jack pointed toward a specific location and walked with Chris and Hannah in that direction, leaving him to deal with the viper on his own.

"This is it," Chris noted, jutting out his chin. "Look here. The top was moved off. There are markings where the vault was damaged."

It was easy to make out what he was pointing at. "I see it." I hunkered down so I could get a better look, holding out my hands as I tried to imagine what I would do if I woke trapped inside the huge cement box. The thought was enough to cause my heart rate to increase. I'd always been a teensy bit claustrophobic. "Do you think someone could move the top from the inside?"

Chris's eyes gleamed at the question. "I don't know. We can certainly perform an experiment to find out. Whose grave was this?"

"I don't have a name," Jack replied, glaring at Laura as she eagerly trailed him toward us. "I just know this was the twenty-nine-year-old woman."

"Then it wouldn't be a proper test for me to climb in to see if I can move the lid," Chris noted. "It needs to be one of the women. Charlie, Hannah and Laura are the only ones who fit the age window."

My mouth went dry.

"There's no amount of money you could pay me to get in there," Laura countered. "I mean ... absolutely none. It's not going to happen."

Hannah looked doubtful as she regarded the grave. "I guess I could do it, but ... I don't want to damage my hands in an escape attempt. I might need to perform an autopsy or two before this is all said and done if we manage to find one of the missing bodies. I don't want to risk it."

"That leaves Charlie." Chris turned to me expectantly. "You won't be in there long. Just see if you can move the lid. If not, I would think that means someone from the outside removed the body."

"You're not putting her in there." Jack was vehement. "I'm serious. It's not going to happen."

"She'll be perfectly fine," Chris countered. "She won't be in there more than a minute. Two tops."

"No." Jack emphatically shook his head. "I'm not letting you put her in there. What if something happens and she's trapped?"

"What could happen?" Chris's expression was blank. "We're all here. You and I will move the lid if she can't move it herself."

"No."

"I believe it's up to her," Chris pressed. His smile was benign when he locked gazes with me. "What do you say?"

"Oh, well ... ." I felt put on the spot ... and vaguely sick to my stomach. "I'm not sure that I think that's a good idea."

"You'll be fine." Chris wasn't backing down. "We'll be right here."

"No." Jack extended his hand and looked at me. "Be truthful. Do you want to go in there? Do you?"

It was almost as if he could feel my fear. "No."

"Then she's not going in," Millie said simply, pushing her way to the front of the group. "It doesn't really matter, Chris. Even if she could move the lid — which is doubtful — you could argue that zombies are stronger because they've been reanimated. There's no proof to be found in this."

"I guess." Chris didn't look happy about losing the argument, but he forced a smile for my benefit. "You don't have to go in."

"She doesn't," Jack muttered, moving me to his right so I was out of Chris's immediate line of sight. "This zombie crap is nonsense anyway. Zombies aren't real."

"Then why do the stories persist throughout history?" Chris challenged.

"There are stories about the Loch Ness Monster, too, and it's not real."

"Oh, it's real."

Jack pressed the heel of his hand to his forehead. "Sometimes I think you're purposely trying to kill me."

"I often feel the same about you," Chris admitted. "I think we're looking for a voodoo practitioner. It could be a priest or priestess. Someone familiar with this cemetery decided to raise the dead. We need to figure out why."

"We don't know that the bodies weren't stolen for medical experiments," Jack shot back. "That's the most common reason for crypts to go empty in this day and age. Well, that and sexual molestation, but we've all agreed we don't want to go there."

"Definitely not," Millie said.

"I like a good molestation every now and again," Laura offered, winking at Jack.

"Ugh." He screwed up his face in disgust. "Stop talking to me. I don't want to hear another word from your mouth."

I tuned out the argument. It wasn't important to me. Jack would always be the naysayer when it came to the paranormal. He couldn't stop himself. Chris would always be the believer. That's simply how he was built. And me? I would err on the side of believing, too. I was magical, so it was easier for me to believe others suffered from similar issues. If I didn't have that to cling to, I would feel like a weirdo alone in a vast ocean of "normal" people ... and nobody wants that.

As the argument between Jack and Chris ratcheted up, I focused on the sarcophagus. Suddenly, I had an overwhelming urge to touch it. I couldn't stop myself.

I extended my hand until my fingers brushed against the cool hardness of the cement and closed my eyes, a series of flashes invading so fast I almost couldn't comprehend what I was seeing.

I heard a noise. It sounded like someone gasping for breath as he or she was running out of oxygen.

I heard scratching, like fingers clawing against a heavy surface as someone tried to escape.

I heard an inhuman whine, like an animal begging for reprieve.

And then, very briefly, I saw a hint of light as a large sheet of rock was moved to reveal an opening.

There was relief ... and fear.

"Charlie?" Millie moved to my side, her voice low.

I shook myself out of my reverie and snatched back my hand. "I'm fine."

"You saw something," she corrected.

"I ... don't know what I saw." I glanced around to make sure no one was paying attention to us. Thankfully, everyone else was too busy watching Jack and Chris go at each other to worry about me.

"Did you see a zombie?" Millie asked with a straight face.

I thought about the scratching ... and whining. "I don't know," I said finally. "It was weird. I'm not sure what I saw."

"You need to be careful when doing this out in the open," she admonished. "Until you tell Jack ... ." She left the rest of it hanging, but I knew what she meant. Until I told Jack my secret, I was vulnerable to being outed before I was ready. That could be disastrous.

"It will be fine," I said after a beat. I hoped I sounded more certain than I felt. "There's nothing to worry about. I'll be perfectly fine."

"If you say so."

"I *know* so."

FIVE

*I*t took us an hour to finish our sweep of the cemetery. While I still found it beautiful, I was unnerved by the vision from the first burial place and wisely opted to refrain from touching the others. I wasn't sure I wanted to see anything. Instead, I spent my time studying the shadows for hints of movement, perhaps a malevolent force watching us.

I came up empty and was happy when it was time to leave.

We returned to the French Quarter for lunch. Chris selected a restaurant about two blocks from our hotel. He'd set up a meeting with a local detective who was supposed to meet us after we'd finished chowing down.

Once seated, menu in hand, I struggled to decide what I wanted to sample for my first meal in New Orleans. Jack seemed determined to make sure I would like whatever I chose, so I wanted to make it good.

"I think you'll like the gumbo," he said as he watched me pore over the laminated sheet. "It's shrimp and rice. Okra. If there's an option, try the mild version."

"Is that authentic?" I had no idea why that was so important, but I didn't want to be the jerk who couldn't handle the local cuisine. "I'm getting it the normal way."

"You'll set your mouth on fire if you're not careful."

"Yeah, well ... I'm still giving it a shot." I offered him a bright smile. "What are you getting?"

"A catfish po' boy."

"And what is that?"

"It's basically a sandwich. Kind of like a regular chicken sandwich with lettuce, pickles and tomatoes. Except I'm getting mine with catfish, because I love catfish."

That sounded interesting. "I've never had catfish before. Maybe I should get that."

"Or maybe I'll let you have a bite of my sandwich to see if you like it first. We know you like shrimp and rice."

He had a point. "Okay." I wasn't in the mood to argue about food. "Tell me about this detective, Chris. Is there a reason he's meeting us here instead of at the local precinct?"

"Now that right there is an excellent question," Jack pronounced. "I would like to hear the answer to that myself."

"His name is Henri Thibodeaux," Chris replied, his attention on the menu. "I'm not sure why we're meeting him here. Uncle Myron had to pull a few strings to make it happen. Local law enforcement was not keen on us being involved."

"I wonder why," I mused. "You would think they'd want our expertise."

"Oh, I can think of a good fifty reasons they wouldn't want word getting out about us," Laura drawled. "The biggest is that we made the news for what happened at St. Pete Beach. Chris was on every station explaining why it was still possible that a Megalodon was out there hunting in the Gulf waters."

Chris frowned. "It's completely possible."

"If you say so." Laura grabbed a carrot stick from the vegetable tray at the center of the table. She was always watching her carb intake and avoided bread as though it contained arsenic. I didn't have that problem, so I immediately grabbed one of the warm rolls and broke it open and slathered butter on it. "I very much doubt the locals want it made public that the giant shark guy is in town looking for zombies."

Sadly, I could understand that. Still, I felt bad for Chris. He was often the laughingstock of his own group, and it didn't seem fair. "I'm with Chris. I think it's totally possible Megalodons still exist. I don't think I ever want to see one after my little adventure swimming with regular-sized sharks, but it's intriguing to think about."

Instead of arguing, Jack smirked as he watched me stuff half the roll into my mouth. He seemed to enjoy watching me eat, which I found odd. "Let's not talk about Megalodons," he suggested. "Let's talk about zombies. We need more information, and he's our best shot. If he can't help us we'll have to track down the families of the missing bodies ourselves. That might take more time than we're comfortable with."

"I don't think Uncle Myron would've gone through the trouble of tapping an old source if he didn't think he could really help," Chris noted. "There's nothing we can do but eat until he gets here. I don't know about anyone else, but I'm looking forward to some old-fashioned Creole cooking."

He wasn't the only one. "Me, too." I smiled brightly as the waitress approached. "I think I'm really going to enjoy this."

"**NOW I KNOW WHAT** it feels like to eat in Hell," I complained thirty minutes later, sweat pouring down my face as I downed my third glass of water. "I think I might be dying."

Jack, who seemed perfectly at ease, sent me a knowing look. "I told you to order mild."

"No one likes a know-it-all," I fired back, frowning when the water did nothing to soothe my scorched tongue. "I seriously think I might be dying."

"You're not dying." Jack waved one of the laminated menus in front of my face to cool me off. "The water won't help you. You need milk."

Milk? Ugh. "Milk is for cereal."

"It's also good for cooling your tongue. Something about the proteins."

I couldn't decide if he was messing with me. Finally, I signaled the waitress and asked for a huge glass of milk. I was willing to put up with the laughter if he was wrong. I was so uncomfortable I was willing to risk just about anything to make the burning sensation disappear.

The waitress — who seemed amused by the show — returned within two minutes. Apparently I wasn't the first guest to bite off more than she could comfortably chew in the establishment. I thankfully took the glass she offered and greedily downed it. I didn't stop until it was all gone.

"You're so classy," Jack teased, using his napkin to wipe the corners of my mouth. In my haste to escape the burn, a bit of milk had sloshed over at the sides. "You should teach one of those manners classes for young women."

My tongue was feeling better, so I stuck it in his direction. That's when I realized a distinguished-looking gentleman was standing near the table and watching the show.

"I'm so sorry," I said hurriedly, recovering. "I just ... had a hot tongue."

Jack chuckled as he focused on the newcomer. "Are you Detective Thibodeaux?"

"I am," he confirmed, his gaze remaining on me for a long beat. "Not used to the spices, huh?"

"Not really." I was rueful. "I think I learned my lesson about asking for the mild version of things from here on out."

"You'll get used to it." Thibodeaux shook hands with everyone in turn and then sat between Chris and me. He was in his forties if I had to guess. He wore a nice suit that somehow looked as if it was freshly pressed despite the humidity. He didn't appear out of place in the establishment, but he didn't exactly look happy to be there.

"Let me start by saying that the only reason I'm here is because I owe your uncle a favor." He directed the statement at Chris. "Personally, I don't see the point of you being here. I'm well aware what your foundation does. There's no reason for you to be here. I guarantee that."

"So, I take it you don't believe these bodies are rising from the dead," Jack offered. He made for an imposing figure as he leaned back in his chair, comfortable and yet formidable. It was no wonder women everywhere — including the waitress who couldn't seem to stop herself from staring from across the restaurant — fell at his feet.

"I don't," Thibodeaux agreed. "Zombies aren't real. I'm sure that will come as a shock to some of you, but it's true." His eyes were on me for the last part. I wanted to argue with his assumption that I was a believer — even though I was — but it didn't seem the right time. All he knew about me was that I spilled milk when I drank it because I couldn't handle spicy food. That wasn't exactly a ringing endorsement.

"Then what happened to the bodies?" Chris queried. He came across as professional, intelligent even. There was a hint of annoyance lacing his words, though. "Surely you must have a suggestion for why people would steal bodies — especially those particular bodies — from one of your cemeteries."

"I have several ideas," Thibodeaux confirmed. "The first is that a medical research facility needed the tissue. It's not unheard of, although usually they aim for cemeteries that get less play in the media. The facilities these people work for pay top dollar for bodies. The fresher the better."

"If you're aware of these medical facilities, why not serve a warrant and search them?"

"We don't have just cause. We have a hunch, but it's not our only hunch. The other is much darker ... and it's not something anyone wants to consider."

"You think that someone grabbed the bodies for sexual purposes," Hannah supplied. "That's what you're saying, right?"

"It is. I would actually prefer it be zombies than that."

"I'm a medical doctor," Hannah explained. "I also did a rotation at a psychiatric hospital. Necrophilia is a real disorder. In sixty-eight percent of cases, the perpetrators state that their reasons for wanting a corpse revolve around a desire to have a non-resisting or non-rejecting partner."

"Oh, geez," I muttered under my breath.

Jack briefly patted my knee as a form of consolation but kept his eyes on Hannah. "What are the other reasons?" he asked.

"Twenty-one percent are reunions with romantic partners," Hannah replied without hesitation. She delivered the statement with a cool precision that I often admired but never coveted. "These are people who lost their soulmates and couldn't move on.

"There is a subset of people who are actually turned on by corpses because they're cold, but that's fairly rare," she continued. "A lot of the time people turn to necrophilia because they believe it's their only option."

"Maybe that's what we're dealing with here," Thibodeaux suggested. "I would have to believe it's not the loved ones of the deceased, because they would obviously be our first suspects — and we've questioned all of them at this point and see no reason to keep looking at them. That means we're dealing with a stranger attracted to corpses."

"I might be able to agree if we were dealing with four women or four men," Hannah said. "But it's a mixture of sexes and ages. That means we're not dealing with a preferential offender, and that seems unlikely when dealing with necrophilia. Of course, I'm not a profiler, so take what I say with a grain of salt."

Instead of being offended, Thibodeaux looked impressed. "No, that's good insight. What else have you got?"

"Just basic information. Necrophiliacs often don't act on their impulses. It's a daunting task to unearth a body. In a weird way, it might make more sense for someone with that compulsion to come to New Orleans because of the way your cemeteries work. It's probably easier to get into a sarcophagus than dig six feet into the earth and break into a vault."

"Go on."

"Necrophilia fantasies are more common than popular belief," she explained. "Most people won't admit to them because of the stigma."

"Oh, you think?" Laura drawled. "I don't understand why everyone doesn't admit to wanting to get it on with a corpse. I mean ... abuse of a corpse makes for awesome romance stories."

Thibodeaux snickered at her sarcasm, which made me dislike him just a little bit.

"An overwhelming percentage of necrophiliacs are men," Hannah volunteered. "We're talking ninety-two percent. That could be because it's more difficult for a woman to get the sexual gratification she needs from a corpse, but I don't have any facts to back up that supposition.

"Also, more than fifty percent of necrophiliacs have access to bodies," she continued. "It might be a common book or television trope, but it's true that a lot of necrophiliacs hide in the funeral home industry."

"So ... you think we should be looking at funeral home workers," Thibodeaux mused.

"Actually, I don't," she countered. "As I said, necrophiliacs are preferential offenders most of the time. They want reunification with a loved one or, if they can't get that individual, they want someone who looks exactly like him or her. That's not what's happening here."

"Unless it is." Thibodeaux obviously wasn't the type to back down. "What if only one of the individuals taken was the target and the others were merely used to cover up what was really happening?"

"I guess that's possible, but that doesn't explain the families seeing their loved ones walking around."

I was impressed with Hannah's fortitude. She often came across as meek, but she was strong when it came to voicing her opinion.

"I believe the families are imagining what they saw," Thibodeaux said. "They heard about the body theft and then told themselves a story that was somehow better than the other possibilities."

"Perhaps, but two of the families didn't know about the body thefts until after they called you with claims of seeing dead loved ones," Chris interjected. "I know. I've got the reports of the calls. Your department didn't check the cemetery for those missing bodies until after the families made the claim."

"I ... ." Thibodeaux worked his jaw. "Are you sure?" He seemed conflicted, which gave me hope that he was a good detective strug-gling with a difficult case and not an uber-douche of the highest order. I was torn about where my opinion would ultimately land.

Chris nodded. "I'm sure. I double-checked."

"I never thought to look at that," Thibodeaux mused, rubbing his chin. "Still, zombies aren't real. I don't understand how you could possibly believe it's zombies."

"We don't know what to believe yet, but there is medical science that backs up zombie stories from the past," Hannah offered. "This is a drug-induced state that mimics death, so when the individual rises it's seen as zombification even though it's something else."

Jack leaned forward, suddenly interested. "How does that work?"

"The first is a powder, French in origin, and it makes people look dead even though they're still alive. This powder has a lethal compound in it that can be found in pufferfish, which are also toxic.

"The second powder includes a series of dissociative properties that makes the victim appear to have no will of his or her own," she continued. "These individuals are extremely open to suggestion. That's how most of the Haitian voodoo legends arose ... at least that's what I believe."

"Is there a way to test for these powders?" Thibodeaux asked.

"Yes. We would need a body first."

"That's high on our shopping list," he admitted. "It would be easy to quell the rumors racing through the Quarter if we could find at least one of the bodies. So far we've come up empty."

"Have any of the families approached their loved ones and tried to hold a conversation with them?" Jack asked. "I mean, I know I can't speak for everybody, but I'm pretty sure that would be the first thing I did if someone I loved suddenly appeared on my doorstep after they'd been reported dead."

"Everyone I questioned was terrified to talk to them," Thibodeaux replied. "Zombies are whispered about in New Orleans on a daily basis because of the religious makeup of the area. We have a little bit of everything here, and it's all mixed together into a stew over the years. A large portion of the population believes zombies are real."

"Technically, if that powder concoction works as Hannah says it does, zombies *are* real," Jack pointed out. "It's not the sort of zombies everyone imagines thanks to pop culture and movies, but it's definitely something to fear."

"It is, but the problem with that scenario is that all of our victims would've had to have been poisoned right before death — and likely by the same person — but we can't find any ties between them," Thibodeaux said. "None of them even frequented the same church, as far as I can tell. Two of them went to the same coffee shop, but Cafe Du Monde is famous in these parts. Everyone goes there."

"It's famous almost everywhere," Millie said. "That's definitely not a tie."

"We're at a loss right now," Thibodeaux admitted. "We're trying to find answers for these families — and to stop a potential panic. If another body goes missing, I'm afraid we're going to tip over into hysteria."

"Then we should try to find answers before that happens," Jack said.

"If you can help, I'm open to it. If all you're going to do is spread zombie nonsense through the Quarter, I would appreciate it if you moved on."

"We won't be spreading nonsense," Chris promised. "I want to get to the truth as much as anyone."

"Then we won't have a problem."

SIX

*J*ack found me on my balcony an hour after lunch. Thibodeaux agreed to share information, but he preferred doing it in Chris's suite ... and without everyone present. Only Chris, Jack and Hannah were allowed at the meeting.

"Hey." He smiled when he saw me sitting with my arms on the railing and staring at the streets. "You look like a little kid who has been banned from playing outside with the other neighborhood kids."

I didn't see that as a compliment. "I'm just watching. New Orleans has a lot of interesting people. Like, for example, the barker is back. He has the same 'the world will end in fire' sign and he's pretty much yelling at anyone who moves past him."

Jack frowned at the sight. "I'll talk to the front desk. Maybe they can move him along or something."

"Don't do that. That's not what I meant. It's just ... he's there. The people obviously realize he's there, but they try to pretend they don't notice because it's easier than dealing with something they don't understand."

He furrowed his brow. "Are you feeling misunderstood?"

"Not last time I checked." At least not openly, I silently added. "I was just thinking about how life is different for so many people."

"Uh-huh." He didn't look convinced. "Well, I'm sorry you got cut out of the meeting. Thibodeaux is understandably leery about sharing too much information. All he knows about Millie is that she's Myron's ex-wife ... and I'm betting Myron told a few tales out of school. Laura is a viper and no one trusts her. And you, well, you were dribbling milk when he met you."

I shot him a look. "Thanks for reminding me of that."

"I thought it was cute." He ducked down and stared into my eyes. "Let me see your tongue."

He was obviously feeling flirty, which warmed me all over. "Why? Are you going to do something to it?"

"Maybe."

I stuck out my tongue and wasn't surprised at all when he swooped in for a kiss. I laughed as he tickled me and then sobered when I realized he had more on his mind than his meeting with Thibodeaux. "What's going on? Has something happened?"

"No, but I'm interested in why you asked that question."

"You looked intense for a moment, as if you had something to tell me."

"I do, but it's nothing bad." His expression was quizzical. "You know, sometimes I think you live in your own head too much. You seem to give a great deal of thought to what others think. You're unique. That makes you stand out. You shouldn't care what others think."

In truth, I mostly didn't. I was still terrified of what was to come when I told him the truth. Obviously that couldn't happen when we were on a case, but I couldn't wait too long to tell him because it would make matters worse if he opted to run in the other direction. With each passing moment I spent with him he owned a bigger piece of my heart ... and I knew without a doubt that I would be crushed if he pulled away from me.

"I'm fine being me." I meant it. "But what did you come in here to tell me?"

"I swear sometimes you're psychic." He grinned as my stomach flipped. "So, I was thinking, Thibodeaux gave us some information, but it's bare bones stuff. We need an in with the local authorities, and I think I know exactly who to go to."

"Oh, really?" I was intrigued. "Do you know another detective in New Orleans? Wait, don't tell me." I held up my hand. "If it's some pretty ex-girlfriend, I don't want to know."

"It's not an ex-girlfriend." He flicked me between my eyebrows. "One of my old military buddies lives here. He's a private detective."

That wasn't what I was expecting. "Oh, well, how do you think he'll be able to help?"

"I don't know that he can. His name is Leon Romero. He's ... a little odd. He used to complain when we were on missions that he missed his mama's beignets something fierce. We all laughed at him. The way he talked about the city was magical, though. He's fairly well respected in the area, so I thought he might be able to offer us some information. I thought you might want to come with me."

The invitation caught me off guard ... and put me in an awkward position. "Oh, um, that's sweet. Do you think he'll want to meet me?"

"Is there a reason he wouldn't?"

"You saw me drink my milk earlier. Sometimes I'm not presentable for public consumption."

He laughed, the sound low and throaty. "You're fine. The milk thing was cute. I figured you would have to learn about the spicy food the hard way. You've got a head like a rock sometimes." He lightly knocked my noggin to let me know he was teasing. "I want you to meet him. You don't have to come if you feel awkward right now. I understand."

"Just so you know, I feel awkward almost every single day of my life. No joke. Sometimes I look in the mirror and wonder how you ever even bothered to look at me."

Jack's lips tipped down. "I don't like that. You're beautiful, Charlie. You may not see it, but I do. Please don't put yourself down."

"That's not what I was doing." Mostly that was true. "It's just ...

you're always smooth and never trip over yourself when you're talking to people."

"I don't feel smooth when I'm with you. I feel awkward, too."

"Bad awkward?"

"No, just ... clumsy. I want to be debonair, but I can't because my heart is always racing and you make me laugh so much I often trip over my own feet."

He was being sweet, which I liked. "I thought I was the only one who tripped."

"No. Not the only one." He leaned forward and gave me a soft kiss. "I want you with me if you want to come."

Part of me wanted to go with him. The other part recognized I had to stick to the plan I'd already made. "Oh, well, while you were busy with Chris and Thibodeaux, Millie came by and invited me on an adventure. I thought it would be fine since I'll be with her."

Jack's smile slipped. "See, the idea of you and Millie together terrifies me. Where are you going?"

"A voodoo shop around the corner. We're going to ask about raising the dead."

"I see." Jack's expression was hard to read. "Is that what you really want to do?"

I felt caught. "I would love to meet your friend. It's just ... I promised Millie."

"And the voodoo shop sounds more fun."

He wasn't wrong. "I've never been to a voodoo shop."

He barked out a laugh and pulled me in for a hug before kissing my forehead. "Have fun at the voodoo shop. It's probably best if I meet Leon on my own this go-around. I guarantee you'll have a chance to meet him before we leave. I want to see how he's doing first anyway."

Something about his tone worried me. "Is there something wrong with him?"

"He suffered from PTSD after our last tour. I heard he needed treatment. He sounded fine when I talked to him on the phone."

On impulse, I pressed my fingers to his pulse point in the hopes of getting a vision of his time with Leon. It worked, and I was rewarded with a picture of the two men sitting in a cozy office and laughing. Everything appeared fine.

"I'm sure he's great. I want to meet him. I just want to go to the voodoo shop first. I think it's going to be fun."

"I think you and Millie are going to terrorize those poor voodoo ladies," he countered. "Something tells me you'll be fine. Do me a favor, though, and don't give them any money. If they tell you a curse is hanging over you, don't pay them to remove it. That's a common grift down here."

"I'll do my best to keep from being taken. Besides, I don't have much money."

Jack immediately reached for his wallet, causing me to balk.

"I'm not taking your money." I was mortified. "I have enough to pay for anything I need."

"You need to get over the money thing," he chided. "Take this anyway because it will make me feel better." He pressed a fifty into the palm of my hand. "If you don't spend it you can give it back. I'll feel better knowing you're covered if you need something to drink or anything ... more milk maybe."

I scowled. "I'm never going to live down the milk, am I?"

"Not as long as I'm around."

I was hopeful he would be around a long time. Fear is a funny thing, though. Now that I had him, I'd never been so afraid of losing anything in my entire life.

"WOW!" THIRTY MINUTES LATER, I raised my eyes to the sign over the ornate purple store and read the hand-lettered advertisement. "'Madame Brenna's Shop of Horrors.' It doesn't sound very welcoming, does it?"

Millie, who appeared to be even more in love with the city than I was, cackled as she put her hand to my back and gave me a shove. "It's going to be fine. Trust me. These are our sort of people."

I opted to take her at her word.

The first thing I smelled when I crossed the threshold was cloves.

It was one of my favorite scents and I closed my eyes as I inhaled. The second thing I smelled was marijuana. No one was smoking, but I had no doubt it was a regular occurrence ... and I was fine with that. Millie obviously smelled it too because she winked at me.

"These are definitely my type of people."

"How may I help you?" a theatrical voice asked from behind the counter. There, a beautiful woman — tall, statuesque, boasting the most magnificent chocolate skin I'd ever seen — stood watching us. She looked to be in her sixties but exuded youthful appeal. She also appeared to be amused ... and maybe a little predatory.

"You must be Madame Brenna," Millie said, not missing a beat. "I've heard wonderful things about you."

"Of course you have. I'm wonderful."

I pressed my lips together to keep from laughing at the woman's response. She was obviously a master at reading people and she pegged Millie as the sort who respected strength, so that's how she greeted her.

"My ex-husband told me about you," Millie started.

"Hold up." Madame Brenna stopped all pretense of being pleasant and waved a finger as she clucked her tongue. "If someone said I was with your husband, I guarantee that didn't happen. I'm never with no one's husband."

"I said he was my ex-husband. I don't care if you were with him. In fact, if you were, I would be impressed. I'm pretty sure you could eat Myron as a snack and spit him out in favor of something better without even working up a sweat. I'm not accusing you of anything."

"Myron?" Madame Brenna cocked an eyebrow. "Are you talking about Myron Briggs?"

"I am."

"Well, well, well." Madame Brenna's smile was so big I could almost count all of her teeth. "I should've recognized you. Myron described you to a T when he was in here last."

"Oh, yeah? How did he describe me?"

"The Devil in Levi's."

Millie laughed, tickled. "I kind of like that."

"I thought you would." Madame Brenna gestured toward the table in the corner of the store. "Have a seat. I need to take a load off. It's been a long day."

Millie led me to the table and we wordlessly sat as Madame Brenna got comfortable. Millie finally broke the silence. "You're probably wondering why I'm here."

"Not really." Madame Brenna tilted her head to the side and smiled. "I know all about Myron. He comes in here every six months for a reading to know his future. He's told me about the Legacy Foundation ... including the bit that his ex-wife and nephew do for it."

"Well, that saves me from having to explain things," Millie noted. "We're here about the zombie thing."

"And you came to me?"

"Myron always told me you didn't deal in bullshit. That's the sort of person we need to talk to, so I figured I should visit you first."

"Okay. That makes sense." Madame Brenna flicked her eyes to me. "Who is your friend?"

"This is Charlie Rhodes. She's the newest member of our team. She's harmless."

Madame Brenna merely shook her head. "She's pretty far from harmless. Obviously she's not ready to embrace who she is, so I'll let her be."

Millie and I exchanged wary looks but didn't comment. There was nothing to say. I wouldn't admit to having powers in front of a perfect stranger and Madame Brenna obviously had other things on her mind.

"We just want to know about the zombies for right now," Millie pressed. "My nephew is gung-ho when it comes to stuff like this and I'm afraid he's going to let his imagination run away with him if we're not careful."

"Why do you think that?"

"Because he's ... a lovely boy with a heart of gold. He would sell his soul for proof of the supernatural, though. It's a sickness with him."

"Really?" Madame Brenna's eyes were heavy when they landed on me. "Imagine that."

I was uncomfortable under her weighted gaze and cleared my throat. "So ... the zombies?"

"I would like to tell you they're not real, but I saw one of them myself," she said, returning to business. "It was an old man. I knew him. He was local, lived in an apartment around the corner. I never knew his name but I heard he died when his wife came in wanting a potion to mend her broken heart. She told me about his passing."

"And you saw him?" Millie queried. "You're positive?"

"I am. More than that, I sensed him. If you operate on a different wavelength like me — and your friend over here — you can feel evil from a great distance. I felt that when I saw him. He was never evil before. Now, he was something else entirely. His eyes were white. He couldn't see anything yet he stared directly at me."

"Did you call the police?" I asked. "I mean ... if I saw a dead man walking around, that's the first thing I would do."

"Really?" Madame Brenna was obviously feeling full of herself as she snickered. "Darling, we both know that's not true. You're a fighter, not a runner. You've been that way your entire life. You'll have to stay that way if you expect to get the things you want — even the man that you want."

I swallowed hard, horrified. Could she see inside my head? It was possible, although I'd learned to shutter at a young age. It was also possible she could merely read the smile on my face when we'd entered. I was still basking in happiness thanks to my encounter with Jack. This woman could very well be a professional grifter like Jack said. I couldn't get a feeling off her, so I wasn't certain.

"Well ... I'm fine with fighting," I said finally.

"And she won't be alone when it comes to that," Millie added pointedly. "Stop trying to show off and make her uncomfortable. She's fine as she is. We want to know about the zombies."

"I don't know what to tell you," Madame Brenna said as she extended her long legs in front of her. It was only then that I realized she was barefoot and a tattoo of a large snake wrapped around her ankle. "I only saw the one. He was there one minute and gone the next. I tried to find him, locked the store up and everything, but he disappeared. I have no idea where he went."

"What about the wife you mentioned?" I asked, my mind busy. "Have you seen her? Has she mentioned seeing him?"

"Now that you mention it, I haven't seen her." Madame Brenna pursed her lips. "I think it's been a good three days since I saw her and I usually see her at least once a day when she crosses in front of the shop when she heads out."

"What do you think the zombies mean?" Millie asked. "I mean ... you must have an idea."

"They mean the end of the world."

I waited for her to whip out a punchline but she didn't. "The end of the world?" I challenged. "Isn't that a bit heavy?"

"It's what I feel. This city is in trouble. I think it could fall thanks to the evil forces working in the shadows to bring it down."

There was that word again. *Shadows.* That word kept popping into my head when we were at the cemetery earlier. "How do we stop the city from falling?"

"I have no idea. If you find out, tell me. I want to help. I love this place. If it falls, I can't help thinking the rest of the world will, too."

"Well, we'll make sure that doesn't happen."

"We will," Millie agreed, retrieving a business card from her pocket. "If you hear anything else, call me. We're at the Royal Dauphine."

"If you hear something, I expect the same courtesy."

"Consider it done."

SEVEN

*J*ack was in a good mood when he arrived at my room before dinner.

"How do you feel about going out to eat?" he asked.

I shrugged. "I could eat ... as long as my tongue doesn't catch fire again."

He grinned. "I thought maybe we would head somewhere on our own. The others are having dinner together, but I already told Chris we wouldn't be joining them."

I was intrigued. "So ... it will be just the two of us? That's fun."

"I thought you might like it."

I glanced down at my clothes. I was wearing simple khaki capris, Nike sandals and a plain T-shirt. "Am I dressed okay? Should I change?"

"You're fine." He gave me a quick kiss. "I figured we would pick a quiet and casual place for dinner and then maybe hit up one of the haunted tours that go through the French Quarter at night."

That sounded interesting. "You don't strike me as a haunted tour guy."

"I've been on tours."

"That doesn't mean you like them."

"I like you, and you're a haunted tour sort of girl. I think I'll survive."

His ho-hum reaction made me grin. "Then let's go."

He watched as I grabbed a few twenties from my purse, making a face when I shoved the fifty he gave me earlier back in his direction.

"You said if I didn't spend it to give it back," I reminded him.

"Yeah, well, I think I need to talk to Myron about how much they're paying you," he grumbled as he slid the fifty into his wallet. "You don't need a purse. I'm buying dinner."

"What about the tour? I need to pay for that."

"That's on me, too."

"That doesn't seem fair."

He looked exasperated. "Just let me pay and stuff your complaints. You don't need a purse, but make sure you put your phone in your pocket."

"Yes, sir. Are there any other orders you would like me to follow, sir?"

He shot me a look. "That's cute only some of the time."

"Is it cute now?"

He looked reluctant to answer. "It might be cute right now," he finally hedged. "I'm starving, though, and I want dinner. I would prefer it if we headed out rather than played games."

"Okay, but I was just gearing up for a round of Monopoly and now you've ruined the fun."

He shook his head. "You have the weirdest sense of humor some-times." He grabbed my hand and tugged me toward the door. "Come on."

"I really do like board games."

"We'll spend our time playing board games if we ever get locked in a haunted hotel for the winter. How does that sound?"

Surprisingly, it was a fun suggestion. "Do you promise?"

He stilled by the door and searched my face, probably to see if I was serious. "I promise," he said after a beat. "If we ever get snowed in — and that's a definite possibility because we live on the East Coast — I will play board games with you all night."

"Do I get to pick the games?"

"This feels as if you're trapping me. Are you into freaky board games?"

"No. Clue is my favorite."

"Then we'll play Clue."

"I even have Golden Girls Clue. I had to save up two months for it, but I got it."

He furrowed his brow. "You had to save up two months for a board game?"

"It's a collector's edition."

"Geez. I'm definitely talking to Myron about how much you get paid. That is ridiculous."

"Don't get me fired." The thought horrified me. "I'll have to leave if I get fired. I won't have a choice if I don't want to be homeless."

"You're not going to be homeless."

He sounded sure of himself. Me? Not so much. "I've been close to homeless." It was hard to admit. "I lived in my car for a month when I was waiting to hear about this job."

Jack looked pained. "How is that possible?"

"I didn't have any money."

"I know that, but ... ." Frustration wafted over his features. "I forget that you've been on your own for the better part of your life. It's what makes you so strong, and I happen to be a big fan of your strength ... even if it makes you reckless. You're not alone now, Charlie. I want to help you."

He was sincere, which caused my heart to ping. "I don't want to be your charity case. That puts me in a position of weakness."

"Is that what you're worried about? I don't see you as weak. I never will."

"Maybe 'weak' isn't the right word," I acknowledged. "Vulnerable might be more apt."

"It's okay to be vulnerable."

"You're not vulnerable."

"I am where you're concerned." He didn't look ashamed to admit it as he rubbed his hands up and down my arms. "I don't want you going without. It bothers me."

"I'm used to going without. In fact, you're the biggest indulgence of my life ... and you're free."

He shook his head. "That was a really weird thing to say, yet it makes me smile." He leaned forward and pressed his forehead to mine. "I'm buying dinner. I'm also paying for a tour. I might even pay for a few rounds of drinks ... or something at one of those little kiosks I keep seeing on the corners. I haven't decided yet. You're going to allow me without complaint."

"I don't remember agreeing to that."

"It's what I need tonight."

He was earnest, which meant I couldn't argue with him ... at least about this. "Fine. You can buy dinner and the tour."

"And whatever else I want."

"And whatever else you want ... within reason."

"I'm forgetting you added that last part."

"I'm not."

I DECIDED TO TRY CRAWFISH for dinner. I had no idea what made me land on that decision — perhaps it was all the movie scenes I'd marveled at over the years — but when the big tray of crawdads slid onto the table I was officially in awe.

"Oh, wow!"

Jack's smirk was obvious when he reached for the pile of napkins the waitress left behind. "These shouldn't be unbearably spicy."

"No. Definitely not." I frowned at one of the dead crustaceans on the platter. "It's staring at me."

He chuckled. "He's dead. He won't feel a thing. I promise." Jack deftly grabbed one of the creatures, pinched near its neck, and ripped the body from the head before popping the meat into his mouth. "They're good."

I was a little grossed out. "Why can't they take the heads off for us? Then it would be just like eating shrimp."

"Actually, that's only an American thing."

"What's only an American thing?" I delicately picked up one of the crawfish and woefully stared at it. "I'm sorry, little bug."

Jack made an odd sound in his throat and snagged the crawfish from my hand. He moved it to his plate and used his knife to cut off the head and remove the shell before spearing the meat with his fork and shoving it in my face. "Eat."

I stared at it, uncertain. "Um ... ."

"Eat," he repeated.

I was the one who'd insisted on crawfish, so I had no choice. I tentatively bit into the meat and started chewing. Surprisingly, it was good. That didn't mean I wanted to behead twenty of the little buggers myself. "I don't suppose you would consider doing that for all of them?"

He didn't look happy at the prospect but he didn't protest. Instead, he simply grabbed three of them and began dissecting. "If you ever go to Europe — which I recommend — they have prawns. It's basically the same as shrimp over here, only bigger. They're all served with their eyes attached."

That sounded disgusting. "Why?"

He shrugged. "That's simply the way it's done."

"I've never been out of the country," I admitted, grinning when Jack slid the headless crawfish in my direction. "Thank you."

"Have some potatoes and corn, too." He pointed toward the vegetables included with the seafood boil. "If you want, I can ask them to add headless shrimp and scallops to the mix if you don't like the crawfish."

"I like the crawfish," I said hurriedly. "I just don't like decapitating them."

"Every meal is an adventure with you," he teased, sipping his sweet tea. It was apparently the only type of iced tea at this establishment. I was a menace when hopped up on sugar, so I figured going with water was a safer bet.

"I never got to try exotic things when I was growing up," I agreed. "This is definitely an adventure."

"I don't consider mudbugs exotic."

"I would prefer you not refer to them as bugs. It grosses me out."

"Fair enough." He leaned back in his chair and regarded me. "If you could go anywhere in the world, where would you go?"

The question caught me off guard. "I don't know. I've never really thought about it."

"I don't believe that. You grew up in a small town. You must've wanted to visit someplace."

"Hogwarts. I fancied myself Harry Potter and thought there was a bigger and better world out there for me. I mean … I knew I was adopted. Once I lost my parents, I started thinking about my birth parents and wondered if they were out there looking for me. I was sure of that."

He frowned. "I'm sorry no one ever came for you."

I internally cursed myself. This wasn't the conversation we should be having on a date. He was well aware that my birth parents disappeared when I was a child, that I essentially had no memory of them, and grew up with wonderful adoptive parents who treated me as if I was their own child. As I grew older, I began to wonder if I was initially abandoned because of the magic.

"It doesn't matter." I meant it. "I'm exactly where I want to be. I know you're upset about the money and everything, but this is the most I've ever made."

"I'm talking to Myron about your salary." He was firm. "If you won't let me help you, then I'm going to make sure that you can help yourself. Myron thinks he can get away with paying you minimum wage because you're fresh out of school. That's not fair."

"It's pretty much what I expected."

"That doesn't mean it's fair." He beheaded three more crawfish and tipped the remains onto my plate. "Eat. You need your strength."

"Okay." I was happy to change the subject. "Tell me about your meeting with your buddy Leon. Did he give you any good information?"

"No, but he's going to start digging. He's heard the stories about the zombies and thought they were exaggerated. Like me, he believes there's a reasonable explanation for what's going on. Zombies aren't a reasonable explanation, in case you're wondering."

I snickered at his serious expression and reached for an ear of corn. "Well, either way, I'm glad we have more help. Our meeting with the voodoo queen wasn't quite as fruitful."

"I was going to ask about that. What did she say?"

"Just that she saw one of the zombies herself and the city is going to fall. You know, the normal doom and gloom stuff."

"Yeah, but ... do you believe her?"

I thought about the way Madame Brenna looked at me. She seemed to recognize there was something different about me and wasn't afraid to comment on it. Of course, it all could've been an act. I simply didn't have enough information to make a judgment.

"I don't know," I said finally. That was the truth. "She was weird. She thought we were there to accuse her of sleeping with someone's husband until Millie explained who we were."

"That's interesting, although I can't help but wonder if Myron had something going with her. She probably jumped to that conclusion for a reason."

"Yeah."

He tapped the side of my plate. "If you eat three more bugs and some potatoes I'll buy you a huge dessert. Whatever you want."

I brightened considerably. "That means I'll be on a sugar high for the tour. You might not like that."

"I'll be fine."

"What tour are we going on?"

"Murder and voodoo. That's what the brochure said anyway. I thought it would be right up your alley."

He wasn't wrong. It sounded like an awesome way to spend the evening.

"I DON'T UNDERSTAND," I SAID two hours later as Jack drank a rum and coke from a plastic cup and we followed our tour group along the sidewalk. "How can you have that on the street?"

He chuckled at my puritan response. "It's New Orleans. There are different rules for living in this city."

"It's kind of freaky."

"Not really."

"No, it's definitely freaky."

He tipped the glass in my direction. "Take a drink."

"I'm good."

"No, seriously. You need to take a drink and chill out. You're a bundle of nerves."

The fact that he'd noticed set my teeth on edge. I was trying to play it cool, but I'd felt … something … following us since we left the restaurant. We went to a place called the Voodoo Lounge to meet with our tour group, and I swore I felt someone watching me the entire time. Even now, in the middle of the city and surrounded by crowds, I couldn't get over the fact that it felt as if something was closing in on me. I knew it on an instinctive level … and yet there was nothing I could do about it.

"Fine." I took a sip and made a face. "That's really strong."

"Why do you think I've been nursing it since we left the bar?" He moved the drink to his other hand and slipped his arm around my waist. "Are you having fun, other than the drink?"

"Yes." It wasn't a lie. Even though I'd been uneasy at the idea of being followed, I couldn't stop smiling. I love history.

"Where do you think we're going next?"

I already knew the answer. "LaLaurie Mansion."

"What's that?"

"It's a house that was owned by a serial killer."

"You'll have to be more specific."

"Do you want the short or long version?"

"Short … but I want you to know that it's a little weird that you know both versions."

I chuckled. "Madame LaLaurie was married three times. Her third husband was wealthy, and they built that house." I inclined my chin toward the huge structure rising into the sky in front of us. "They had attached slave quarters, and there are stories about how she treated her slaves."

"Meaning she did horrible things to them." Jack wrinkled his nose. "I'm not sure I want to hear this."

"There are mixed stories," I offered. "In some, she kept her cook chained to the stove and whipped her daughters if they tried to feed the slaves. In others, she actually freed a few slaves. Another story says that she experimented on slaves in the uppermost room of her house."

"Which story do you believe?"

That was a good question. "I'm guessing there has to be some truth in the torture stories. They had to originate from something."

"Well, I don't want to go inside and see the torture room." He was adamant. "We can wait on the street."

"It's a private residence now anyway. We can't go inside. In fact ... ." I felt it again. Someone was watching me. When I turned, I found a man standing in the middle of the road. I didn't recognize him. And yet, despite that, I couldn't help thinking he was there for me.

He appeared to be older, although guessing an age was difficult, and wore ragged clothing. He almost looked homeless. I knew what it was like to struggle financially, and I wanted to help him. "He shouldn't be in the middle of the road like that," I volunteered, taking a step into the street. "In fact ... ." I trailed off, uncertain.

Something was very wrong. Like ... even worse than normal.

"He's going to get hit," Jack muttered, shifting away from me and toward the road. "I wonder if he's drunk. I'm going to ... ." He never finished what he was going to say. At that exact moment, a car barreled around the corner and smacked directly into him, knocking him backward. The driver never slowed, let alone stopped.

"Oh, no!" I covered my eyes to block the horror.

Jack stepped off the curb and into the road, the color draining from his face. "Stay here, Charlie," he ordered when he found his voice.

I wanted to argue with him but I was too busy fighting the urge to retch. "Jack ... ." He was gone. I felt his absence before I turned. When I reluctantly shifted my eyes to the road, to where the man had fallen, I found Jack on his knees trying to help. I also found traffic continuing to blow past him.

"Why won't they stop?" I stormed onto the road, my temper getting the better of me. The first car that neared the scene and made as if it was going to keep going around Jack and the fallen man fell victim to a set of unfortunate circumstances. The front tire blew, causing the car to swerve into the curb and roll to a standstill. It just so happened to occur in such a fashion that no vehicles could eke around it.

Jack arched an eyebrow as I rushed to his side. "That was ... weird."

I caused the blowout, so I couldn't exactly argue. "It's karma." Revulsion ripped through me as I caught my first full glimpse of the man on the ground. He was still, his right arm bent at a ridiculous angle, and his eyes were open and sightless as he stared at the night sky. "Oh, no!"

"Yeah." Jack reached over and grabbed my hand. "He's dead. I don't think he even felt it. It happened too fast."

That was a nice possibility, but I wasn't sure I believed it. "We need to call the police. I'll do it. I ... ." I stilled when reaching into my pocket for my phone, my eyes trained on the dead man.

"What's wrong?" Jack was sympathetic as he patted my back. "It's okay. I'll make the call. You don't have to be out here."

That's not what gave me pause. "Jack ... ." It happened again. One of the man's legs moved. It was only a few inches, but it was movement all the same.

"What?" He was looking at me and not the body.

Out of instinct, I grabbed the arm hanging at Jack's side at the same moment the man's head moved in that direction and he bared his teeth. I had no idea if he was trying to bite Jack — that was my guess, though — but I jerked Jack's well-muscled arm away before it could happen.

Jack's eyes went wide when he realized the man was moving. "Is he ... ?"

"Come here." I refused to let go of Jack's arm and dragged him further away from the hissing and spitting man. "I'm calling for help. Just ... don't let him bite you."

Jack made a face. "He's not a zombie."

As if on cue, the man started growling again.

"Are you sure of that?" I challenged.

He let loose a sigh. "Get help out here right now. I don't even know how to explain this."

That made two of us.

EIGHT

*I*t didn't take long for a team of paramedics to arrive. I decided I was going to warn the emergency responders ... even if it made me look like an idiot.

"He's foaming at the mouth and trying to bite people," I offered as they hurried in our direction. "Also ... I'm pretty sure he was dead and came back to life."

The team consisted of a man and a woman. It was the man, the nametag on his coat read "Randy," who shot me a withering look. "Oh, geez. Is this another zombie story? I wish this rumor would just die. I can't tell you how sick I am of hearing it."

"She's not making it up," Jack countered, moving to my side. "The guy was dead. We both saw it."

"Well, he's obviously not dead now." Randy shoved Jack to the side so he could make a path. "Please don't make this more difficult than it already is."

"Then don't say we didn't warn you if something bad happens," Jack shot back.

"You have my word. If I turn into a zombie, I promise not to blame you."

Jack's annoyance was obvious, but he managed to hold it together.

"We've done our due diligence on this and will have no sympathy if you're bitten."

"Yeah, yeah, yeah." Randy knelt next to the frothing man. "Hello, sir. It looks like you've had one heckuva night." He pasted a ridiculous smile on his face. It would've been out of place even if we weren't dealing with a zombie. "Can you tell me where it hurts?"

The injured man's only response was a series of grunts and growls as he tried to latch onto the hand that moved to his forehead.

"He's altered," Randy said to his partner, a woman who looked to be in her thirties. Her nametag read "Jessica," and she seemed more wary than her partner.

"Oh, you think?" Jessica's dark eyebrows hopped up her forehead. "He's trying to eat you."

"Don't you start," Randy warned. "I don't want to hear another word about this zombie nonsense."

Jessica didn't continue protesting, but she did shift her eyes to us as she moved to the man's weak side and began running her hands over his arm "Did you guys see what happened?"

Jack nodded. "Yeah. We were on a tour, just getting to the LaLaurie Mansion. Charlie was explaining about the history of the house when we turned and saw the guy in the street. He was just standing there, not moving."

Jessica furrowed her brow. "Did he say anything?"

"No."

"Did he look as if he was in distress? Maybe he was grabbing his left arm or holding his head."

"No." Jack drew me closer to him, as if he wanted to make sure we were sharing warmth. "He was just standing there."

"Was he watching your girlfriend?" Randy inclined his head toward me. "I mean ... she's a pretty girl. Maybe he was drunk and thought he had a chance or something. He might not have realized she was with you."

"That's not how he was acting." Jack searched for the right words. "I'm not sure how to describe the way it went down. He just stared, but it wasn't as if he was seeing anything."

"Kind of like he was a zombie," I added.

Randy shot me a look. "Don't go there. You have no idea how many zombie stories I've heard the past few days. It's ridiculous."

Jack slid me a sidelong look and smiled. "I don't want to encourage her, but it was a little weird. He was very clearly dead on the pavement after the car hit him."

"Speaking of that, did you get a plate?" A police officer appeared on the curb and started moving toward us. I hadn't even seen him arrive. "A few of the witnesses over there described it as a blue car and said it didn't slow down."

"It was a blue Ford Focus," Jack confirmed. "I definitely saw that."

"What happened to that car?" The officer asked, gesturing toward the vehicle with the blown-out tire.

"I have no idea," Jack replied. "Traffic wasn't slowing down when we came out to help, and somehow that car ended up with a flat and blocked traffic. It's probably not convenient for the drivers, but it was much safer for us."

"I would say you got lucky there," the officer agreed. "I'm Officer Pete Pasquale. I heard the call come in. Are you the one who called it in, ma'am?"

His question was aimed at me so I nodded. "Yeah. He was dead, though. I'm telling you. We're not imagining it."

"Well, he obviously didn't come back to life," Pasquale prodded. "That means he wasn't dead."

"No." I was firm as I shook my head. "You can tell when someone is dead. He wasn't moving ... and his eyes were open and he wasn't blinking. He was dead."

"Ma'am, he's breathing." Pasquale gestured toward the man who was still snapping his teeth at Randy. For his part, the paramedic seemed to be an expert at avoiding a potentially dangerous bite because his hands were deft as he worked to triage the man's injuries. "He's clearly not dead."

"But ... he was."

"I think you're imagining things."

69

Jack cleared his throat. "She's not imagining things. I was with her and saw the same thing."

"Are you perhaps drunk?"

"No. I had one rum and coke and I didn't come close to finishing it. I'm not drunk."

"I was simply asking because ... well ... this is New Orleans. The question wasn't meant as an insult."

"And yet it felt like an insult," I muttered under my breath.

Jack tightened his grip on me. "I'm not a hysteric. I saw what I saw. He was dead. And I know you're not inclined to believe this because of the nature of this situation, but I'm the last person who would be predisposed to believe in zombies."

"That's true," I confirmed. "He tells me I'm crazy for believing in stuff like that all the time. I mean ... just ask him about the Megalodon incident."

Pasquale made a face. "I'm sorry ... what?"

"Ignore her." The look Jack shot me was full of admonishment. He clearly wanted me to be quiet. I could manage that – maybe just barely, but I could – and I wisely zipped my lips. "I'm not saying he's a zombie. I'm just saying ... maybe test his blood for pufferfish poison."

"That's a very specific suggestion," Pasquale noted. "Do you have any reason to believe that he was poisoned?"

"No, but a scientist I know explained earlier today about pufferfish poison and how it mimics signs of death, and now I can't get it out of my mind."

"It's not as weird as it sounds," I interjected when Pasquale made an incredulous face. "We were talking about the zombie stories that people are spreading and she told us about the pufferfish poison. He's not saying this guy was really poisoned with pufferfish toxin."

"Uh-huh." Pasquale didn't look convinced.

"He's really not," I reassured him. "It's just ... I swear that he was dead." I adopted what I'd been told was my most trustworthy smile. People tended to believe me regardless, probably because of my age, but I was desperate to find an opening for us to leave. I was uncomfortable being out in the open like this, especially with a potential zombie snapping away at our feet. "We're not telling you how to do your job, but it's probably best that you not let him bite you."

"I think we can manage that, ma'am." Pasquale forced a smile that didn't make it all the way to his eyes and then pointed toward the curb. "I'm going to need to take a formal statement. You'll have to wait about ten minutes or so while I organize efforts here. If you could just step over there, I promise to be with you as soon as possible."

"Sure." Jack kept me close to his side as he headed toward the curb. "We'll be right over here."

I waited until it was just the two of us to ask the obvious question. "Do you believe in zombies now?"

"I still don't believe in zombies." He was firm. "It is a weird situation, though."

"He was dead. You and I both know it. We saw it. You're not even remotely an alarmist and you saw it."

"I ... don't know." He was conflicted as he pulled me against him. "It was definitely weird."

"Zombies are always weird."

Jack shook his head. "I can't get to zombies, Charlie. Don't push it."

"Fine." I slipped my arms around his neck and offered a hug, which he gladly took. My eyes drifted to the LaLaurie Mansion. Our tour group was gone, disappeared into the night. Only one or two people remained behind to answer questions. I found that telling. "Do you know what happened to Madame LaLaurie?"

"No." His voice was a whisper close to my ear. "What?"

"When rumors started circulating about what she'd done to her slaves, a mob attacked the house."

"I'm pretty sure that was deserved."

"Oh, without a doubt. But she escaped. The mob set a fire and she ran. She managed to get out of the country and fled to Paris."

"That doesn't sound like much of a punishment. Of course, this was the 1800s. It's not as if police had computers to track people down back then."

"Yeah."

"How did she die?"

"There are two stories. The first is that she died in a boar-hunting accident in France."

"That sounds like karma."

"The other says that a sexton of St. Louis Cemetery No. 1 found a copper plate in the cemetery with her name on it. This was in the 1930s, I believe, so it would've been years after she supposedly died."

"Meaning ... what?"

"Meaning that no one knows how she died. All they know is that she got away with torturing her slaves. Her persona has grown larger than life in the years since and it doesn't matter that the copper plate had her dying seven years before officials in Paris registered her death. She's still infamous."

"That's kind of a depressing story, Charlie."

"I don't deny that. Her house is still standing. It's a testament to horror."

"And you say people live in it now?"

"They do. They won't allow tourists inside."

"Do you blame them?"

"Not even a little. The house was restored in the late 1800s, long after Madame LaLaurie died. It's been used as a high school ... and a music conservatory ... a bar ... and a furniture store ... and even an apartment building. None lasted because the history of the house made people believe it was evil."

Jack pulled back so he could stare into my eyes. "Do you believe a house can be evil?"

"I don't know. I believe people can be born evil. I also believe people can be made evil. Maybe if someone really evil owns a house it's forever tainted because the memory simply can't be washed away."

"This sounds like a nature vs. nurture argument."

"You don't believe that people are born to be something?"

"No." He was firm. "I believe people make themselves. I mean ... look at you. You spent most of your childhood wondering about your birth family. You said you always knew you were adopted, and while you loved your adoptive parents, there was still a hole where your birth parents should've been. You didn't see a lot of happiness. You could be terrible to deal with because of that, bitter and mean. You're not. You're warm and open. Laura is bitter and mean, and she grew up with everything handed to her. That's proof right there that we make ourselves."

"That's a good point and I mostly believe it. I also believe some people are sociopaths and they're born that way. They simply have something disconnected in their brains."

"Okay, I can get behind that. I'm not sure what it has to do with what happened tonight."

"Maybe nothing. The thing is ... if someone is controlling these people, or stealing bodies, we're dealing with an evil individual. We need to figure out exactly what sort of person we're dealing with."

"I agree." He gave me a soft kiss. "You're good, though. Don't ever doubt that."

"I wasn't doubting it."

"Sometimes I think you do. I don't want you worrying about things like that. Bad people don't care what others think about them. You're not a bad person."

"Even though I believe in zombies?"

"Ugh." He sounded exasperated as he rubbed his cheek against mine. "I just knew you were going to take it back to zombies. I can't get behind that idea, Charlie. I mean ... zombies are ludicrous."

"They are. But it's a story that endures, like Madame LaLaurie. Somewhere in there, you have to wonder if there's a bit of truth."

"I guess."

"Does that mean you agree with me?"

"That means I'm too tired to debate. We'll revisit this conversation in the morning when I've had some sleep and the trauma of watching a man get hit by a car is a few hours behind us."

"Fair enough."

IT WAS AFTER MIDNIGHT WHEN we returned to the hotel. People were still reveling on the street, but I could barely keep my head up as Jack and I wandered down the hallway that led to our rooms.

"Are you going to be able to sleep?" he asked as he paused outside my room. "I mean ... you're not going to have nightmares, are you? I can sleep with you if that's the case."

My cheeks burned at the suggestion. "Oh, well ... ."

"Not that way," he added hurriedly once he realized what he said. "I wasn't suggesting we do ... that."

For some reason his embarrassment made me feel better. "Well, we wouldn't want that," I teased, amused. "Never that."

"You know what I mean." He wagged a finger. "I definitely don't think this is the time for that discussion."

He wasn't the only one. "No. I can only deal with so much, and I'm at my limit."

"Yeah." He gently slipped a strand of hair behind my ear. "Do you want me to sleep in there with you? I promise it will just be sleeping."

"Oh, well ... ." I was caught off guard by the offer. "Do you want to sleep in here? I mean ... I'm okay with it. Do you not want to be alone?"

He chuckled. "Not particularly, but I think this conversation is proof that we shouldn't have this particular chat when we're both so tired. I'm right across the hallway. If you need me, don't hesitate to call out. Until then ... let's table this discussion."

That was a relief. "Okay. I ... okay."

He leaned forward and brushed his lips against mine. "Go to bed. We'll have more information tomorrow morning. I'll make sure to call the hospital first thing to catch up on the status of our dead guy who turned out not to be dead."

"That sounds like a plan."

"Lock your door and make sure the balcony door is locked, too." He was adamant. "You're on the third floor, but I don't want you taking any chances."

"I'll be a good girl."

He gave me another kiss. "That would be a nice change of pace."

I DIDN'T THINK I WOULD sleep. In fact, I was certain I wouldn't.

Surprisingly, I was out before my head hit the pillow. I slept long and hard, which is why I was groggy when I opened my eyes three hours later and stared at the ceiling.

There was nothing there. No one was in the room. I figured that out when I struggled to a sitting position and glanced around. Still, something woke me.

"Jack?" I called out his name, briefly wondering if he'd used the extra keycard I gave him to check on me. He wasn't here. I would've felt him. Still, it was better to think of him breaking in than someone else.

Then I heard it, a scratching noise near the door that led to the hallway. I frowned as I snapped my head toward the door, confused. Someone scratched again, and that's when I realized the door handle was turning.

Someone was trying to get in.

As if in slow motion, I tossed off the covers and climbed out of bed. I felt as if I was mired in quicksand as I padded toward the hallway. I stilled on the other side of the door, jolting when the handle moved again. Someone was definitely trying to get in.

I pressed my ear to the door and listened. "Jack?"

I knew in my heart it wasn't Jack. He would never try to gain entrance to my room this way. Speaking made me feel better, so I called out to him again. When there was no answer, I sucked in a breath and pressed my trembling hands against the door.

"Who is it?" I reached out with my magic, brushing up against a physical body but finding an emotional void. It was almost as if a shell of a human being was outside rather than a real person. "What the ... ?" I had no way to explain what I was sensing.

I drew another deep breath and turned the handle, preparing for what I was certain would be a horrific sight. To my utter surprise, the entity waiting for me wasn't a monster from another realm or some grotesque creature that had climbed out of a cemetery to haunt me. It was the man who was struck on Royal Street in front of the LaLaurie Mansion.

"Holy ... !" I jolted back when the man jerked in my direction.

There was only one thing I could do, so I did it. I called on my magic and drew the painting from the opposite wall toward the man as he blindly grabbed for me. It hit him in the head with a loud thud, knocking him to his knees.

Then, because I didn't know what else to do, I hit him again, releasing the painting only when I heard Jack fumbling with his door across the hall.

His eyes were bleary, confusion etched across his handsome face when he met my gaze. "What's going on?"

I was shaking as I pointed to the body on the floor. "Now do you believe in zombies?"

He was clearly dumbfounded when he realized what was happening. "Son of a ... !"

NINE

*J*ack stood frozen for a long moment and then he rushed
to me.

"Are you okay?"

I couldn't tear my eyes from the man on the floor. He wasn't
moving. He'd played possum at least once that we knew of, so I didn't
trust him not to start moving again.

"Charlie, are you okay?" Jack shook me by the arms. It was only
then that I realized he was dressed in nothing but pickle print boxer
shorts, his chiseled chest completely bare of hair.

"Do you wax?" It was a stupid question, but it was all I could think
to ask.

"What?" he gave me a long look. "Are you okay? You haven't been
bitten, have you?"

That shook me out of my reverie. "Aha!" I jabbed a finger at him.
"You think it's zombies, too. Admit it."

He captured my finger and gave it a squeeze. "I'll admit nothing of
the sort. I'm simply covering my bases. You haven't been bitten,
right?"

I shook my head. "No. I'm fine."

"Good." He pulled me in for a hug and kissed my forehead,

frowning when a door down the hallway opened and Laura poked her head out.

"Ugh." She made a disgusted face. "I don't even want to know what you two perverts are doing. I get it. You're happy and blah, blah, blah." She wore a skimpy negligee and planted her hands on her hips in such a manner that her cleavage was on display ... even from four doors away. "Do you have to rub it in?"

"Go back to bed," Jack ordered. "This doesn't concern you."

"You're darned right. I don't roll that way. I don't care if Charlie does ... although that would explain why you chose her over me."

It took me a moment to grasp what she was saying. "Oh, gross!"

"Gross is right," Jack agreed. "Go back to bed, Laura. We've got this under control."

That was a bit of an overstatement. As far as I could tell we didn't have anything under control. Instead of pointing that out, I bobbed my head. "We're awesome." I shot her a fake thumbs-up. "We've never been better."

"Apparently he gets off on fuzzy sleep pants with unicorns on them," she groused as she shut her door. "How do you compete with that?"

I glanced down and frowned. "I forgot I packed these."

"The pants are cute." He swept me toward his door as he gave the fallen man a wide berth. "I need to call the police. They deal with ... whatever this is."

"What do you want me to do?"

"Lock yourself in there and be safe."

"I was asking in a broader sense."

"Yeah, well, tough." He pushed my hair from my face and stared into my eyes. I thought he was going to say something profound, maybe even romantic. I thought he might even profess how much he adored me and was thankful I was okay. Instead, he took me by surprise ... as he always did. "He's not a zombie."

"Yeah, you keep telling yourself that."

. . .

I WOKE TO WARMTH AND QUIET. It took me a moment to remember where I was, and when I did I almost slammed my forehead into Jack's jaw in my haste to bolt upright.

"Whoa." I grabbed my head to keep it steady from the rush of blood.

"Go back to sleep," Jack ordered, rolling to his back. "It's not time to get up."

That's when I remembered the previous evening. The cops showed up right away, Pasquale leading the charge. He seemed confused by the turn of events, which only worsened when Thibodeaux arrived. In short order, they declared the man on the floor dead, asked how I managed to remove a painting to clobber him — which I denied — and then packed him up for an autopsy. They claimed the last they heard my attacker was at the hospital and promised to check on his prognosis in the morning. Then, just like that, they disappeared and left us to grapple with the remnants of the evening.

By that time it was almost four and we were both exhausted. Jack locked my room and pointed me toward his bed. I wasn't worried that things were about to turn sexy because we were both too tired to lift our heads, let alone anything else. Instead, we merely crawled under the covers and passed out.

Now, four hours later, I was plagued by questions ... and really weird hunches.

"It's eight," I said, glancing at the clock on the wall. "We're expected downstairs for breakfast in an hour."

"Okay." He moved his hands to my waist and tugged me toward him. "We'll get up in an hour."

He was warm, his face serene as he tried to convince me to settle in next to him. Part of me wanted to surrender. The other part couldn't contain my worry.

"We have to tell Chris about the zombie."

"Why?" He made fake crying sounds as he tried to push the pillow over my face, which made me laugh. "Do you have any idea how obnoxious he's going to be when we tell him what happened last night?"

I had a few ideas. "Yeah. He's going to be really mad we didn't wake him to see the zombie."

"Stop calling him a zombie." He flicked my ear. "You'll make things worse if you call him that."

"You can't stop me from using that word. I mean ... a guy who already died once yesterday somehow found my hotel room even though he should have no idea how to do that because he was nowhere near the police officer when I revealed that information, and then he died a second time. If I can't call him a zombie, then this is the worst job ever."

He tickled me until I gasped. "Promise me you won't call him a zombie."

"No."

"Promise me."

"No."

He dug harder. "Promise me, Charlie."

"No!" I was firm. "I'm not giving in on this one. He's totally a zombie."

Jack let loose a long sigh. "I'll never be able to live this down, will I?"

"Not even a little," I agreed, enjoying myself far too much. "We should get up and shower. I'm starving. I'm going to need food for when you tell Chris that he missed the zombie."

"You're a horrible girl." He dragged a hand through his shoulder-length hair and cast me a sidelong look. "Are you showering in here or your room?"

The question was simple, and yet I had no idea how to answer. "Oh, well ... ."

He grinned at my discomfort. "Here's the deal: Every time you say the word 'zombie,' I'm going to start questioning you about things in our relationship that you're not ready to discuss. How does that sound?"

Honestly, it sounded painful. That didn't mean I was willing to back down. "Do whatever you want. I'm not going to give in on the zombie thing. I've earned the right to say whatever I want."

"Fine. Then I've earned the right to tease you about our sleeping arrangements."

I didn't like that one bit. "Do you have to? It feels weird given everything that's going on. Why can't you just be a gentleman?"

He stared at me for a long beat and then shook his head. "I can't even torture you when you're polite enough to ask in that way. It sucks."

"Does that mean we can get ready for breakfast? I'm not joking about being hungry."

"Yes, we can get ready for breakfast." He was utterly defeated as I moved to climb out of bed.

I stopped myself before I moved too far away, and pressed a quick kiss to the corner of his mouth. "Thanks. By the way, they don't have anything weird I need to know about for breakfast, right? I'm safe ordering eggs and hash browns?"

"Yes. Just stay away from grits. You won't like them."

"Good tip."

"Stay away from the hot sauce they bring, too. You won't like that on your eggs."

His response made me laugh. "You know what's funny? A few months ago we didn't even know each other and now you know what I like to eat ... and more importantly, what I won't like, even better than me. Life is kind of miraculous sometimes."

He rubbed his forehead and shook his head. "There are times I think you're the most earnest person I've ever met."

"Is that bad?"

"No, Charlie, it's not. Don't ever change for anyone."

"Oh, that's kind of sweet." I moved toward the door. "If you hurry and get ready we can split breakfasts like we do when we're home and one of us can get pancakes and the other can get eggs and hash browns."

"Just get ready." He was clearly overthinking what he considered my cuteness. "I'll pick you up before we head down. I would rather tell Chris the zombie story together, if you don't mind."

"Is that because you're worried I'll get him riled up?"

"Oh, I know you'll get him riled up. I want to make sure I'm there when the conversation goes down. Just ... hurry up. Now that you've brought up breakfast it's all I can think about."

"Aye, aye, Captain." I kicked my heels together and offered him a saucy salute.

"I think you're going to be the death of me one of these days."

"And I think you're more dramatic than me. Buck up, camper. We're going to have a busy day hunting zombies."

"Yup. Definitely the death of me."

EVERYONE WAS ALREADY GROUPED AROUND the table in the dining room. Unfortunately, we had a visitor. It was Thibodeaux, and he was sitting next to Chris, clearly mired in a deep conversation as everyone else nursed coffee and tea, and considered menus.

"There they are." Millie beamed at me as I took the chair across from her. "We wondered if you guys were going to make it down after your busy night."

"You heard about that, huh?" I slid my gaze to Jack and found him frowning at Chris and Thibodeaux. "What exactly have you heard?"

"Well, according to Detective Thibodeaux, a dead man knocked on your door last night and asked for a bit of romance," Millie replied. "According to Laura, you two were practically naked in the hallway with the dead man, and she's convinced you were doing something wicked."

My mouth dropped open as Jack shifted in his chair. "What?"

"First, we were not naked," Jack snapped. "We were in our pajamas. And we didn't even come from the same rooms when she saw us. We met in the hallway because of the dead guy. Second, he wasn't dead when he knocked on Charlie's door. In fact, he didn't knock. He tried to force his way in. It was a traumatic event for her."

"I wasn't really traumatized," I corrected, smiling gratefully at the waitress as she delivered a fresh cup of coffee. "Oh, this smells great. I'm excited. I need the caffeine."

"I bet you do," Millie teased.

"Stop that." Jack shot her a warning look. "This is not the time for your nonsense. We have other things to discuss. For example ... what are they talking about?" He inclined his chin toward the distracted detective and our boss. "Apparently we should've gotten down here earlier if we wanted the scoop."

"I believe I told you that," I offered.

He shot me a look. "Order your blueberry pancakes and sausage."

"I was actually thinking of French toast today."

"Oh, shaking it up. Nice." Even though I could tell he was agitated, he smiled ... and then narrowed his eyes when Thibodeaux shifted in his chair and finally turned his full attention on us. "Oh, great. Good morning, detective. How are you this fine day?"

I recognized the sarcasm and knew Jack was walking a fine line. That was the only reason I opted to keep my mouth shut.

"Mr. Hanson." Thibodeaux let loose a smile that was more grimace than grin. "I hear you had an adventure last night. I was on the scene, but I didn't get a chance to talk to you for very long."

"What I want to know is why I'm only hearing about it now," Chris complained. "Don't you think I should've been made aware of what was happening with my own people?"

"I planned to tell you this morning." Jack was calm as he dumped cream in his coffee. "It was late when we got back last night. It was after midnight. I figured everyone was already sleeping, which is exactly what we wanted to do because we'd had a long day. I had no way of knowing that our friend would escape from the hospital and follow us. In fact, I'm kind of curious how he managed it."

"That makes two of us," Thibodeaux supplied. "We're not sure how he ended up here either."

"I'm assuming he somehow heard the responding officers talking at the scene. We told the officer we were talking to — I believe his name was Pasquale — where we were staying when he questioned us. That guy wasn't close when we did so we figure Pasquale told one of the other officers."

"I guess that's possible, but that doesn't change our real problem," Thibodeaux noted.

"And what's our real problem?" I asked.

"The fact that the gentleman in question was declared dead at the hospital about twenty minutes after he was transported from the scene. He didn't get up and wander away from the hospital. He was locked in a meat locker at the coroner's office."

I was officially flabbergasted. "What?"

"You heard me." Thibodeaux's tone turned accusatory. "What do you have to say about that?"

"Wait a second ... you're not blaming her for this, are you?" Jack's eyes flashed with anger as he stared down the detective. "She didn't do anything, so if you're trying to blame her for this you can just walk yourself right back through that door."

"Calm down," Chris ordered, shooting Jack a curious but cautionary look. "I don't think Detective Thibodeaux is blaming Charlie."

"Not Charlie alone, certainly," Thibodeaux agreed. "I am, however, curious about how you arranged for this to happen. I'm asking you that question, Mr. Biggs, not Ms. Rhodes. I don't think she has the capability to set this up on her own. She needed help."

"Help for what?" I was still confused. "What did I set up?"

"This hoax."

"Hoax?" I looked at Jack to see if I was misreading the conversation, but the fury on his face told me the exact opposite.

"Don't accuse her of something like that." Jack's tone was icy as he gripped his coffee mug. "She was the victim last night. She woke up to someone trying to get into her room."

"And yet you and Ms. Rhodes are the only ones who saw this man actually on his feet," Thibodeaux countered. "I asked the night doorman. He didn't see anyone fitting the description of our dead man – who still hasn't been identified, mind you – entering the premises. I find the fact that members of your group are the only ones who saw him rather suspect."

Chris pinned Laura with a look. "You saw him, right? I know you're part of our group and that doesn't do much to shake his argument, but you saw him."

Laura was clearly uncomfortable with the question. "He was on the ground. I wasn't really paying attention. I was more interested in the fact that Jack was practically naked and Charlie was wearing fuzzy unicorn pants."

"I was not naked," Jack snapped. "And Charlie's pants were fine."

"Right." Laura rolled her eyes. "I wasn't paying attention to the guy on the floor, but I'm pretty sure I didn't see him moving."

"See." Thibodeaux threw his hands in the air, as if Laura had just proved his point.

"That doesn't matter." Chris refused to back down. "Jack and Charlie saw him. That's enough for me."

"Technically, Jack didn't see him," I interjected, realizing too late that I should've kept my mouth shut.

"What do you mean?" Chris's face was blank.

"I had already knocked him down by the time Jack got to the hallway," I replied, my heart sinking at the look on my boss's face. "He only came out because he heard the noise from the painting falling. I grabbed it and hit the guy over the head with it after it fell the first time, but Jack wasn't around for any of that."

"It's even worse than I thought." Thibodeaux made a clucking sound with his tongue. "She did orchestrate this on her own."

"She did not." Jack found his voice. "She was minding her own business when someone tried to get into her room. She didn't somehow manage to sneak out of the hotel, break into the morgue, drag a body back here and then set up a fake attack. That's more ludicrous than believing in zombies."

Thibodeaux's expression darkened. "Obviously she didn't do it on her own. Someone had to help. I'm guessing it was someone in your group. The two of you are always joined at the hip, so I'm leaning toward you."

"I'm pretty sure they're joined at other places," Laura muttered.

Millie didn't say anything, but the way she moved her arm — and the small yelp Laura let loose — told me she was probably pinching Laura by way of punishment.

"We didn't fake this," Chris said, folding his arms over his chest.

"That's not what we do. The Legacy Foundation is about finding scientific proof, not lying to create a media firestorm."

"Really? Would the people in St. Pete Beach believe the same thing? Weren't you just there looking for a prehistoric shark?"

"After someone killed an author and tried to make it look like a shark attack," Chris confirmed. "We didn't create that situation. We were called there to investigate. We proved it was a human killer. If we were all about creating news coverage for ourselves, why would we do that?"

"That's right." Jack sounded bitter as he leaned forward and pinned Thibodeaux with a dark look. "Charlie figured out who the killer was there, too. She was in danger at the end. Don't start accusing her of unethical actions. You don't know anything about her."

"Fine. I apologize." Thibodeaux held his hands up in surrender but his gaze was filled with fire. "I think we need to come to agreement, though. You people need to stay out of my investigation. That's the only way we can coexist."

"No." Chris immediately started shaking his head. "That's not how we operate. We're going to keep up our end of the investigation. If you don't like it, well, that's just too bad. We don't work for you. We're going to do exactly what we want. If you don't like that, well, take it up with my uncle. He's the boss."

"I will take it up with him."

"Go for it," Millie suggested. "I think you'll find that Myron isn't as easily bullied as you believe. If he were, we'd still be married."

"Well ... then I guess we're at a standstill." Thibodeaux slowly stood. "I'll be in touch."

"We're looking forward to it," Jack drawled, slapping a menu into my hands before focusing his full attention on me. "So ... pancakes, French toast and hash browns?"

I knew he was trying to lighten the mood and I appreciated it. Still, I could feel Thibodeaux's eyes burning into me and I felt even more awkward than usual. "Sure. Sounds good."

TEN

*C*hris was so annoyed with Jack and me that he suggested we investigate the case on our own. He added a passive-aggressive "since that's what you really want to do anyway because you guys clearly consider yourself the A team," which I found frustrating but knew better than to argue.

For his part, Jack didn't seem bothered by Chris's huffy attitude. He pulled out his phone, held a finger up that indicated I should wait for him to tell me what to do, and then disappeared in the lobby to place his call. Only Millie and Hannah were still at the breakfast table, which was a relief, because I didn't want to deal with Laura's mouth again.

"It sounds like you had quite the adventure last night," Millie noted. She was calm. I could tell she wanted to ask invasive questions — like if I used my magic — but she was smart enough not to do it in front of Hannah. I didn't worry that Hannah would start screaming "witch" and try to run from me. That's not how she was wired. However, she was a scientist. I'd suffered horrible dreams about her trying to lock me in a cage so she could experiment on me multiple times since joining the group. I had no idea if she would actually do that, but I wasn't willing to risk it.

"It wasn't supposed to be an adventure," I argued. "We were supposed to have dinner, eat bugs he had to rip the heads off of before I could stick them in my mouth, and go on a haunted tour. It didn't really end up that way."

"You went on a haunted tour?" Hannah looked interested. "Which one? Chris will need something to get him out of his funk. That's right up his alley."

"Here." I dug in my pocket and came back with a business card. "It was really good."

"Did you learn anything?"

"Yes. I learned when a zombie gets hit by a car to keep walking. Never stop."

Millie snorted as Hannah got to her feet.

"Thank you for this," Hannah offered. "As for Chris, he's disappointed he missed out. He'll be over it in a few hours. Just stick with Jack and everyone will be working together again before you know it."

"I appreciate that." I meant it. "We didn't go out looking for zombies. Trust me. That's not ever going to be on Jack's to-do list."

Hannah cracked a smile. "No, I don't suppose so. Everything will be fine."

Once she was gone and it was just Millie and me, the older woman wasted no time getting to the heart of matters. "What really happened in the hallway?"

"How do you know we're not telling the truth?"

"Because you have one of those faces that tells every truth without saying a word if you know how to read it. When Thibodeaux mentioned the painting falling on the dead guy's head, you had the look. I'm guessing that means you used your ... gift ... to make that happen."

I glanced around to make sure nobody was listening. "He took me by surprise. It was the only thing heavy enough to use as a weapon. I smacked him over the head with it three times and then he fell down."

"What did you tell Jack?"

"I didn't tell him anything. He just assumed we were grappling and somehow the painting fell. I didn't really confirm or deny it."

"Well, that's good." Millie leaned back in her chair, contemplative. "What are you going to do next?"

That was a good question. "Jack doesn't want to hear it, but that guy was acting odd from the start. I think he was already a zombie when he was struck in the road. He was just standing there, staring, and yet not seeing anything.

"The car hit him really hard," I continued. "It was gross. Like ... so gross. And I actually covered my eyes. Jack immediately went to check on him, but it was obvious it was too late. You can tell when someone is dead."

Millie nodded in understanding. "Then he came back?"

"He did. He kept trying to bite people."

"I thought our idea of zombies trying to gnaw on human beings wasn't real." Millie looked perplexed as she rubbed her cheek. "If these things are trying to eat people ... half the city would be infected by now. We've all seen how that works in television and movies."

"We have," I agreed. I thought back to the way the man reacted. "I don't know how to explain it. He wasn't moving across the street in an effort to eat someone when we first saw him. The biting thing only happened after he was hit and on the pavement. Maybe the blow somehow jarred his brain, made him feral."

"That's a lovely thought." Millie pursed her lips and turned her eyes to the open archway where Jack stood, phone pressed to his ear. "He seems okay despite the fact that he wanted to rip Thibodeaux's head off his shoulders. I thought he might be more freaked out because his core assumption about zombies not being real was threatened."

I followed her gaze. "The first thing he asked me when he stepped into the hallway last night was if I'd been bit."

Millie chuckled. "So much for not believing."

"I think it was instinct."

"Charlie, I know you're worried that he's going to fall apart when you tell him the truth, or even walk away, but I'm here to tell you that won't happen. He's Jack. He'll listen and stand by you. That's what he does."

"I hope so, but this is not the time to tell him. It has to wait until this is behind us."

"It definitely has to wait," Millie agreed.

Jack was apparently finished with his call because he lowered his phone and picked his way back to us. He was considerably happier when he slid into the chair next to me. "Are you done feeding your face?"

I shot him a dirty look. "You suggested we get three entrees and split them," I reminded him.

"Yes, that was adorable," Millie intoned, her expression reflecting amusement as she watched us. "I thought Laura's head was going to implode from watching you share food. The fact that Jack actually dunked a slice of toast in an egg yolk before handing it to you, Charlie, was particularly adorable."

I shifted in my seat, uncomfortable. "I didn't even realize you were watching that."

"You guys have obviously been having a lot of meals together. I think it's cute. Hannah and Chris are in the same honeymoon stage, but they're nowhere near as snarky as the two of you so it's a different phenomenon to observe. There are times with Chris and Hannah that I actually think they might turn into spun sugar. You two are far more likely to turn into Sour Patch Kids."

Jack didn't appear bothered by the comparison. "You say the sweetest things, Millie."

"Yeah, well, I should probably get going." She groaned as she used the table as leverage to stand. "It's hell getting old, kids. Enjoy your youth. I'll talk to Chris and calm him down. By the time you see him next he'll be back to normal."

"Tell him Jack was the one who wanted to keep him from the zombie," I suggested, refusing to back down when Jack scorched me with a look. "What? He won't fire you. I need this job."

"He won't fire you either." Jack waved to Millie as she made her escape but kept his eyes focused on me. "How do you feel about visiting another cemetery?"

The question caught me off guard. "I don't know. Which cemetery did you have in mind?"

"St. Louis Cemetery No. 1."

"And why are we going to that cemetery?"

"My friend Leon heard whispers about strange activity at that one last night. I thought we should check it out with him — you did say you wanted to meet him. And that will give Chris time to cool down."

I liked the suggestion. "I definitely want to meet him."

"Good. I think you'll like him."

"Do you think he'll like me?" That was the thing I was most worried about, after all. If he was important to Jack it would be better if he became a fan of mine.

Jack smirked. "I think he'll fall all over you and try to embarrass me, because that's how he is. You'll be fine." He squeezed my hand. "As for Chris ... you know not to take what he said to heart, right? He's just upset."

"You're the third person to tell me that. I still feel bad."

"Well, don't. We'll work everything out."

I hoped that was true. "I'm excited to see your friend," I offered, deftly changing the subject. "Will he have embarrassing stories to tell about your days in the military?"

"Not if he knows what's good for him."

LEON TURNED OUT TO BE THE gregarious sort. He had a booming voice and he made me laugh within minutes of meeting him. He was waiting for us at the gate. He had a woman with him, which confused me until he explained you couldn't enter the cemetery without a guide. The young woman, who had long braids and fierce eyes, looked to be of Haitian descent ... and I didn't just suss that out by looking at her. When we clasped hands in greeting I got a gander at her extracurricular activities, and there was a lot of dancing and ritual chanting involved. It was intriguing.

"This is Cassandra," Leon said by way of introduction. "She can get us into the cemetery to look around."

"I thought all the cemeteries were open to tourists," Jack countered. "I see shows where people are allowed to tour them all the time."

"Yes, but to make sure the companies make money on that — and the tomb desecration is kept to a minimum — guides are now required in some cemeteries. It's simply the way of the world. Cassandra doesn't mind if we look around."

"I really don't," Cassandra said dully. "I care about my payment. I'm going to school and I need the money."

"You'll get your money when we're done with our tour," Leon shot back, annoyance evident. "I'm not giving it to you now, because I know you. You'll take it and run, and then we'll get in trouble for being here without a babysitter."

"Whatever." Cassandra rolled her eyes. "Just do your thing and stop talking to me."

I found their interaction strange. "Are you guys related?"

"Give the young lady a cigar," Leon teased, shaking his head. "She's my niece. How did you figure that out?"

"Yeah, how did you figure that out?" Jack asked.

I shrugged. "Only family could get that exasperated with one another. I saw it growing up. Not with my birth parents or endless relatives, mind you, but with the Rhodes ... I saw a lot of it."

Jack worked his jaw and I thought he was going to say something. He must've changed his mind, because instead he flashed a smile. "Let's look around," he said.

"What are we looking for?" I was genuinely curious.

"Supposedly there was noise in here last night," Leon explained.

"Do you think it was zombies?" It was an honest question ... that made Leon snicker.

"I don't believe in zombies."

"You might change your mind once I tell you about our night," Jack said, his eyes flicking to me. "Go ahead and look around. Try not to wander too far. I don't want to go looking for you."

"I'll see if I can take care of myself for a whole hour in the middle of the day," I drawled as I set off. "It will probably be a terrible hardship."

"I like her," Leon said to my back. "She's cute and feisty."

"She has her moments," Jack agreed.

MOST PEOPLE WOULD'VE BEEN uncomfortable in a cemetery. That was not my experience. I'd been drawn to them since I was a child. The house I lived in with the Rhodes was near a cemetery, and I always walked through it on my way home from school. There was something calming about the headstones and mausoleums. Of course, that cemetery was much different from the one I prowled through today.

At some point, and I wasn't even sure how it happened, I found myself moving toward a specific tomb. Once there, I stood directly in front of it, staring for a really long time. Someone had scrawled graffiti across the walls, and yet I didn't read it. I just stared at the relatively nondescript tomb for a long time. So long, in fact, that I lost track of time.

"Do you know what this is?"

I jolted at Leon's voice, turning quickly to find him watching me with curious eyes. "Um ... what?"

He gestured toward the tomb. "Do you know what it is?"

"It's a tomb," I answered perfunctorily.

"It's Marie Laveau's tomb. Do you know who she is?"

I couldn't hide my surprise. "I know who she is." Reverence pinged through me as I turned back to the tomb. "I didn't realize she was entombed in the city. That's ... neat."

"It's definitely neat," he agreed, grinning. He seemed amused. "You're kind of neat, too."

His intense gaze caused me to shift from one foot to the other. "What do you mean? I'm just a normal woman."

"No, you're definitely something other than normal. You're ... different."

"Different good or different bad?"

"Good. I'm a hundred percent convinced of that."

"Oh, well ... thanks. I guess."

His grin only widened. "You're also good for Jack. I haven't seen him this happy in ... well ... forever."

"You've known him a long time."

"Ten years. We went through basic training together."

"He obviously respects and likes you. That means I do, too."

"Because whatever he says goes?" Leon's dark eyes mischievously twinkled. "I don't think that's how you roll. You're an independent thinker. You exude confidence ... and energy ... and a certain sweetness that I never would've thought would attract Jack. You seem perfect for him."

The avalanche of compliments made my cheeks burn. "I like him a great deal."

"He likes you a great deal, too."

I smirked. "I know."

He laughed at my simple response. "You're a kick, girl. I can't even tell you what a kick you are. You're awesome."

"I don't feel awesome." That was true. "I feel ... out of my depth."

"Because people are talking about zombies? I don't think fear of the unknown stymies you. In fact, I think you're drawn to it ... the same way you were drawn to this tomb."

"Oh, I wasn't drawn to the tomb. I just ... happened upon it."

"No, you cut through fifty other tombs and headed straight for this one. It's as if you knew where you were going."

"I ... ." Was that true? I couldn't remember how I got to the tomb. "Um ... I was just meandering."

Leon didn't look convinced. "Well, you're here now. What do you think?"

I turned back to the tomb and frowned. "I think it's a shame that people wrote on the tomb. Why would they do that?"

"And now you know why people aren't allowed in here on their own." He winked at me and glanced over my shoulder, his smile widening when he realized Jack was coming to join us. "Your girlfriend is pretty funny. She found Marie Laveau's tomb without even looking at a map. That's pretty impressive."

"Who is Marie Laveau?" Jack asked.

I shot him a look. "She was a voodoo queen. In fact, she's the most famous voodoo queen. She's revered in certain circles."

"She is indeed," Leon agreed.

"Oh, well, great." Jack didn't look impressed as he moved to my side. "Why have people written on her grave? That's awful."

"Why have people spray-painted Stonehenge?" Leon countered. "There are idiots everywhere."

"I guess so." Jack's eyes were thoughtful as he stared at the tomb. "Marie Laveau would be a draw for anyone trying to pretend they were raising the dead, right?"

Leon cocked an eyebrow. "What are you asking?"

"If Marie Laveau's tomb has been messed with."

"No, this tomb is locked up tight," Leon replied. "Trust me. They're not going to risk some nutbag stealing her bones for a ritual or anything. That would cause people to freak out."

"What about over there?" I asked, pointing toward a tomb that looked to be gaping open. It was only about fifty feet from where we were standing. "Is that supposed to look like that or has someone broken in?"

Leon furrowed his brow as he started in the direction of the tomb. "I haven't been here in years, but I'm pretty sure that shouldn't be like that. He stopped in front of the tomb, glanced around, and then poked his head inside. "Hmm."

"What?" Jack asked, his hand automatically going to my back. "What is it?"

"It's empty."

"Meaning?"

Leon held his hands out and shrugged. "Meaning it's empty. If there was a body in here, it's gone now."

I felt sick to my stomach. "Do you think it got up and walked away on its own, or do you think someone stole it?"

"I think we have no choice but to call the police," Leon answered, digging in his pocket for his phone. "The cops aren't going to be happy to hear about this."

ELEVEN

Thibodeaux arrived twenty minutes after we placed the call. His expression was dark as he stomped over to us, never changing as Jack explained the situation. Once Jack was finished, the detective turned on his heel and stormed into the tomb. The curses he let loose once inside were enough to singe my cheeks as I remained rooted to my spot.

"Did you do this?" he demanded when he returned, his eyes aimed directly at me. I'd swear he was almost frothing at the mouth.

"What?" I looked around, confused. "Do what?"

"Did you steal the body that was entombed in there?"

"Of course not."

"You just assume I should believe you, but I don't." His hands landed on his hips. "You've been in the thick of this from the start. Where is the body that belongs in this tomb?"

"Don't yell at her." Jack smoothly slid in front of me, his eyes wild. He looked ready for a fight, which caught me off guard because he was usually calm and collected when dealing with law enforcement. "She hasn't done anything. She was minding her own business when we discovered the open tomb."

"And you expect me to just believe that?" Thibodeaux looked as if he was teetering on the edge of derangement he was so angry. "This is the second time in two days she's been involved in something hinky."

"I was involved with both those incidents, too," Jack reminded him.

"Yeah, but she's the one who ... ." He didn't finish the sentence. Instead, he clenched his hands into fists at his sides, his cheeks flooding with color, and took a long moment to collect himself. In my mind he was counting to ten in his head. "Tell me what happened."

Jack was calm when he launched into the story, but I could tell that he was prepared should Thibodeaux start yelling again. It was as if he was daring Thibodeaux to call him a liar. If that happened, I was terrified Jack would be hauled off to jail and I wouldn't have the money to pay his bail. Then I would have to call Millie, she would make inappropriate jokes and things would be so much worse ... if that was even possible.

"We've only been here for an hour," Jack volunteered as he wrapped up the tale. "There are cameras at the exits. I saw them when we were coming in. I'm sure you can access the feeds. All you'll see is us wandering in. We very clearly didn't have a body with us."

"If there are cameras, can't they just check and see who actually did steal the body?" I asked.

Leon offered me a pleasant smile. "Except there's no way of knowing when the body was removed. It will take a lot of hours to go through the feed. I'm sure Detective Thibodeaux will be happy to do that, though, because he's obviously a slave to the truth."

If Thibodeaux could shoot lasers from his eyes, Leon would be dead ... or at least on fire. "I'll happily go through the video feed myself. Don't you worry about that."

"That's good." Leon didn't back down as he regarded the detective with cool eyes. "Until then, unless you have other questions, we should be going."

"You think I'm just going to let her walk away from this after what she's done?" Thibodeaux jabbed his finger in my direction. "She's stealing bodies."

Jack made a move, as if he was going to jump Thibodeaux. Anticipating his friend was about to lose his cool, Leon stepped forward and put a hand on Jack's arm. "You have no proof she was stealing bodies. Be reasonable, Henri, she weighs, like, a hundred thirty pounds. She's not familiar with the area. There's no way she managed to break into a tomb, drag a body through the cemetery and then come back and set up this entire show."

Henri? I chewed my bottom lip as I watched Leon. He didn't seem overly friendly with Thibodeaux, but calling him by his first name seemed to indicate they knew one another. I made a mental note to ask Leon about it when we were free and clear.

"She's been present for two very odd occurrences," Thibodeaux shot back. "She claims a dead man tried to get in her room last night."

"Don't say 'claims' like that," Jack snapped. "She's not a liar."

"You should look at things from where I'm standing."

"I don't care where you're standing. She's not a liar."

I was grateful for the fact that he felt the need to stand up for me, but I was also ready to escape. The longer Jack dug in his heels, the more likely we were to be held for questioning. I wasn't an expert at law, but I knew enough to understand that Thibodeaux couldn't hold us without taking us into custody. If he did that, things would spiral rapidly ... and I very much doubted that's what he wanted.

"Jack." I took a chance and leaned forward. "It's okay. Detective Thibodeaux is just upset. There's no reason to get worked up."

"Oh, I can think of a reason to get worked up," Jack snarled. He was a bristling mess. The fact that he was reacting this way because he was standing up for me was interesting ... and frustrating at the same time.

"Jack." I kept my voice gentle. "We should go. How about we find some place to get lunch? I'll buy."

"That a good idea," Leon seconded. "We need to find Cassandra — she's around here somewhere — and skedaddle. There's no reason to hang when we're obviously not needed."

"I didn't say you could leave," Thibodeaux pointed out.

"Then arrest us," Leon suggested. "You can't keep us without placing us in custody and we both know you won't do that because you have no proof. We've told you what happened. The evidence will back our story. There's nothing left for us to do here."

"And what if I don't want you to leave?" Thibodeaux challenged. "What if I demand you stay?"

"Then I'm going to insist you make us." Leon's tone turned dark. "If you want us to stay, you're going to have to arrest us. If you do, make no mistake, I'll hang so many lawyers on you that you'll never shake them all off. Is that really what you want?"

Initially, Thibodeaux didn't say anything. He just glared. Finally, he started shaking his head. "Just go. I'll be in touch when I have more evidence."

"I'm sure you will." Leon nodded. "When you have that evidence, we'll be expecting apologies from you as well."

"Don't hold your breath."

Leon motioned for Jack to fall into step with him. "Come on. I'll text Cassandra and have her meet us at the front gate … if she's still here. She might've run when she heard the sirens."

Jack reached out and grabbed my hand so he could pull me along. "Come on, Charlie."

I followed without complaint, waiting until we were around the corner to say anything. "That is not a happy detective."

"He's not," Leon agreed. "There's a story behind that … but I can't tell it here. Let's find a spot for lunch and I'll lay it all out for you there."

"What about your niece?" Jack asked. "Where did she go?"

"Oh, well, she was probably carrying." Leon's smile was rueful. "She likes her pot. I'm pretty sure she took off the second she realized the cops were coming. I'll text her to make sure, but I wouldn't worry about her."

"You know some colorful people, don't you, Leon?" I queried.

He laughed. "I do. Just wait until I tell you about Henri. Talk about colorful."

THE RESTAURANT LEON PICKED for lunch was quaint and

homey. The menu wasn't fancy — something for which I was thankful — but I was still determined to try local fare.

"I'm going to have a poor boy."

Jack, who shared a booth bench with me, slid me a sidelong look. "Po' boy," he corrected automatically. "If you call it a poor boy the waitress will laugh at you ... and then probably lick your food."

I knit my eyebrows. "What's a po' boy?"

"I already told you. It's a sandwich."

"Yeah, but ... where does the name come from?"

"That I can't answer."

"I can, if you're really interested," Leon offered, sipping his sweet tea.

"I don't think we care that much," Jack replied.

I shot him a look. "Speak for yourself. I like learning new and interesting things."

"We're talking about a sandwich here, but I'm happy to oblige." Leon offered me a wink. "Back in the 1920s, it's said that a restaurant owner served his former colleagues free sandwiches during a strike against a streetcar company. The story goes that the people handing out the sandwiches to hungry friends called them 'poor boys.' That has since been shorted to po' boys."

"Ha!" I waved a finger in Jack's face. "I told you they were called poor boys."

"Not anymore they're not." Jack grabbed my finger and gave it a squeeze, smiling. "I won't feel sorry for you if you call it that and they lick your food."

I rolled my eyes. "I'm not going to call it that. I want a chicken one, with extra pickles."

"Oh, good. I love it when you have pickle breath." He held my gaze for a moment before turning back to his friend. Leon was watching us with amusement, which caused Jack to snap to attention. "I mean ... pickles are good."

"Oh, don't bother." Leon let loose a dismissive wave. "You can't cover for that charming little exchange. You two are so ... sweet."

Jack glowered at him. "We're not sweet. We're ... what's the word I'm looking for?" He looked to me for help.

"Sexy," I automatically answered. The instant the word popped out of my mouth I regretted it. The look on Jack's face was speculative ... and then some. "I mean ... we're sassy. Yeah, that's the word."

"You're definitely sassy," Jack agreed, leaning back and extending his arm so it rested across my shoulders along the back of the bench. "So, you said there was a story about Thibodeaux. We're dying to hear it."

"You just want to change the subject from your sweet little girlfriend," Leon teased. "Well, I'll oblige ... but only because I'm afraid I might get a cavity if I don't focus on something else."

"I'll never live this down, will I?" Jack whined.

"Nope." Leon's grin widened. "As for Henri, his story is interesting. He's famous in police circles for what happened during Katrina."

My interest was officially piqued. "Hurricane Katrina?"

Leon nodded. "That was in 2005, so it was fourteen years ago, but it's still fresh in the minds of a lot of people."

"My understanding is that neighborhoods are still recovering," I noted. "I read a few articles on the plane that said a lot of the buildings that were damaged are still being rebuilt, and some neighborhoods look completely different."

"That's true," Leon confirmed. "But the French Quarter wasn't hit as bad as other wards and, because of tourism there was a priority to get this area back up and running. The poorer areas are still struggling."

"That's too bad."

"It is, but this city is strong and I love it," Leon said. "Henri feels the same way. We've known each other a number of years. He's older than me — a good eight years or so — but he went to school with my brother, so I was aware of him growing up.

"He wasn't a bad kid," he continued. "He was quiet and kept to himself. His father was the former New Orleans Police chief and was very strict. Henri wasn't allowed to hang around with anyone unless they were properly vetted by his father ... and I'm betting you can guess how that went over."

"Not good, huh?" Jack's fingers moved to the back of my neck, tracing light circles. "We knew a few guys who were raised in law enforcement families when we were in the military. They were the craziest guys."

"In general," Leon said. "That's not how Henri was, though. He followed all the rules and did exactly as his father demanded. He never put up a fuss and made sure he didn't miss curfew. He wasn't a hell-raiser like my brother. He was a rule follower and good boy. It was no surprise to anyone when he decided to become a cop.

"The thing is, his upbringing was weird for another reason." Leon stretched in his seat as he got comfortable. "Henri's mother was his father's second wife. She was a voodoo priestess, supposedly of some renown in this area, and it was some big scandal when his father took up with this woman because he was married and had two other kids.

"This was obviously before my time, but people were still talking about it when I was growing up," he continued. "Some scandals never die, and this was one of them. So, the chief's first wife left him because she was embarrassed. Racial politics were still a thing back then — and technically still are today — so being thrown over for a black woman who made money reading palms on Bourbon Street was considered the height of embarrassment.

"She packed up and left the state. The rumor is she moved to Virginia, but I don't know that it matters. My understanding is the chief never got to see the children he had with her again. That was their choice, I guess. He immediately took up with this voodoo priest-ess, married her, and together they had Henri."

It was an interesting story, but I wasn't sure where he was going with it. "Did he get picked on because he was mixed race? It's not his fault, after all."

"I don't know that he was picked on," Leon replied. "I don't think it was all that bad, but it doesn't matter. The most important part of the story is that the voodoo priestess picked up and left when Henri was eight or nine, leaving him with his father, who was extremely strict.

"I don't know what happened to the voodoo priestess and I don't even know her name," he said. "She just disappeared. I once heard a rumor that Henri's father killed her because she was conducting black magic in their house, but I don't believe that — and Henri's whole life was his father."

"Are you trying to make me feel sorry for him?" Jack asked blandly. "If so, it's not working. He's still a jerk."

"I'm simply trying to explain why Henri is the way he is," Leon corrected. "Like I said, Henri had a relatively normal childhood. His father was ridiculously overprotective, though. For example, Henri wasn't allowed to hang around at any of the voodoo shops. Most of the locals don't, but occasionally, if there's beer and fun to be had, it's been known to happen.

"Henri was never allowed to party with the other kids and was restricted from hanging around in what his father deemed 'rough' areas," he said. "He was relatively popular, but he wasn't wild and crazy. He followed the rules, became a cop and fulfilled the destiny his father set out for him.

"Then Katrina hit," he continued, his voice darkening. "Some of the cops ran because they were afraid. I don't blame them. Most stayed. It was a terrifying time. Some of the people who remained behind were poor and got trapped.

"In one of the buildings in the 9th Ward, several children were in an apartment when their mother got separated from them because she was out trying to secure food." He turned morose. "The building started flooding and the kids couldn't find a way out. Henri took a boat and got into the building and saved all five children. He did it on his own and without any backup."

I felt a grudging respect growing for the man. "That was nice of him. He was a hero that day."

"He was. The feat also made him famous ... especially when news hit that his father died in the storm."

My eyebrows flew up my forehead. "Oh, wow! That's horrible. How did he die?"

"No one is sure how, but he drowned," Leon replied. "It was a tragedy. He stayed behind to help and it ended up costing him his life. What's interesting is that once his father was gone, Henri all of a sudden started acting out.

"He wasn't mean or anything," he added hurriedly. "He just suddenly discovered he had an ego. I always theorized he thought he had to live up to his father so he channeled the man's personality. It doesn't matter, though.

"What's important to note is that this city believes Henri is a hero," he said. "They believe he saved five children at the time he could've been helping his father. He gave of himself to save innocents. That's helped him grow to almost mythical proportions."

"I don't understand what that has to do with his attitude today," Jack persisted. "Just because he's a hero doesn't mean he gets to be a jerk."

"That's what I'm saying. Henri believes his own hype. He does whatever he wants and often gets away with it. Quietly, though, he's amassed quite a few reprimands. His future in the department isn't secure because of some of the things he's pulled.

"I guess what I'm trying to say is that he's a wild card," Leon continued. "He's not a bad man and he will help if he thinks it will benefit him. He's mostly interested in what people think of him, and he most certainly doesn't want to be the guy who let zombies take over on his watch. That won't go over well given the whole 'his mother was a voodoo priestess who abandoned him' thing. I don't think he ever got over that and he has attitude when it comes to the hoodoo and voodoo folk. It doesn't matter if they're the real deal or grifters."

"Oh." Realization dawned on me. "He doesn't want to believe in any of it because his mother abandoned him and voodoo was a part of her belief system. That makes sense."

"Well, it doesn't make sense to me," Jack groused. "He doesn't need to be a jerk for no good reason."

"No, he doesn't," Leon agreed. "That won't stop him from going after you if he thinks you're a threat to his perfect world. I just thought I should make you aware of his past."

"Thank you for that." Jack smiled at his friend. "It explains a few things. I'll have to make a call to Myron and tell him what's going on. There's a chance he might be able to rein in Henri."

"I wouldn't count on that," Leon said, "but good luck with it. I'll be interested to see if you can get it done."

"That makes two of us."

TWELVE

I felt better after the sandwich. The food bolstered my energy level to the point I was almost bouncing when it came time to leave.

"Where are we going next?"

Jack looked amused when he slid his eyes to me. "Where would you like to go?"

"I'd like to go on one of those swamp tours where they take you out to look at gators and bayou gas that's supposed to look like ghosts. But I doubt we have time for that."

"Swamp tour?" He arched an eyebrow. "I'll see what I can figure out for later. For now, we have to stick to the French Quarter."

"I've never been here before. I don't know where to suggest going. You can pick."

He exhaled heavily as he absently brushed my hair away from my face. "We're supposed to meet the others at the hotel at two. That gives us a full hour. How would you like to see a voodoo store?"

"I saw one when I went out with Millie," I reminded him.

"Yes, but this is a store I know about."

Leon snickered. "I believe I know which store you're talking about. That's a fabulous idea."

I was confused. "Is there some joke I'm missing out on?"

"Yes." Jack's eyes twinkled. "But you'll like it."

VIXEN VOODOO — THAT WAS its real name — wasn't what I expected. The second we walked through the door I could tell the atmosphere was different. The women behind the counter weren't exactly women, you see. They were something else entirely.

"Oh, they're drag voodoo priestesses." I was excited. "This is awesome!"

Jack grinned. "I thought you'd like it." He snagged me by the back of my shirt before I could take off and search the store. "Don't break anything. They have a strict 'you break, you buy' policy."

"How do you know that?" I was legitimately curious. "Have you been here before?"

"Let's just say that I know the owner and leave it at that."

That sounded ... intriguing. "How do you know the owner? Is he here? Wait ... she? Am I supposed to say she? I've never understood the correct way to refer to a drag queen. Or ... is that a rude term? Am I not supposed to say that?"

Jack merely shook his head. He looked tired. "I think you're okay just being you. They'll understand that you're not being rude as much as honest. As for the he-she thing, I would go with she."

"She." I nodded. "Good tip."

"Don't break anything," he repeated.

"I'm not that clumsy."

He chuckled. "Maybe I should go with you just to make sure."

He sounded so certain that I wanted to elbow him ... hard. I was fairly certain that would result in me accidentally knocking something off a shelf, so I refrained. "Whatever."

Jack stuck close but didn't crowd me as I looked around the store. At a certain point I realized Leon wasn't with us, which threw me off. I found him at the counter talking with one of the workers.

"How do you know the owner of this place?" I asked as I glanced over my shoulder. I was confused. "You're not the judgmental type —

I appreciate that, by the way, so keep it up — but this doesn't seem the sort of place where you would spend time."

"It's a long story."

"Which means you don't want to tell me," I deduced.

"It means that I don't want to tell you right now," he clarified. "I have no problem telling you later, when it's just the two of us."

"Okay." I understood what he was saying. He didn't want to risk anyone overhearing us, especially since it could be potentially misconstrued. "You can tell me later."

"Thank you." He leaned forward and I thought he was going to kiss me in the middle of the store, which was unlike him when we were working. Instead, he pointed his nose toward the shelf and smiled. "Louisiana chicory. That is the best coffee. Remind me to take you to Cafe Du Monde so you can try it ... and beignets. You'll love their beignets."

"Sure. You know me. I'll try anything."

"Yes, but this is something you'll actually like, and your tongue won't catch fire when you eat them."

"Then I'm on board."

He laughed, but he wasn't alone. Another voice, a rich baritone, joined in from behind me.

"How cute," the voice pronounced, causing me to swivel quickly.

Jack grabbed me by the shoulders before I could careen into the coffee mug display and send it crashing to the ground. "Hold up, Charlie. It's okay," he murmured as he pressed my back against his chest and moved his eyes to the individual wearing a purple turban, ankle-length skirt and shirt that revealed a decent amount of fine chest hair. "Hello, Max ... or are you going by a different name now?"

"I'm Max," he replied. "I don't really live the life as fully as others. I'm more of a dabbler, although everyone is welcome here. I still enjoy the game." He flicked his eyes to me. "And who is your friend?"

"This is Charlie Rhodes," Jack replied without hesitation. "Charlie, this is Max Nettle. He served with Leon and me overseas."

"He ... you ... ." I was confused, but I forced myself to get it together. "It's nice to meet you, Max." I held my hand out. "You make a fabulous Marie Laveau."

He laughed as he shook my hand. "How did you know that's who I was going for?"

"I've read a lot about her."

"So have other people. I could've been going for any number of famous faces."

"Yes, but she's the queen for a reason," I noted, relaxing a bit at his gregarious smile. "Am I supposed to refer to you as he or she?" I blurted out before thinking.

Instead of being angry, Max snickered. "I'm fine being a he or she. It doesn't matter to me. I essentially live my life as two people and am comfortable as both. Others prefer being female. It was thoughtful of you to ask."

"Jack says I have a busy brain," I explained. "I don't think he means it as a compliment."

"Rarely," Jack agreed, slipping his arm around me and holding it out so he could shake Max's hand. "It's been a long time."

"It has," Max agreed. "What are you doing in my neck of the woods?"

"Looking for zombies," I answered for him.

Jack sighed, his breath hitting the side of my face. "See. She does have a busy brain."

"Oh, well, I'm dying to hear about this." Max took a step back and gestured toward a set of heavy drapes. "Come into my parlor. We can have privacy there ... and chicory. I believe that's a favorite of yours."

"It definitely is," Jack agreed, nudging me forward. "I think Charlie will be a big fan, too."

"Good for Charlie." Max chuckled as I moved past him. "Ain't she just cute as a bug?"

"I've never understood that expression but she's definitely cute," Jack agreed. "She's got a mouth without a mute button, though."

"That's what makes her cute."

"It's only one of the things that makes her cute ... and only sometimes."

"I guess I'll have to accept your word on that."

IT TOOK TWENTY MINUTES TO GET settled in the back room. Max was the consummate host. He made sure everyone was settled in comfortable chairs with chicory coffee — or tea for me, because I wasn't sure I wanted to try something new when it came to hot beverages — and he put a huge plate of cookies at the center of the table before sitting.

"What brings you to New Orleans?" he asked, his gaze bouncing between faces. "Leon, I always see. You, Jack, I wasn't sure I would ever see again."

"I always had plans to come back for a visit," Jack countered, grabbing a cookie from the tray and breaking it in half to share with me. I gratefully took the shortbread offering and dunked it in my tea, happy to let Jack lead the conversation. "I'm working with the Legacy Foundation. Do you know what that is?"

"Not last time I checked."

"It's a corporate think tank deal up in the Northeast. It has a foothold in a multitude of different things. That includes investigating stories involving paranormal phenomenon. Our boss, Chris Biggs, is the nephew of the man who runs the foundation. He basically gets free reign to do whatever he wants ... and right now he wants to investigate zombies in the French Quarter."

"Ah." Max nodded, recognition blooming. "I've heard the stories. People say bodies are going missing, the dead are returning to their families, and the sewers are filling with the walking dead."

"I haven't heard the part about the sewers," Jack admitted. "We're not going down there to check. I don't care how adamant Chris is. We're staying clear of filthy tunnels that could cave in at any moment."

I looked at him as I reached for another cookie. "You're claustrophobic. I didn't know that."

His fingers brushed against mine as he took the cookie from my hand and I saw a flash. It was brief, and only one scene. I saw Jack. He was younger, hair shorter, and he looked to be trapped in an enclosed space as he struggled for breath. The image was gone almost before it had a chance to settle. "I'm not claustrophobic," he corrected as he broke the cookie in two and took half before giving me the rest. "I just ... there's no need to go underground."

Leon and Max both reacted with sympathy, which made me think they knew what had happened to him. I opted to let it go. "Okay." I forced a smile for his benefit. "I don't want to go underground either. Unless ... well ... if we can go back underground to find the Chupacabra again so I can prove to you I wasn't seeing things, I would do that."

Jack frowned. "I don't like being reminded of the time you fell two stories into a basement and almost died."

"And saw the Chupacabra," I added.

"You didn't see the Chupacabra."

"I did so."

"Whatever." Jack made a dismissive waving motion with his hand as Max chuckled. "She has a big imagination," he explained.

"She's got a big heart," Max corrected as he winked at me. "She would have to if she expected to get you to open that iron cold heart you were carrying last time I saw you."

"I didn't have an iron cold heart."

"Not to mention the huge chip on your shoulder. It seems she's managed to get rid of that, too." Max's smile was wide when it landed on me. "Honey, you're a miracle worker."

I laughed. "I don't think his chip was all that big when we met."

"Then you weren't looking hard enough. As for the zombies, we've all heard the stories. So far, they're just that. Stories. Do you have reason to believe they're something more?"

"Well ... ." Jack licked his lips and slid his gaze to me. "Kind of."

"One of these things showed up outside Charlie's hotel room last night," Leon volunteered. "She heard a noise, like someone was trying to get inside, and when she opened the door it was a guy they saw hit by a car earlier in the night. He went after her, she somehow managed to get a painting off the wall and smack him in the head with it, and then he died for what they say is a second time. I didn't get to see him die either time, but I'm taking their word for it."

"You always were loyal." Max shot him a thumbs-up but his expression was thoughtful when he turned to me. "You weren't hurt, were you?"

"No," I replied hurriedly. "I'm fine. I'm tougher than I look."

"She is," Jack agreed. "This isn't the first time she's found trouble. Still, I'm bothered by the fact that this ... guy ... managed to track us back to our hotel. We weren't even near him when we told the police where we were staying."

"I see." Max steepled his fingers. "Charlie, it sounds as if you're the only one who saw this man before he died — perhaps for a second time. What did you see?"

"Oh, well ... ." The question caught me off guard and I shifted in my chair.

"It's okay," Jack prodded. "I never really asked you specific questions either. We were so tired after we were done with the cops that we just crawled into bed and passed out. What did you see?"

"I don't know." That, sadly, was the truth. "I was dead to the world when I woke. At first I thought it was you because you have my extra key card, but then I realized that wasn't what I was hearing."

"Hold up." Jack held up his hand, annoyance obvious. "I can't believe you thought I would just use my key card to sneak into your room in the middle of the night like that."

"I can't believe you two aren't sharing a room," Leon countered. "What are you, like twelve? You're so cute."

"I know, right?" Max chuckled.

"We're handling things our own way," Jack shot back. "Mind your own business."

I was sorry I'd brought it up. "Um ... that's not the important part of the story," I reminded them. "I was confused when I woke. I'd been sleeping hard."

"And apparently dreaming — and only dreaming — about Jack," Leon replied cheekily.

"Leave her alone," Jack ordered, wagging a warning finger in his friend's face. "Don't pressure her."

"Wait a second ... is that what this is about? Are you actually being a good guy and not pressuring her?" Leon snorted, and then sobered quickly. "Wait ... you are. How did this happen? The Jack I know was a total ladies' man who romanced every woman who crossed his path ... and on the first night."

"Don't worry about it!" Jack practically jumped out of his seat. "Leave her alone."

I felt put on display in a way, but not to the extent Jack seemed to be worried about. "It's fine." I patted his arm. "They're just messing with you. I thought that was the guy way of doing things. They don't mean anything by it."

"We really don't," Max agreed. There was something in his eyes I couldn't quite identify. I almost thought it was recognition. Of what, I had no idea. "We're sorry." He held up his hands in capitulation. "Tell us the rest of the story, Charlie."

"There's not much to tell," I said, keeping one eye on Jack as he worked overtime to put himself back together. He was angry, but I didn't understand why. I told the rest of the story, leaving nothing out. When I finished, Leon and Max were more perplexed than ever.

"Well, that sounds like a zombie," Leon said finally. "I still don't know that I'm comfortable using that word."

"That makes two of us," Max said.

"Three," Jack muttered. "I can't wrap my head around zombies either."

Max smiled at him. "At least there we agree."

WHEN IT WAS TIME TO LEAVE, I excused myself to use the restroom. Max was waiting for me in the hallway when I exited. He flashed a smile when he saw me, but I read trouble in his eyes.

"What's wrong?"

"Nothing is wrong," he replied quickly. "I just wanted a moment alone with you to apologize for what occurred earlier. I didn't mean to make you feel uncomfortable."

"You didn't. Jack was uncomfortable."

"Yes, but I didn't realize why right away. I do now and ... I'm very sorry." He sounded sincere, which I found baffling.

"You don't have to apologize. You didn't do anything wrong." I meant it. "Jack and I haven't been dating all that long. We're just not there yet."

"I know. What you don't know is how ... miraculous ... that truly is. Jack has never had a girlfriend."

I snorted. "Please. Look at him. He's had hundreds of girlfriends."

"No, he's had hundreds of dates," Max corrected. "You're his first girlfriend and it's all kinds of cute."

I didn't know what to make of that. "I don't understand."

"I know. But you will. One day, things will simply click into place when it's time. Don't rush yourselves. Things are obviously going well for the two of you. Jack is perfectly content with how things are, so don't change yourself to try to keep up with him. He's waiting for you."

I understood what he was saying and it made my cheeks burn. "Oh, well ... ."

"And I've embarrassed you again." He made a clucking sound as he patted my shoulder. "I'm sorry. That wasn't my intention. Jack absolutely adores you. I find it ... marvelous. I don't know that I would've picked you as his type, but you're perfect for him."

"Oh, yeah?" I fanned my face to cool my embarrassment. "Why is that?"

"You challenge him. You trust him. You have faith in his abilities. You're his equal even though he tells himself he has to protect you. You're just unbelievably cute."

I pressed the heel of my hand to my forehead. "This is weird to talk about."

"Definitely cute," he echoed, shaking his head. "I can't wait to see how this all plays out. I think it's going to be amazing. As for Jack, don't do anything differently than you're already doing. Things will happen when they're supposed to happen. You'll know when it's the right time."

"Okay."

"Also, be careful." His tone darkened. "I don't know what's going on with the zombies, but I'm going to start digging for information. I don't like the sound of any of this and I don't know what to make of it. We'll work together to solve it. You and Jack are not alone."

"We have a whole group of people. We're never alone."

"You know what I mean."

"I do." I beamed at him. "You're not what I expected. I thought all Jack's friends would be buff ego machines. I'm happy to be wrong. You're a lot of fun."

He chuckled. "You're not what I expected for Jack's girlfriend. I'm also happy to be wrong. We're definitely going to have a lot of fun."

I had no trouble taking him at his word.

THIRTEEN

*W*e made it back to the hotel with five minutes to spare. Jack steered us toward the bar, where everybody was waiting, and introduced Leon as we sat. Everyone greeted him cordially. Laura went so far as to look him up and down like a piece of meat, which wasn't lost on him as he gave her a saucy wink for her efforts.

We jumped into things right away, so there was no time for flirting.

"What have you got?" Chris asked. His tone wasn't nearly as cold as it was earlier in the day, but he wasn't exactly his normal gregarious self either.

"Well, we have a little of something and a lot of nothing," Jack replied. "We went to St. Louis Cemetery No. 1 this morning and in one of the vaults near Marie Laveau's tomb the door was open and a body was missing. Apparently it's a family vault. We're getting the name."

I knit my eyebrows, confused. "When did you do that?"

"͏you were in the bathroom at the voodoo store. Leon has a ͏͏d he managed to track down his niece, who has a map ͏͏Γhat particular vault belongs to the LaFleur family. The

116

body that's missing was a recent addition. Apparently they had one more space and he paid for it a long time ago. He was elderly. His name was Martin. That's all we know right now. We're waiting for further information so we can track his family."

This was all news to me. Apparently Jack and Leon had been busy while Max and I were discussing relationship issues in the hallway. "Oh, well, good."

"So ... a body was missing?" Chris leaned back in his chair, his expression unreadable. "Do you think we're dealing with another zombie?"

Jack grimaced. "I don't believe we're dealing with zombies."

"Because your girlfriend is the one who said she saw a zombie?" Laura asked. "I don't blame you. I think she's full of crap, too."

Jack scowled. "Because zombies aren't real. I think something else is going on."

"Well, getting to the bottom of this mystery is definitely at the top of our list," Chris said. "With that in mind, Hannah managed to get invited to the autopsy of our dead friend from the hallway last night. She couldn't participate, but she was allowed to watch." He turned to his girlfriend expectantly. "What have you got?"

"I don't know." Hannah shrugged. "The entire thing is weird. I've been a witness to strange autopsies before, so I shouldn't be surprised when things like this pop up, but this one ... there's a lot of weird stuff to talk about.

"First, there's no way that our dead guy — who still hasn't been identified — managed to get himself to the hotel, climb the stairs and then try to get into Charlie's room. He died from massive internal organ failure. The thing is, I'm not sure the organ failure was due to being hit by a car."

I was understandably confused. "What killed him?"

"He had cancer. He was riddled with it. I'm not an oncologist, but I'd estimate he'd have been bedridden at least three weeks ago. Given his age and poor health, it could've even been a month ago."

I ran the possibilities through my head. "Doesn't that essentially mean that he was up and walking when he should've been dead?"

"I don't know about 'dead,'" Hannah clarified. "He was very sick and didn't have long to live. I've seen people with cancer linger before, but I don't see how he was walking around."

"He was a zombie." That seemed like the simple answer to me. "Zombies can walk around because they don't feel anything. I mean ... what more proof do you need?"

"Charlie." Jack made an exasperated sound deep in his throat and pinched the bridge of his nose. "What else did you find, Hannah?"

"He had weird marks on the bottom of his feet," she replied, pulling out a photograph that made me very uncomfortable. It was obviously a shot of the dead man's feet. They were devoid of color, and there were ugly red welts on the heel and outer rim of the top pad.

"Ugh." I cringed. "That is so gross. I don't ever want to die and have people take photos of my body. Make sure that doesn't happen."

Jack slid his eyes to me. "You're not going to die. Don't say things like that."

"Eventually I'll die." I'd never been all that fearful of death. I knew about ghosts, that our souls went on. It wasn't that I had a death wish or anything. It was more that I recognized that death wasn't always the worst possible outcome. "We're all going to die."

"Let's not talk about death," Jack suggested. "You're not going to die for a long time."

"We're not that lucky," Laura chimed in as she angled her face toward Leon and smiled.

"You, on the other hand, can die any day," Jack muttered.

I knew he didn't mean it, but I still shot him a quelling look. He was antsy this afternoon, and I couldn't help wondering if it was because of the things Max had said. The more I thought about it, the more I realized that Jack was amped up because of the next step in our relationship. He was just as nervous as I was ... and for some reason that made me feel better. I wasn't the only one freaking out

⁻ᵗ step.

ᵒut Laura," Chris instructed.

118

"Let's definitely forget about Laura," Millie said. "That should be our group motto."

"We need to focus on what we can prove." Chris was insistent. "Was there anything else of note in the autopsy, Hannah? What do the marks on the feet indicate?"

"Well, without going into detail that will gross everybody out, the marks are significant because they show where blood was pooling," Hannah answered. "The thing is, this man was probably bedridden. There's physically no way he was walking around. The marks on his feet seem to indicate he was doing a lot of walking. So much so that there are the early formations of blisters, which means he covered a great distance."

"Wait." I leaned forward so I could grab the photo and give it a better look. "If he was walking, I understand why he might have the blister on the bottom part of his foot like this. But why would he have it on the top?"

"Some people who have a weak side get blisters like that," Hannah explained. "For example, people recovering from a stroke might have a weak left side so they put more weight on their right foot, making it dip to the side a bit. That's what this looks like to me."

"That he had a stroke?"

"That he had a weak side," she corrected. "He was obviously struggling to walk. I can't guess as to why. They're running further blood tests. The initial ones they ran were ... troubling."

"How so?" Jack asked. "What was off about them?"

"They're calling the original blood draws tainted because, under a microscope, the blood looks older than it should."

Ah. We were finally getting somewhere. "Are you saying the blood looks like it was drawn from a corpse?"

"It *was* drawn from a corpse," Jack reminded me.

"Let me rephrase that," I countered. "Are you saying the blood appears to have been drawn from a corpse that was dead for more than a few hours?"

Hannah nodded once. "That's exactly what I'm saying."

"I can't believe I'm going to ask this question, but I don't see where I have a choice," Jack groused. "How old did the blood appear?"

"About two weeks old."

"Oh, geez."

I leaned forward, excited. "That means he was really a zombie. There's proof."

"There definitely is," Chris agreed, his eyes gleaming. "Good job attracting a walking dead killer, Charlie. We're finally going to find the proof we're looking for."

"Yes, good job, Charlie," Laura drawled. "You're everyone's favorite pet."

Leon made a face as he leaned closer to Jack. He obviously meant to whisper his question, but he spoke loud enough that I could hear. "What's her deal?" he asked his longtime friend.

"She's evil," Jack replied, rubbing the back of his neck.

"She's kind of hot."

"She also probably has chlamydia because she gets around."

"That's what condoms are for."

"Ugh. Do what you want." Jack slid his eyes to me, his lips curving down when he saw my smile. "You're not going to let this zombie thing go now, are you?"

"I wasn't going to let it go before Hannah told us what she found. Now I'm just really excited."

"Well, if you're really excited ... ." He trailed off, tapping his fingers on the tabletop. "We need to talk to the family of the most recent missing body. If we can get to them before the stories of zombies make the rounds, we might be able to figure part of this out."

"I've got a name for you," Leon offered. "I'm willing to give it to you if you let me stay behind with your friend Laura."

"I'll take Charlie. Just give me the information."

"Somehow I knew you would take Charlie. You guys are so cute."

"Yeah, yeah, yeah. Just give me the information."

ELIZABETH "BETSY" LAFLEUR LOOKED to be in her early seventies and beaten down by life when she opened the door. That made her younger than her husband, who was in his nineties, but the exhaustion weighing her down was palpable.

"Can I help you?" She looked fearful as she glanced between faces. "If you're selling something, I'm not interested. I don't like solicitors."

"We're not selling anything," Jack replied, digging in his pocket for the badge he carried. It didn't identify him as a police officer but it looked official, which he often found helpful in situations like this. "I'm with the Legacy Foundation. We're investigators, and right now we're looking into some of the missing bodies that are being reported around the French Quarter."

"Oh." Betsy pushed open her door to allow us entrance. "I wondered when someone was going to stop by. I've been expecting the police ever since I was notified that Martin's body was gone."

Jack and I exchanged quick looks. That was both good and bad news. It was good that we would be able to question her when she was fresh and hadn't had time to prepare answers. Things would turn bad when Thibodeaux realized we'd beaten him to the man's wife. We couldn't think about that now, though.

"We don't want to take up much of your time," Jack offered as she led us through the modest house, stopping when we reached a brightly-painted kitchen. "Oh, wow!" I turned a circle when we hit the room and I realized the ceiling was made up of what looked to be greenhouse panels. "This is ... neat."

"Martin designed it for me," she said as she pointed toward the table. "It's my favorite room in the house for obvious reasons. The glass filters out harmful UV rays, but I can grow anything in here, even during the dead of winter when we sometimes get hard freezes. I absolutely love growing things. You should see my garden when it's in full bloom."

"This is amazing." I meant it. "I've always thought it would be cool to garden, but I don't have a yard."

"You don't have a yard?" Betsy looked horrified. "How is that possible?"

I shrugged. "I live in an apartment ... and I just moved to the

Northeast. I think it's going to be quite a while before I have a house of my own."

"You could always rent one of those community parcels that they have on building roofs," Jack suggested. "If you really want to try, that would be the way to start. Just one small plot to see if you can handle it."

"That's a good idea. I'll have to research how expensive they are."

He looked as if he was going to argue, perhaps go off about how I shouldn't constantly be worried about money, but he changed course quickly. He clearly remembered that we were working with a limited timetable and it was important we get our information — and then get out — before Thibodeaux came calling.

"Ma'am, we really don't want to bother you when you're going through a trying time like this," Jack started, choosing his words carefully. He smiled when she poured hot water from a teakettle into a cup and pushed it in front of him. "Thank you."

"You're welcome." She managed a weak smile. "I've been grappling with Martin's death for what seems like forever. He only died ten days ago, but it's been coming for months. It's strange to say, but I was mourning him before he died. It got much worse when he finally passed.

"Even when he was sick and in hospice care, I could still talk to him," she continued. "He didn't have much energy. He could stay awake for twenty minutes at the end and then sleep for eight hours. I didn't mind waiting, because those twenty minutes meant everything.

"You wouldn't think I'd miss him the way I do." Her expression turned wistful. "But I do. I miss him so much. I would give anything to have those twenty minutes back."

She was so sincere that I felt tears pricking the back of my eyes. When I glanced at Jack, I found he looked as miserable as I felt.

"It's good that you have memories of him," he said finally. "I wish there was something I could do to make you feel better. The thing is, we do have a few questions."

"Because you need to capture the grave robbers." Betsy nodded. "I understand. What are your questions?"

"Well, for starters, were you practitioners of voodoo?"

Whatever invasive query she was expecting, it wasn't that. Betsy made a face that I would've found comical under different circumstances. "We most certainly were not! We're Catholics. He had Last Rites and everything. Actually, Martin had Last Rites four times because he came so close to death and then rallied. That's neither here nor there, though. Why would you ask if we were involved in voodoo?"

Jack licked his lips and I recognized the debate going through his head by the way his eyes gleamed under the light.

"Because there are rumors going around the French Quarter," I volunteered, drawing Betsy's eyes to me. "They're horrible rumors, the stuff of nightmares really, but we have to ask about them. We're trying to figure out exactly what's going on because we're hearing conflicting tales."

"And what stories are you hearing?"

"Well, your husband's body is not the first to go missing. Quite a few have gone missing."

"Do you think the bodies are being sold?" Betsy looked disgusted at the thought. "I mean ... I can't imagine what else is being done with them. It's awful to think about."

"It's definitely awful." I had no problem agreeing with that. "The thing is, some people — and I'm not talking about everybody affected — are reporting that they've received visits from their loved ones after their deaths."

Betsy's forehead wrinkled as she absorbed my words. "Wait ... are you talking about bodies getting up and walking around?"

"No," Jack replied hurriedly.

"Yes," I supplied emphatically. "That's exactly what we're talking about."

"Charlie," Jack groaned, covering his eyes. "We need to work on your tact."

Betsy ignored him and remained focused on me. "Are you talking about ... zombies? You are, aren't you? Is this a joke?" She looked around, as if searching for hidden cameras. "I don't see what else it could be but a joke. Zombies aren't real."

"We're not saying it's zombies," I offered. "We think something else may be going on and perhaps someone is trying to make people believe it's zombies."

"And how are they doing that?"

"Yeah, Charlie, how are they doing that?" Jack asked.

I pretended I didn't hear him. "We're not sure how or why anyone would want to do anything like this. It's troubling because there has to be a reason people are going after those grieving. We want to make sure that whoever is doing this doesn't get away with it ... whatever their end game may be."

"Oh." Understanding blossomed on Betsy's face. "You think that someone who owns a voodoo shop is trying to make people believe the dead are walking around. I guess they think they can get money out of the bereaved by saying they can bring their loved ones back. That's diabolical."

I was pretty sure I said nothing of the sort. I was even more certain I didn't believe that. What was important was that she believed it, which is why I immediately began nodding. "We don't know how or who, but we're looking into it. You haven't seen Martin, have you?"

"No, and now that you've told me it might happen I'll make sure I'm ready."

She sounded so determined I had to swallow ... hard. "How will you do that?"

"I'm going to get my gun and wait for him to show up. When he does, I'm going to take down whoever is pretending to be him. They'll have to be close. I mean ... it's not as if they can just prop a body on the fence and then walk away."

"Definitely not," I agreed. "It's just ... do you think a gun is the right answer? Perhaps it might be smarter to just lock yourself in the house and call the police."

"Nope. I'm going to shoot them."

I cringed as I turned to Jack, who was vibrating with annoyance.

"Now I know why you always admonish me to keep my mouth shut when we're doing things like this."

"Oh, really?" He was shrill. "Don't you think it's a little late for that particular epiphany?"

"I guess. I'm going to turn things over to you."

"Well, great." He didn't look thrilled with the prospect. "You opened the barn door and let the horses out, and now I'm supposed to corral them without a rope. This should be interesting."

I couldn't have agreed more. I was interested in how he was going to fix my mess. I decided to sit back and let him get to work. I was officially done inserting myself into the investigation ... at least for today.

FOURTEEN

*B*etsy was relatively calm by the time she let us out of her house. We took a moment to claim our shoes in the foyer and then stepped out onto the front porch with her in tow, where something shiny caught my attention at the base of the walkway.

"What's that?" I hopped down the steps and bent over, brushing some of the dirt out of the way and came up with an odd coin. It was silver and looked to have a weird series of squiggles and dashes on the front. "Is this yours?" I held it out to Betsy, who made a face when she saw it.

"That's not worth anything," she said, shaking her head dismissively. "In fact, that's worth less than nothing. Martin had four or five he used to carry around in his pockets. They were trinkets handed out at one of the Mardi Gras parades."

I studied the coin with interest. "Even if it's not real silver, it has to be nostalgic for you."

"I have all the rest." She waved me off. "You keep it. I didn't even know it was out here. It's not worth any money."

"Are you sure?" I didn't want to take something, especially if she might regret it later. Still, the coin intrigued me.

Her smile was benign. "I'm sure. You look the sort to enjoy something like that. Just don't try to spend it. They're really worth nothing. They're iron, not silver. They just polish them up something pretty."

Jack peered over my shoulder at the coin. "It's kind of neat. Keep it for good luck, Charlie."

"It wasn't good luck for Martin," Betsy said bitterly. "He still died."

Jack nodded, a pitying look washing over his handsome features. "Oh, I don't know. You guys spent decades together. You loved each other a great deal. That's obvious. That seems pretty lucky to me."

Betsy's smile turned watery. "I guess you're right. This thing is just ... I think it's too much for me to bear."

"It would be too much for anyone," Jack conceded. "We'll be in contact if we have any information. Until then, just remember, that's not your husband. He left his body. While it's still a crime what's happening here, he's not going through it. He's someplace better."

"Thank you. That helps a great deal."

I waited until Betsy shut the door to speak again. "You're good with people, Jack. I don't know why that always surprises me."

"You're good with people, too, when you don't speak before you think."

"Yeah, well ... ."

"Come on." He gestured for me to follow him. "I want to get out of here. I feel ... heavy. This is New Orleans. We shouldn't be feeling this heavy."

I was right there with him.

JACK WANTED TO WALK THROUGH THE French Quarter to let me look around after our depressing conversation. I had the distinct impression he was trying to butter me up before dressing me down, but he didn't say anything about my words to the widow. Of course, that meant I had to say something, because I was uncomfortable at the thought of it hanging over my head.

"If you want to tell me I was stupid to say what I did, I'm ready for it."

He arched an eyebrow. "I don't particularly enjoy calling you stupid."

"You're thinking it, though."

"How do you know? Are you suddenly a mind reader?"

That was an interesting question. It also reminded me of the flash I got off him earlier. "Maybe I am. Will you immediately discount it if I tell you I can occasionally read people?"

His lips curved. "I don't know. What am I thinking right now?"

"That you want to mess with me." That was easy to read and I didn't need to tap my magic to do it. "You want to put me at ease and you're trying really hard not to yell about the things I said earlier. Before we started dating you used to yell at me all the time. You don't any longer."

"Well, there's a reason for that."

"We're dating."

"And you haven't done anything ridiculous in weeks." He grinned as he watched my reaction. "You're new to this, Charlie. Believe it or not, when I yelled at you I did it because I was worried. I'm not always great at reining in my temper, but I've been trying."

"I get that. I shouldn't have said what I did. I don't know why I always realize that after it's too late to take it back."

"You're young."

"You're not that much older than me ... and I'm not a child."

He let loose a low chuckle. "Oh, I know. I tried to look at you as a child for the first few weeks because I didn't like the feelings you were stirring up. I thought if I could paint you a certain way in my head that I would stop being attracted to you."

"How did that work out?"

He swooped over and gave me a quick kiss. "How do you think?"

I laughed at his expression. It was a cross between annoyance and acceptance. "You can still yell. I shouldn't have said what I did, especially the way I did. I'm an idiot sometimes."

"You're enthusiastic," he corrected. "And I don't want to yell at you, Charlie. I don't want you to ever be afraid of me."

The naked emotion he was emitting caught me off guard. "I would never be afraid of you. I promise."

"Well, I'm glad about that. I still don't want to yell."

"Okay."

"That doesn't mean I won't yell if I think you're putting your life on the line and doing something stupid. I probably won't be able to stop myself."

"That seems fair."

"Good." He linked his fingers with mine. "We have an hour until we have to be back at the hotel. What do you want to see?"

"Well ... I wouldn't mind riding one of those trolleys." I pointed at the quaint transportation vehicle that was pulling to a stop. "It looks fun."

"Trolley it is." He tugged me in that direction. "During the ride, you can tell me what you and Max were talking about in the hallway. Don't bother denying it. I saw you with your heads together."

"We weren't talking about anything serious." That was mostly true. "He just kept saying how cute we are."

"I have a feeling he said more than that."

He did, but in this particular case, what Jack didn't know couldn't hurt him.

WE WERE BOTH IN REMARKABLY high spirits when we hit the hotel. Millie and Bernard sat in lobby chairs, seemingly amused when we arrived.

"Your hair looks a little crazy, Charlie," Millie noted. "Has someone been running his fingers through it?"

Jack shot her a warning look. "We were working."

"Whatever." Millie was much more interested in messing with me than Jack. "Where have you been?"

"We went on the trolley," I replied, flopping on the couch across from them. "It was fun. I've never been on a trolley."

"Down here I think they're referred to as streetcars," Jack corrected.

I opted to ignore him. "They were really great trolleys."

Millie's smile was indulgent ... and then she sobered. "Are you serious?"

"Where would I ever ride on a trolley in Michigan?"

"I don't know." She slid her eyes to Jack. "Is it wrong that I now want to get a list of things she's never done and make sure she can cross everything off in the next year?"

Jack shrugged as he sat next to me. "I'm kind of there with you. I've never considered myself much of a streetcar person, but she had so much fun I now love them."

Millie snickered. "You're a softie at heart, Jack. I never thought I would see it –let alone say it, but you are."

"Yes, well ... ." He turned his eyes to the other side of the lobby, to where Laura and Leon were sitting together looking at a tablet. "How long has that been going on?"

"Since you left," Bernard replied. "She's flirting with him as a way to annoy you and he's flirting with her because he's curious to see how far she'll take things. He doesn't especially like her — heck, no one does — but he seems amused by the game."

"How do you know she's flirting with him because of me?"

"Because we've met her," Millie answered. "Oh, and she keeps asking him questions about how he knows you and whether or not he thinks you and Charlie will last. She's convinced you're only with Charlie as a way to drive her crazy. She actually told him that."

Jack frowned. "She's delusional."

"Yup." Millie shifted her gaze to the front door as movement stirred there and then her face fell. "Speaking of delusional, Chris found an expert for us to talk to. He secured a conference room and everything."

Jack shifted so he could look in that direction, his mouth falling open when he realized the man in question was wearing shiny pants that made noise when he walked ... and a cape. No, really, he had a cape.

"What the ... ?"

"That's Marius Garret," Bernard volunteered. "He's a local psychic of some renown."

Immediately my insides began to crawl with worry. "Psychic? Why do we need a psychic?"

"Because Chris will believe anyone if they tell him what he wants to hear," Jack groused. "I can't believe he went this route again."

I was understandably curious. "Again?"

"He's done it before." Jack didn't look happy when he turned back to me. "He calls whatever psychic has the most juice in the area — even when the guy is obviously a charlatan, like what we're dealing with now — and then believes whatever he says. He'll start making decisions based on what this guy says. And it always ends in disaster."

I flicked my eyes to Millie. She always stood up for Chris. Jack tended to lean toward the pessimistic. Even Millie looked agitated, though. "Has he ever managed to stumble across the real deal?"

"Nope." Millie shook her head, her eyes keen when they latched with mine. "Not that he knows of anyway. I'm sure this guy is just as bad as the others. Whatever he says, don't react. That's how these guys make their money. They read people. Don't wear your emotions on your face, Charlie."

It was a pointed warning, one I didn't take lightly. "I'll do my best."

GARRET HAD A LOT OF RESTLESS energy and it was on full display as he prowled the conference room Chris had secured. He seemed to be putting on a show, and even though I was naive and young and hadn't crossed paths with a lot of other psychics — real or imagined — I could tell right away he wasn't the real deal. That was a relief, although I still felt exposed.

"Someone here is not a believer," he announced, suddenly standing ramrod straight in the center of the room and lifting his chin as high as it would go. "Someone is draining the positive energy from the room. Who is it?"

Jack immediately raised his hand. "That would be me."

"I'm not sure I believe in zombies either," Leon offered. "If you need a positive-energy environment, perhaps Jack and I should leave. We can wait for the rest of you at the bar."

I didn't like the sound of that and turned quickly to see if Jack was going to agree. Instead, he merely sat in his chair, arms folded across his chest, and glared. "Just do your thing so we can go to dinner. I'm not in the mood to sit here and watch you practice your soliloquy for whatever theater troupe you're participating in this week."

Millie snickered and Laura shot him an appraising look. Me? I simply felt sick to my stomach.

"The end of the world is upon us," Garret announced, his tone grave. "We're at a crossroads. The world could fall into the abyss if we pick the wrong path. We cannot let that happen."

"Wouldn't there be more dead people wandering around and biting people if we were really in the middle of an apocalypse?" I asked, giving in to my baser urges and speaking before thinking. I knew better, but I couldn't seem to stop myself. "I mean ... we have a lot of missing bodies, but not many deaths. Every movie I've ever watched about the apocalypse leads with millions of deaths.

"From *The Walking Dead* to *The Stand* to *I am Legend*, the one thing that's needed to kick off an apocalypse is the demise of ninety percent of the population," I continued. I'd come this far, I saw no reason to turn around. It was already too late to keep Garret from focusing on me. "All we have are people who seemed to have died of natural causes and might be wandering around so their relatives can see them. That's not really an apocalypse."

"I hate to agree with Charlie — mostly because she's using movies and television shows as proof — but she has a point," Jack noted. "I mean, think about it. If the world is coming to an end, why aren't we seeing more signs?"

"This is just the start," Garret shot back. "Every apocalypse has a beginning. They can only be shut down if you manage to find a solution before things get out of hand."

"That seems like a convenient answer," Laura argued. "Basically you're saying it might be the apocalypse."

"No, it's definitely the apocalypse."

"But why?"

"Because it is."

"You still haven't said why."

"Because it is."

This conversation was getting us nowhere fast and I found I was suddenly struggling with a headache. "Tell us what you're seeing," I suggested, rubbing my forehead. "You must be reading certain signs. What are they?"

"And what do you mean by signs?" Chris queried. "I don't think I'm following you."

"He's made a pronouncement about the end of the world," I explained, impatience making me bold. "There are often fifteen paranormal harbingers of doom. We're talking the Mothman, the black bird of Chernobyl, Nain Rouge, the Flying Dutchman, demon cats and so on. There are tons of them and they're all supposed to warn us of horrible things that are about to happen. If Mr. Garret is seeing signs that point to an apocalypse, I would like to know what they are."

Jack gave me an appraising look that was also tinged with worry. "Do you feel okay? You look a little pale."

"Believe it or not, I have a headache that only popped up with this guy." I jerked my thumb in Garret's direction. "That doesn't change the fact that I want an answer. What harbingers are you seeing?"

"Not everything in life is a harbinger, young lady." Garret was haughty. "I believe there are other things we should be worried about."

"I'm with Charlie," Millie interjected. "I want to know what signs you're referring to."

"Is that really necessary?"

Chris looked uncertain as he glanced between Millie and me, but he ultimately nodded. "I would like to hear about the harbingers, too."

"Fine." Garret tapped his foot, as if he was impatient and we were wasting his time. "I've seen the white stag."

"Is that a sort of bachelor party for white dudes?" Leon asked. "If so, it sounds deathly boring."

Jack smirked but managed to hold in a laugh. "What's the deal with the white stag?"

"It's a Celtic legend," I answered before Garret could. I knew he would draw out his answer for dramatic purposes, and I had no interest in that. "Supposedly, if you see the white hart — or stag, in this case — then something bad is about to happen. There's nothing in the lore about an apocalypse, though."

"I know how to read the signs." Garret was defiant. "That's hardly the only sign, though. I've also seen black-eyed ghosts. You know what that means."

Jack looked to me for an answer.

"Black-eyed ghosts have been seen in almost every country," I explained. "Supposedly they sneak into people's houses but only show up when something bad is supposed to happen in that individual's life. They're not harbingers of the apocalypse."

Garret made a sound that was halfway between a growl and a snort. "And what about the running of the foxes? I've seen them in the streets right before dawn."

That one was trickier. "That's also an Irish legend," I said finally. "It's about the death of the head of household. Do you guys have foxes here?" I asked Leon.

"I'm sure we do, but I've never seen any in the city," he answered.

"That's why it's a harbinger of our doom," Garret intoned.

"Or a pack of dogs running the street," I argued. "I want to know what specific things you've seen that would lead you to believe we're facing the end of the world."

"I've heard the cries of the banshees," he snapped. "How can you explain that?"

"You live close to Bourbon Street. I'll bet you hear banshees every night. Where we come from you just call them drunken morons having a good time."

A huge grin cracked Jack's face as he regarded me, emotion pouring out of him. The dominant one was pride, and it threw me for a loop.

"What?" I asked, self-conscious.

"That was amazing," he said as Garret began cursing under his breath and railing at Chris. "Even though you believe we're dealing with zombies, you totally dismantled him."

That hadn't been my intention. I only realized after the fact that I'd managed it with minimal effort ... and in spite of the fact that my headache was growing. I had no idea where the discomfort had originated from, but I was steadily becoming sicker.

"So, you're happy?" I asked finally.

"I'm thrilled."

"Great, because I'm going to throw up." I knew I couldn't make it to the bathroom. Instead, I stumbled to my knees and grabbed the nearest trash receptacle before immediately vomiting.

"Oh, geez!" As Laura squealed and Hannah hurried over to help, Jack held my hair from my face as I lost the remnants of my lunch. "You don't have to be so brave next time if it's going to make you sick. I'm proud of you no matter what."

It was nice to hear, but that didn't change the fact that I was shaking with sickness. What in the world was going on now?

FIFTEEN

"I got a cold cloth."

Jack's fingers were gentle on my neck as I knelt on the floor and rested my head against the toilet seat. I'd managed to make it into the bathroom, but just barely. "Here." He dropped the washcloth into place and moved his fingers to my forehead. "You're not hot." He was talking to himself more than me.

"I'm okay, Jack." I hoped I sounded strong, but the way my voice croaked told me I was anything but. "I'll be okay. It must be something I ate."

"You just had a po' boy for lunch. I had the exact same thing. I'm fine."

"Maybe I have a weak stomach."

"Maybe." He didn't look convinced and his hand was back on my forehead before I could protest. "I think I should take you to the hospital."

That sounded like a terrible idea. "How does this warrant a trip to the hospital?"

"You're sick."

"Lots of people throw up without going to the hospital."

"Yeah, but ... ." He trailed off when the bathroom door opened to allow Hannah entrance. If she was disgusted by the sight in front of her, she didn't show it.

"I came to make sure Charlie is okay." Hannah's smile was encouraging as she crouched next to me. "Can I examine you?"

"I'm just sick. I'm sure I'll be fine tomorrow morning."

"Well ... I want to be sure." She moved her fingers to my throat and asked me to tilt my head up. I did, but it made me feel worse. "I don't notice anything that's swollen. That's good."

I flicked my eyes to Jack. For the first time, something akin to panic rolled through me. "It's just a quick bug. I'll be fine."

"We just want to make sure," Jack assured me as he brushed my hair from my face. "You went down fast, Charlie. You have to understand, that frightened us."

Oddly enough, he looked shaken. I couldn't remember the last time I saw him react this way. "I'm fine." I felt the need to reassure him. "I just got hot really fast ... and then sick, which you were a witness to. I swear I'm fine. You don't have to worry."

"Let Dr. Hannah tell me that," he teased. "You're many things: smart, sarcastic and funny among them. But you're not a doctor."

I was frustrated. "This is ridiculous."

"Shh, baby." Jack stroked his hand down my head, his eyes on Hannah. "Should I take her to the emergency room? I don't care what she says. I care what you say."

Hannah looked amused at the declaration. "I don't see anything terribly wrong with her right now. She might be dehydrated. In this heat and humidity that's a real concern. You two were wandering around. Was she drinking water?"

"I ... don't think so." Jack glanced at me. "I guess I'll need to keep you hydrated from here on out, huh?"

I was still marveling at the fact that he called me "baby." No one had ever called me that. "I just want to rest for a little bit," I admitted. "You guys can go to dinner and I'll close my eyes. I'm sure I'll be better by the time you get back."

"I'll stay with you," Jack offered.

I managed to hold off a groan, but just barely. "I think you should go with everyone else. All I'm going to do is sleep."

He opened his mouth to speak, but I cut him off. On this one point I was firm. "You can't sit in the room and watch me sleep. That's weird."

Jack looked to Hannah for confirmation.

"Totally weird," she agreed, bobbing her head.

He made an exasperated sound. "What if you need something while I'm gone?"

"I'm going to sleep." I meant it. Exhaustion was seeping into every bone. "You're going to go out, have a good time and leave the worrying behind. I'm fine. I just ate something funny. Maybe they really did lick my sandwich because they heard me call it a poor boy."

"Fine." He slipped his hand around my waist. "I am getting you upstairs and settled whether you like it or not, though. I want to make sure you're safely in bed before I go."

"Sure. Whatever makes you feel better."

"I heard that sarcasm."

"I wasn't trying to hide it."

JACK HAD TO BE TOLD TWICE more that sitting by my bedside and watching me puke wasn't acceptable before he finally left. He was reluctant — which was sweet — but all I wanted to do was close my eyes. Finally, he tucked me in with promises that he would check on me before disappearing.

I drifted off quickly. I was fairly certain I was dealing with a bug that would pass after a few down hours. Part of me predicted I would sleep straight through until morning. Apparently, that wasn't in the cards. I was barely down thirty minutes when I heard a strange noise.

"Jack, if you came back I'm going to kill you," I muttered, rolling so I could look in that direction. I expected to see his sheepish face staring at me. Instead, I found a blonde in a ponytail — pants so tight they had to be painted on — watching me with curious eyes. "Who are you?" I scrambled to a sitting position and made a face when my stomach lurched. "Ugh. Now is so not the time to puke again."

"I really wish you wouldn't puke," the woman agreed after as she walked into my bedroom. She didn't strike me as threatening. She was about my size, young, and looked to be carrying enough snark on her shoulders to feed a small village. "I'm a sympathetic puker. If you puke, I'll puke. That's a whole heckuva lot of puke."

I wasn't in a position to disagree. "Who are you?" There was something about the woman that was off, but I couldn't put my finger on it. "You look ... familiar. I'm almost certain we haven't met."

"I'm certain we haven't," she replied, matter-of-fact. "I'm sure I would remember you if we'd crossed paths. You smell like ... blueberry muffins." She lifted her nose. "What are you?"

"Funny. That was going to be my line." She was ridiculously pretty, boasted one of those bodies that looked as if she stepped straight off a Victoria's Secret runway. I still felt as if I should know her, which was beyond weird. "Why do I feel as if we've met before?"

"I don't know." She sat on the edge of the bed. "I've been watching you all afternoon. Maybe you sensed me on the periphery. That's not unheard of for people with powers like yours."

"Powers?" I glanced around to make sure we were really alone. It was a ridiculous reaction, but I couldn't stop myself. "Why would you say something like that?"

"Oh, you're cute." The blonde got to her feet and moved around the room, not stopping until she found the jeans I'd been wearing earlier in the day. She dug in the pocket until she came up with the coin I'd picked up in Betsy's garden. "I was called by this."

Confusion washed over me. "That was some sort of coin that was given out to people during a Mardi Gras parade. It's useless."

"No, that's what Martin told his wife," she corrected. "It's much more than that. It's a calling coin. Do you know what that is?"

Vaguely. I believed I'd read the term in a book once. I couldn't remember where, though. "What are you?"

"My name is Harlequin Desdemona Stryker."

My mouth dropped open. "That is the worst name ever. It's a cross between a porn name and a video game vixen."

"It is," she agreed. "You can call me Harley."

"That's a little better." I was grudging with my compliment. "You still haven't told me what you are."

"I'm a crossroads demon." Her smile deepened when my eyes widened. "I see you've heard of my kind. That's good. It'll save us some time."

"I know what a crossroads demon is in theory," I admitted, licking my lips as I leaned forward. "Ugh. Why am I so sick?"

"It's the coin." She flipped it around her fingers. "You're sensitive to the magic. A lot more sensitive than a normal person. I'm curious about that because I smell magic on you, but it's impossible for me to determine what you are. I've never had that happen."

"Well, I've never been in this position before, so I guess we're both all sorts of lucky," I drawled, causing her to laugh. "It's not funny."

"It's a little funny. May I?" Harley gestured toward my hand, which was resting on top of the comforter. I immediately snatched it away.

"What are you going to do?"

"I want to touch you to see if I can learn something that way. If you won't tell me what you are, I'm curious to discover it for myself. I always love a good mystical find."

She was far too cheerful. I hated that. Still, she didn't strike me as something to fear. She seemed like a straight shooter. "I don't know what I am." I opted for the truth. "I was raised away from my birth family. I had a great adoptive family, don't get me wrong. I don't know anything about my origins, though."

"Which means they're probably good." Harley's eyes sparkled as she held out her hand again. "Just let me try to touch you. It probably won't work, but it's worth a shot."

"You're a demon."

"I know."

"If I let you touch me, will you be able to steal my soul? I don't want to lose my soul. I just got a boyfriend and everything. Losing my soul will be depressing."

She barked out a laugh so loud it caused me to jolt. "I'm not here for your soul. If I thought I could get my hands on it, I might try. I'm guessing you're valuable. I also recognize it's a losing effort with you. You won't trade your soul for anything I have to offer."

Reluctantly, I held out my hand. Harley's fingers were warm when they clamped around my wrist. "Hmm. You have power. You're not a mage. There might be hints of mage in your blood, but they're buried deep. That means if you had a mage ancestor it was at least four cycles ago."

I stared at her blankly. "Is that good or bad?"

"It just ... is." Her smile was bland. "There's no shifter in here. No lamia." She leaned close and sniffed around my ear, which caused a chill throughout my body. "No succubus. No demon. There's some witch, but it's fifty percent of your bloodline, which means whatever is fueling you is larger than those genes. Hmm. You are interesting."

I was annoyed she insisted on talking about me as if I wasn't right there. "Um ... you're interesting, too," I said, my eyes flashing. "You're rude, barge into rooms when you're not invited, and that sniffing thing is weird."

She laughed. "I like your attitude, but I can feel your fear." She moved her hand to my forehead. I wanted to pull away, but I managed to remain strong. "You're afraid of what the man will think, aren't you?"

I opted to play dumb. "What man?"

"The one who wanted to sit by your bedside and hold your hand as you slept. The one who, even now, is worried that he should rush back and make sure you're all right. He's holding it together for form's sake — doesn't want the boss to think he's weak — but he'll be back in twenty minutes or so. We don't have much time."

"And you know all that from just touching me?"

"I have a unique set of skills," Harley replied. "As for you, you're not sick because of the food ... although you might want to learn to eat in moderation occasionally. You don't always have to stuff your face until you're ready to burst."

I stared at the bedspread. "Sorry. I didn't realize random people were watching me eat."

"You eat like that because you were once hungry," Harley noted. "I understand. You won't go hungry again. Jack won't let that happen. More importantly, you won't let it happen either. You're stronger than you give yourself credit for ... whatever you are."

"I'm guessing you can't point me toward answers about my past?"

"I could ... for a price."

I frowned. "I'm not selling you my soul for answers. I'm not an idiot."

She chuckled, seemingly genuinely amused. "Good. Don't make that mistake in the future. It's never worth it."

That was an odd thing for a crossroads demon to say. "Aren't you supposed to try to get me to sign over my soul?"

"Yes, but I'm not very good at my job." Harley flipped the coin over. "The man who had this before, Martin LaFleur, you're in search of him, correct?"

I nodded. "Why did he have so many of those coins? And why did he tell his wife they were trinkets from a parade?"

"Martin sold his soul to us ten years ago. He didn't ask for riches or fame. He asked for more time for his sick wife, who had cancer eating away at her."

I felt sick to my stomach when I realized where the story was going. "Oh, geez. Are you saying that you made him sell his soul to you to save his wife?"

"He didn't strike a bargain with me," she corrected. "He struck it with one of my co-workers. He was a real butthole. Jericho. I haven't seen him for years because he got busted for doing something inappropriate with a member of the Devil's harem. You know how that goes."

I had no idea. "Someone claimed his soul all the same, even though this Jericho was off the clock."

"*Someone* did," Harley agreed. "I was dispatched to collect his soul. I felt bad for him. I really did. I would've given him more time. Of course, I'm considered soft in this field. That's why I've never been promoted."

"And why you're looking for a way out?" I queried.

"Could be." She flashed a tight smile before flipping the coin so it landed on the bed. "Put that away. You can't be around it for too long without getting sick. You're sensitive. Wrapping it in something silk should protect you well enough. Don't access it unless you really need something ... and if you ever make that choice, be darned sure what you're trading for is worth it forever, not just at the moment."

"I'm never going to sell my soul. I promise you that won't happen. I'm not an idiot."

"Not everyone who trades his or her soul is an idiot," Harley chided. "Martin wasn't. He was simply a man who loved a woman for a very long time. He wasn't ready to lose her and was willing to trade his life for hers. He got another ten years with her and then we came to collect. He wasn't ready to go, which is why he was collecting the coins. He wanted to make a second deal. That never happens, for the record."

I felt inexplicably sad. "His time ran out. That's what you're telling me."

"His time literally ran out," she agreed.

"Is that why he ended up the way he did?"

Her eyes reflected curiosity when they shifted to me. "How did he end up?"

"He's a zombie."

She stared at me for a long beat, unblinking, and then burst out laughing. "Girl, there's no such thing as zombies. What have you been smoking? You didn't take a funny drink from someone on Bourbon Street when I wasn't looking, did you?"

I tried to keep from taking her words to heart. "It's true. The dead are rising in New Orleans. I saw a guy die twice yesterday. He might've technically dropped three times because I have no idea what happened before I saw him on the street, but I know he died at least twice."

Harley's smile disappeared as the wrinkles in her forehead deepened. "Are you serious?"

"Yeah." I bobbed my head. "Didn't you know?"

"No. Tell me what you know."

Because I didn't see any harm in it — she was a demon, after all, so she might be able to help — I launched into the tale. It took a good ten minutes to relate. When I finished, she was flustered.

"I didn't think that was possible." She slowly got to her feet and glanced around. "You think there's more than one body walking around?"

"I do. I think Martin is walking around, too. His body is missing from its vault."

"That is not good news." Harley tapped her bottom lip and moved to the window. Frustration was practically pouring off her. "Your boyfriend is back. He's on the main floor and getting ready to enter the hotel. We don't have much time."

"Can you figure out what's happening and get word to me?"

"I don't know. I can try to figure out what's happening. As for getting word to you ... all I can do is keep watch and listen to the whispers. Keep the coin with you, but cover it in silk. It will keep making you sick otherwise. I wasn't lying about your sensitivity."

"Okay. What are you going to do?"

"I'm going to try to find answers."

"And then what?"

"I have no idea." She shrugged and smiled as she turned. "I have to go. Romeo won't be kept away from you for another minute. Hide the coin away from you and don't lose it. I'll need to follow it to find you again."

"I've got it. I ... um ... thanks for trying to help." I felt ridiculous saying the words, but that didn't dissuade me. "You're kind of nice for a demon that trades souls and has a weird name."

"You're kind of nice for a magical hybrid, too."

I frowned. "What sort of hybrid?"

She didn't answer because she was already gone. I cursed under my breath and flopped back against the pillow as I studied the coin.

Now what?

SIXTEEN

I had already wrapped and hidden away the coin by the time Jack entered my room. He was like a ninja, stealthy feet and quiet breathing. He looked surprised when he found me sitting up in bed with my laptop.

"Why aren't you asleep?" His tone was accusatory.

I shrugged. It wasn't as if I could tell him about my visitor. He would think I was hallucinating and insist on taking me to the hospital. That was the last thing I wanted. "I'm feeling a little better." That was true. The second I wrapped the coin in a pair of silk boxers that I often slept in and hid it in my suitcase the nausea evaporated. "I decided to do some research."

"On what?"

"Hoodoo."

"Why?"

"Because New Orleans is a melting pot of religions and beliefs. So is hoodoo ... and voodoo, for that matter. I just thought I might as well do something useful if I'm going to be stuck in bed."

"You could sleep," he suggested.

"I'm not tired." In fact, I was feeling energized since hiding the coin away. Plus, Harley's appearance had my mind working at a fantastic rate. "I'm fine, Jack. I really am feeling better."

"Yeah?" He kicked off his shoes and climbed onto the bed next to me. "If that's true, go in the bathroom and brush your teeth."

I was caught off guard. "Why?"

"Because I want to kiss you and can't until you brush your teeth. You've been throwing up."

"Ah." His response made me smile. "I guess I can do that."

"I'll make it worth your while."

"I'm sure you will."

JACK WAS KNEE-DEEP IN RESEARCH when I exited the bathroom. In addition to brushing my teeth, I took a quick shower and I smelled like coconut shower gel when I climbed back into bed. It seemed natural, as if we did it every night. Sure, we'd shared a bed for sleep several times on assignments. This felt somehow different.

"I thought hoodoo and voodoo were the same thing," he admitted as he held the laptop so I could get comfortable next to him. He leaned in close and sniffed, momentarily reminding me of Harley. "You smell good. Do you still feel okay?"

I ignored the impulse to roll my eyes. He was simply showing he cared. "I'm fine. I told you. It came and went fast."

"Do you want something to eat? I can order room service."

It was a nice offer, but I didn't want to risk it. "I'm good for now. Thank you."

"Just tell me if you change your mind. While you're debating, break hoodoo and voodoo down for me. I think I understand the difference but I want you to explain it as if I'm stupid. I'm a bit out of my depth with this stuff."

He was adorable, but that observation would have to wait until we were finished with work. "Voodoo is a religion practiced by millions of people. It has two main branches. There's Haitian voodoo and New Orleans voodoo. They have much in common, but they're different.

"Hoodoo is something else entirely," I continued. "Hoodoo isn't a religion. It's more a way of life, or practices. It originated in West Africa and also tends to be popular here. Hoodoo is based on folklore and magic. It involves calling on gods called loas and saints from Roman Catholicism. Voodoo uses loas and African deities, but doesn't worship Catholic saints."

"That sounds complicated." Jack slipped his arm around me and tugged me closer. "Tell me if you feel sick. I'm not kidding. If you throw up on me, this relationship is going to have a massive hurdle to overcome."

"Thanks for the warning," I said dryly.

"I'm just trying to make sure I don't get sick."

"Are you a sympathetic puker?"

"Maybe. Are you?"

"Actually, I am. I don't know how to explain it."

"Well, now at least I don't feel as much of an idiot."

"There's that." I briefly rested my hand on his and smiled. "You didn't have to come back early because of me."

"Yes, I did."

"I'm perfectly capable of taking care of myself."

"I don't doubt that, but this wasn't a normal situation. When you're sick, someone is supposed to take care of you."

"Really?" I didn't remember anyone taking care of me after my parents died. When I was sick, I was basically left to my own devices. Of course, I rarely got sick. That was probably a blessing. "Well, thank you. It wasn't necessary, though. I really am feeling better."

"Good." He pressed a kiss to my temple and then tapped the computer. "Go back to what you were saying about hoodoo. There must be a reason you're zeroing in on that."

I had been visited by a crossroads demon. That was the one and only reason. He wasn't ready to hear that much truth.

"Hoodoo involves root doctors, or root healers in some cases. It's often likened to being a religion of personal power. Roots, herbs, animal parts like chicken feet, crystals and blood are often part of the spells," I volunteered.

"That sounds freaky. I'll never trust anyone who uses blood in a spell."

"It's actually quite normal."

"I still don't like it."

"Fair enough." I held up my hands in capitulation. "From the research I've done, I found that voodoo was brought to Louisiana via Haiti when it was a French colony. Hoodoo was brought by slaves from Africa."

"Were the slaves trying to cast spells on their masters to escape?"

"I'm sure that was part of it. Obviously I wasn't there. It makes sense, though. If I was treated as less than human I might want to embrace a religion that promised I could make my oppressors pay."

"Yes, but we're dealing with something that enslaves people," Jack pointed out. "Doesn't that go against the very tenets hoodoo was created to fight?"

He had a way with reasoning. "Yes, but it also makes sense on a different level. I mean, think about it. Slaves were used for physical labor, treated like cattle. They would've been looking for a way out. They probably knew there was no way they would ever escape from bondage if they didn't have other ways for the work to get done."

"Oh." Realization dawned on Jack's face. "You think this spell — or whatever it is — was created as a way to give the overlords an alternative workforce."

"Why not?"

"Because they were desecrating bodies in the process."

"Sure, but what's worse? Is mistreating live human beings better than enslaving dead bodies that should, at least in theory, be soulless?"

"That's a very interesting dilemma."

"It was a harsh world," I supplied. "It's still a harsh world. Maybe the roots of what's happening now extend back to that time. I mean ... maybe someone is trying to raise an undead army for a specific reason."

"And what reason would that be?"

"I don't know." And that was the most frustrating part of all of this.

We had no answers. "I don't think it can be anything good, but none of the bodies that have been raised have attacked anyone."

"That we know of."

"Don't you think word of that would've spread like wildfire?"

"I guess." He dragged a hand through his hair and cast me a side-long look. "You're good at this."

"What?"

"Thinking things through. When you first joined the team, I wasn't happy. I asked Chris to get someone older. I thought you would be a distraction."

I pursed my lips. "Aren't I distraction?"

"Oh, you're definitely a distraction." He let loose a hollow chuckle. "You're all I can think about sometimes and it drives me crazy."

"Do you wish I hadn't joined the team?"

"No." He immediately started shaking his head. "You're good for the team. You think outside the box. You're willing to embrace Chris's crazy theories. You're also willing to break from him if the evidence suggests he's on the wrong track. You're good for us."

"For you?"

He broke into a charming grin. "You're definitely good for me ... even though I told myself you should be the last thing I wanted. I couldn't make myself pull away from you. I tried. I mean ... I really tried. I think you were inevitable for me."

He was baring his soul and it felt nice. "Do you believe that there's only one match for everybody?"

"No."

I arched an eyebrow. "No?" That was a bit disappointing. "I thought maybe you believed in fate."

"I didn't say I didn't believe in fate. I simply don't think there's only one possible match for everybody. If that were true, there would be no love. I don't believe things are predestined. I think sometimes things happen that can make life so much better. You're that for me."

I went warm and gooey all over. "I can't believe you just said that. I feel as if I'm in a romance novel."

"Do you want to be in a romance novel?"

149

It was a sincere question and I was caught off guard. "I don't know how to answer that without looking like a doofus," I admitted.

"Just tell me the truth. What do you want?"

"What do you want?"

"No, no, no." He wagged a finger. "This isn't about me. It's about you. I want to make sure you're comfortable, Charlie. I don't want to push you before you're ready. There's a natural progression to a relationship, though, and I feel as if I'm caught in limbo."

I graced him with a sloppy smile. "You mean that you want to make a move but don't want to do it too soon. It must be difficult to be a guy. You have a lot of expectations hanging over you."

"I just want to do the right thing by you."

And that's what sealed it for me. "I think we should finish researching for the night." I carefully closed the laptop and moved it to the nightstand.

He swallowed hard. "Do you want me to go?"

"No."

"Do you want me to stay?"

I was exasperated. "Do I have to say it out loud?"

"Yes. I need to hear it."

"I want you to stay." Once I'd said it, some of the trepidation I'd been carrying around for weeks disappeared. We still had a winding road ahead of us, but it was going to be okay. I honestly believed that in the depths of my soul. "I want you to stay all night and ... you know."

He smirked. "I should make you say that part, too."

"If you do, we'll never get anywhere."

"I figured." He leaned in close. "Okay. I guess it's time to wow you."

My eyebrows flew up my forehead and a giggle, unbidden, caught in my throat. "You have a very high opinion of your abilities. I hope you can live up to the hype."

"Me, too."

I WOKE THE NEXT MORNING and stretched languidly. I felt

remarkably good for a woman who had spent an hour throwing up the previous day while her boyfriend held her hair. I felt reborn. I was naked as the day I was born, so that was a good thing.

Jack made a muffled groan next to me. He was on his back, one arm thrown over his head, and he was caught somewhere between consciousness and slumber. He was ridiculously beautiful in the morning sunlight.

As if feeling my eyes on him, he slowly turned and greeted me with a smile. "Morning." He gave me a soft kiss. "How do you feel?"

Leave it to Jack to immediately go to the practical. "I'm not sick, Jack. How many times do I have to tell you?"

"That's not what I'm talking about."

"Oh." My cheeks burned. "I'm good. How are you?" The question came out a lot more stilted than I intended.

Instead of being offended, he chuckled. "I'm good." He moved his arm around my waist and tugged me so my head rested on his chest. "We only have a few minutes before we have to get up. You should rest."

"I'm not sick."

"No, but you must be tired after last night."

If it was even possible, my cheeks burned hotter. "You have a ridiculously high opinion of yourself. Has anyone ever told you that?"

"Yes."

"I don't want to know who."

"I tell myself that every day." He tickled my ribs, causing me to gasp. The levity was welcome. "I have a really high opinion of you, too. You should feel proud."

"Oh, yeah?" I laughed as he tickled me again, this time rolling so I was on my back and he was on top of me. His eyes were earnest when they met mine.

"You're okay?"

I nodded. "I'm good, Jack. In fact, I'm great. You don't have to worry about me. I swear that I'm fine. I don't think I've felt this ... great ... in a really long time."

"Yeah, well ... me either." He lowered his mouth to mine and gave me a long kiss. "I love that you smell like coconuts in the morning." He buried his face in my hair and I wrapped my arms around his back so I could hold him for a bit. "You're so warm. Are you always this warm in the morning?"

"I think that might have something to do with sharing a bed with you," I pointed out. "We practically slept on top of each other."

"I slept good. I can't remember when I last slept that hard." It was almost as if he was talking to himself. "Usually I dream about being overseas, having to run. Sometimes my sleep is more tiring than my work. Not last night. Last night I only dreamed about you."

That was an unbelievably flattering comment. "Oh, well ... ."

He laughed, his breath tickling my ear. "You are slow in the mornings. It takes that sarcastic tongue of yours some time to catch up."

He wasn't wrong. "I guess I'll have to work on it."

"I like it. In fact ... ." He broke off, frowning when he heard someone futzing with the door. "What time is it?"

I immediately turned my attention to the clock on the nightstand. "It's not even eight yet. We're not expected to be downstairs for breakfast for an hour."

"Wait here." All traces of romantic Jack fled when he hopped to his feet. He had the foresight to grab the boxer shorts he'd discarded on the floor the night before, but he didn't bother with more clothing than that. He strode toward the door with a purpose, ready for a fight.

I sat up, clutching the sheet to my chest. I felt caught. If something was on the other side of the door getting ready to attack, I would have to step in and use my magic. I wasn't ready for that conversation yet. I wanted to bask a bit longer. It seemed I didn't have a choice.

Jack threw open the door, his body ready to pounce. The look on his face, which I could only see in profile, went from predatory to mortified in a blink. "Millie!"

"I wondered if you were in here." Millie breezed past him and into the room, pulling up short when she caught sight of me in bed. "Well, well, well. Look what we have here."

I glanced down to make sure I was completely covered and then pinned her with a furious look. "What are you doing here?"

152

"Chris sent me to make sure you two were up. We're moving early this morning." Her gaze bounced between Jack and me. "You guys look radiant ... and you're glowing!."

"We are not." Jack shut the door and stalked toward the bed. "Why can't this wait a freaking hour?"

"Chris is convinced he's about to prove zombies exist," Millie replied. "I'm sure if he knew he was interrupting your morning-after bliss he would've delayed his urges to give you more time to cuddle."

"Shut up," Jack growled. He flopped on the bed, but he didn't crawl under the covers, his cut torso on full display. "Go ahead and do your worst. I don't care how much you tease us."

"I'm not going to tease you."

I waited, not believing her for a second.

"Okay, I'm not going to tease you just now," she corrected, her grin mischievous. "I need to wrap my head around this. Last time I checked, Charlie was sick. This wasn't the scene I expected this morning. In fact, I thought there was a chance I was going to have to fight with Jack to get him to leave you."

"I'm fine," I supplied. "I feel much better."

"Obviously."

"What is going on that requires our attention first thing in the morning?" Jack asked. "It had better be good. Otherwise I'm going to track down Chris and shake him for an hour, until I burn up every ounce of frustration that he's caused."

"I'm honestly sorry for interrupting you." Millie looked contrite. "It's just ... there was a disturbance at one of the cemeteries. Apparently someone reported multiple people walking around last night and Chris is convinced a bunch of zombies were raised."

"Ugh." Jack slapped his hand to his forehead. "I can't even ... he's a menace."

"He's a believer," Millie corrected. "You used to understand that, accept it."

"I do understand. It's just ... he ruined my morning." Jack wearily rolled to a sitting position. "How long do we have?"

"Thirty minutes."

"We'll be ready."

Millie's lips curved. "I'm sure you will." She grabbed the door handle. "By the way, you two are so adorable I just want to bottle whatever it is that you've got going and sell it because I would make a million dollars off your essence right now."

"Goodbye, Millie," Jack snapped.

"See you soon, Jack."

He slid his eyes to me as soon as she was gone. "Well, so much for our morning."

"It's okay." I tossed off the covers. "We'll have a lot of mornings … at least I hope we will." I shot him a smile. "I want to prove that zombies are real."

He let loose a world-weary sigh. "Of course you do. Let's get to it."

SEVENTEEN

*A*ll eyes were on Jack and me when we reached the lobby. The look on his face practically dared anyone to say a word. Bernard, Chris and Hannah were wise and did nothing but smile in an absent sort of way. Perhaps they didn't care. Millie's lion-that-ate-the-hyena grin wasn't easy to dismiss. It was Laura's expression, though, that raised my hackles.

"It's about time," she sneered, hands on her hips.

"We're here, aren't we?" Jack shot back.

"Like it matters."

"What is your problem?"

"I don't have a problem. You're the one with the problem you ... you ... fornicator."

That wasn't the word I expected to escape her lips. "Wow! A four-syllable insult," I muttered, causing Millie's smile to widen.

"Mind your own business, Laura," Jack instructed, turning his attention to Chris. "Do we have vehicles?"

"They're arriving right now," Chris replied. Either he was oblivious to what had gone down or he simply refused to engage. "We have reports that at least ten people were seen shambling around Lafayette

Cemetery in the Garden District. We can't walk there so I thought it was best to arrange for drivers."

"That's fine." Jack steadfastly refused to meet Laura's petulant gaze. "Do we know what these people were doing in the cemetery?"

"That's just it. No one saw them go in. They only saw them leave." He looked almost gleeful as he leaned forward and lowered his voice. "They were walking in a line, moaning, and they didn't pay any attention to the people watching from across the street."

Jack blinked several times. "And in your mind that means they're zombies? Have you considered it was regular people playing a prank?"

"Nope. It was zombies."

"Of course it was." Jack dragged a hand through his hair and found me watching him. He was clearly frustrated, but the second our gazes met he grinned. It took him a minute to realize what he was doing, and then he collected himself and went back to scowling, but his happiness was hard to miss. I wondered if I looked the same way.

A quick look at Millie told me I probably did, because she moved closer when the first sports utility vehicle pulled up. "I'm going with Jack and Charlie," she announced. "You guys can take Laura."

Chris made a face. "Fine. I guess I can deal with that."

"Hey!" Laura was incensed. "You should be so lucky to have me in your vehicle. I'm a delightful co-worker."

"Yes, that's what we all whisper when you're not around," Millie agreed, giving me a small shove toward the door. "Come on, Charlie. I can't wait to bend your ear."

That sounded like an uncomfortable ride, but I didn't see where I had much choice. It was either her or Laura — one form of torture or another — and Millie was much more pleasant than our resident harpy. "Sure. I'm looking forward to it."

Bernard joined our group and sat in the front seat, leaving Millie, Jack and me to scatter throughout the middle rows of the SUV. Jack moved to take the spot next to me, but Millie expertly hip-checked him out of the way.

"I think you should sit behind us," she ordered, her magnificent smirk coming out to play. "I would hate for you to lose your head and develop a case of wandering hands when we're on the clock."

Jack growled but slid into the backseat. He winked at me as he fastened his seatbelt, but otherwise remained silent.

"So ... how are you feeling?" Millie's presence was hard to ignore as I stared out the window to my left.

"I'm fine, Millie."

"You look ... shiny and new."

"Is that a compliment?" I couldn't quite work it out.

"It's most definitely a compliment. I kind of want to bottle whatever you use on your hair to make it so glossy. I swear, it's almost as if you're glowing."

"Oh, geez." I slapped my hand over my eyes even though it was my ears giving me issues. "How far is the Garden District from here?"

"Not far," Jack replied. He had his phone out and was reading. "Lafayette Cemetery was founded in 1833. It's the city's first planned cemetery and notable because of its cruciform layout, which is perfect for parades and second lines. Who throws a parade at a funeral?"

"I want a parade at my funeral," I offered.

"You do?"

"Yeah. I don't want people to mourn me. I want them to celebrate my life. I want them to say, 'That Charlie Rhodes is going to be missed, but look what she did while she was here.'"

Jack furrowed his brow. "How about you just don't die until after me — like when we're ninety — and I don't have to think about it? How does that sound?"

Millie chuckled. "Oh, I think I might overload on the cuteness."

"Shut up, Millie," Jack barked. He was genuinely fond of the woman, went out of his way to help her and share conversations that I wouldn't normally believe entertained him. However, she was obviously on his last nerve today.

"Stop being such a spoilsport," Millie shot back, seemingly unbothered by his tone. "This should be a happy day. The fact that you keep smiling between snarls tells me you think so, too."

"Shut up," Jack repeated, with less vehemence this time. "We need to focus on work. Not ... other things."

"What other things could we be focusing on?" Bernard asked from the front. He was the quiet sort, and had a longstanding relationship with Millie that they didn't broadcast because her ex-husband was everyone's boss. He also was inquisitive, and I didn't miss the hint of mischief weaving throughout his words.

"There is nothing else to focus on," I said hurriedly. "All we care about is work ... and the zombies."

I didn't miss the way the driver flicked his eyes to the rear-view mirror, as if trying to ascertain if I was purposely being ridiculous. I held his gaze for a moment, until he went back to watching the road, and then turned to look at Jack.

"What else does it say about the cemetery?"

"*Interview with a Vampire* and *Double Jeopardy* were filmed there."

I perked up. "Really? That's kind of cool."

"It was also damaged heavily during Hurricane Katrina, and apparently there's some 'Save Our Cemeteries' group fighting for conservation. It's supposedly architecturally significant."

"Then I'm excited to see it." I meant it. This day was going well. I couldn't wait to see what was around the next corner. "I've never been to the Garden District. This should be fun."

He shook his head. "Life is an adventure."

"It is," I agreed, risking a glance at Millie, who looked so happy I almost wanted to shove a slice of cake in her mouth to get her to stop grinning. "I'm looking forward to it."

THE FEELING LASTED FOR the entire ride and only grew when we reached our destination. The overblown houses, kitschy bars and sprawling trees took my breath away as I climbed out of the SUV.

"Wow!"

Jack caught me before I could trip over my own feet. "Watch where you're going," he admonished, although he looked more amused than alarmed. "I take it you like what you see."

"It's ... I don't even know what to say. Look at that house." I pointed toward an ancient-looking behemoth. "I read a lot of Hollywood stars live here."

"I read that, too," Jack said, his hand automatically moving to my back. He seemed happy with the brief touch, making sure not to linger, but I found the covert way he moved cute.

"There are definitely a lot of stars here," Millie agreed. "Myron was going to buy a house here for me because he knew I loved the city. We did some research. That was before we divorced, of course. I still check from time to time because this is my end goal. I would love to end up here."

Bernard shot her a fond smile. "Then I have a feeling you'll end up here."

"And not alone," I teased, poking her side before moving around her to get a better look. "What stars live here?"

"Sandra Bullock, John Goodman, Brad Pitt, Drew Brees, Nicolas Cage."

"Is Nicolas Cage still a star?" Jack asked. "I'm not all that impressed with him. John Goodman, ... him I would love to call a neighbor."

I laughed as the second SUV pulled up. Laura, her expression just as sour as when we left the hotel, was the first to climb out. She glared directly at me as she crossed to us.

"I'm glad to see you waited for everyone to arrive before entering," she sneered. "I thought for sure you guys would take off and ... play games or something."

"I rarely play games in cemeteries," Jack countered. "It's not respectful to the dead."

"Let's go in," Chris said. He was practically overflowing with excitement. "I want to see this place. It's famous."

"Movies were filmed here," I agreed.

"I don't care about that. I care about the dead people who rose and walked out of here. Those are the people I want to see."

"Yes, we're all dying to see them," Jack deadpanned. "I don't suppose you know which direction we're supposed to look?"

"I only know that it's in there ... somewhere." Chris threw out his hands in a wide arc to signify the whole of the cemetery. "Let's find some dead people, shall we?"

IT WAS EASIER SAID THAN DONE to find tombs and mausoleums that had been messed with. This particular cemetery was rough around the edges in some parts. Some of the edifices looked as if they were one stiff breeze from collapse.

"It's sad," I noted as Jack followed me through the cemetery. We'd split into groups, essentially pairing off as couples. Someone had ended up with Laura, of course, but it wasn't us, so I refused to worry about her.

"What's sad?" Jack asked, his eyes on the window of a mausoleum.

"People put their loved ones in here because they thought it meant they would be remembered forever. The problem is, so many people die that few can be remembered forever. Even famous people get forgotten."

"Are you worried about being forgotten?"

"No. I'm just thinking about life and death."

"For now, I prefer you focus on life."

I turned my eyes to him and found a smile waiting for me. "I'm not being maudlin," I reassured him. "I just think about these things sometimes. I can't help it."

"And you don't think that's maudlin?"

I shrugged. "I wonder if my parents are dead. Maybe that's why they left me. Then I wonder if they're alive, and it's almost worse to think about that because then it makes me wonder why they didn't want to keep me. Maybe there was something wrong with me and they knew it."

I hadn't meant to say the last part aloud. I wasn't fishing for sympathy. I often lost myself in "what if" scenarios. Maybe my parents realized I was different from the other kids and that made them abandon me. Or, in more fanciful moments, I imagined they abandoned me to keep my abilities a secret from some unseen enemy. I much preferred that daydream.

Jack crossed to me and snagged my hand. "I don't know what happened to your parents, but if they purposely left you they don't deserve another thought. I don't know why anyone would leave you."

There was one reason, but he was still in the dark about that. The longer I let things go like this, the more I would regret it. I would have to tell him ... and soon. It could wait until after this investigation. After that, though, I had no choice. It was time.

"Maybe they just didn't want me," I suggested. "Or maybe they did want me and changed their minds at a certain point."

"We can try to find out," he offered, somber. "If you want, I can do some digging. There must be records from when you were found. A search was likely conducted. I can try to get those files."

It was an enticing offer. It was also terrifying. "Maybe," I said after a beat. "I need to think about it first. Is that okay?"

"Absolutely." He dipped in quickly and gave me a kiss. "Whatever you want."

I smiled at his earnest expression. "Right now, I just want to find a zombie. I think it would make Chris really happy."

"Yes, well ... ." He scuffed his foot against the hard-packed earth. "I think Chris is going to be disappointed. I don't see any zombies running around."

As if on cue, an excited voice called to us from across the cemetery. "Over here!" It was Chris, and he was waving excitedly.

When we reached him, the reason for his enthusiasm was obvious. The doors of four tombs, all standing wall-to-wall, gaped wide. It looked as if someone had come through and ripped the doors off their hinges to get inside.

"What the ... ?" Jack forgot about me and moved to the nearest vault. "Someone definitely wanted in here," he said, his hands running over the door.

I left him and Chris to explore and focused down one of the narrow aisles. I was almost certain I'd seen a hint of movement and wanted to reassure anyone — whether it be a visitor or security — that we weren't up to no good. The aisle appeared to be empty, though.

On a whim, I moved down another aisle, increasing the distance between my co-workers and me. Sure enough, a man stood alone. He wore simple jeans and a black hoodie. He was white, unbelievably pale in fact, and he looked to be staring directly at me.

My heart skipped, and I raised my hand to wave at him. He didn't wave back, instead disappearing behind another mausoleum. I walked to the next aisle and looked, but he wasn't there. That propelled me to go down another aisle.

This time he was there, and he'd moved closer. His blue eyes were pale, almost icy, and the look he graced me with was dark. A nervous tingle ran down my spine and my throat dried to Death Valley humidity level. I decided to call out to him despite the fear.

"Hello."

He didn't respond.

"It's a nice day, huh?" It was hot and humid, just like the day before. That begged the question of why he was wearing a hoodie. Of course, we were from the Northeast. This might feel cool to a local.

"We're just looking around because we heard there was a distur-bance here last night," I offered, doing my best to memorize the man's face. He had dark hair that looked dirty. His cheekbones were high, his eyes sunken. He looked like a meth addict almost, although that association didn't feel right.

"Do you need something?" I asked. "Are you hungry? I can buy you a meal if you're hungry."

He didn't answer, instead turning on his heel and walking in the opposite direction.

"Where are you going?" I called to his back.

He didn't answer. By this point I didn't expect him to. I took one step to follow and then stopped. What if he was trying to entice me to give chase, perhaps isolate me from the others? What if he was some-thing other than human?

I opened my mouth to call out a final time, but he'd already disap-peared. I checked one aisle over but he looked to be gone. When I turned back, I realized I'd put quite a bit of distance between me and the rest of the group. Only Laura was close, and I got the distinct impression that she'd been following me. That left me unsettled for a different reason.

"Do you need something?" I asked finally.

"No. I just wanted to make sure you didn't wander off. Poor Jack would be despondent if we lost you."

I was in no mood to put up with her attitude. "There was someone walking between the aisles. I wanted to check him out."

"Right. You wanted to find the zombie so you would be the big hero. I know how your mind works."

"I definitely wanted to find a zombie," I agreed. "I don't care about being a hero."

She grabbed my arm when I moved to brush past her. For some reason, the simple act of aggression — she'd done far worse things to me since I'd joined the group — was enough to set me off. "Don't put your hands on me!"

"Oh, so sorry." She rolled her eyes and released me. "You think you're hot stuff, don't you? You think that because you got Jack you're higher in the pecking order than I am. Well, I'm here to tell you you're wrong. You're still the intern."

"Fine. I'm the intern. Will you excuse me?"

"We're not done talking." Disdain dripped from her tongue. "This isn't going to last. You know that, right? You're just a momentary distraction. He'll get bored. When that happens, he'll drop you."

I shook my head. "Your infatuation with Jack is getting sad. You need to let it go."

"Maybe you should let it go."

"Why would I do that? I'm happy. He's happy. The only one who isn't happy in this arrangement is you. That seems to indicate you're the one holding on when you should let go."

"I'm going to win."

"Is that what you're worried about? Winning isn't everything." I felt inexplicably sad for her. "Besides, you can't win a person. You should try to better yourself. What you're doing now is only going to blow up in your face."

"And what am I doing?"

"Nothing good. But I don't really care." I was forceful when I pushed her to the side. "Laura, I don't know what you expect to get out of life, but all you're doing is making yourself miserable. I'm not going to let you hurt me ... and Jack won't let you hurt him. So who are you helping by acting like this?"

"I'm not acting like anything."

"You are. You're acting like a spoiled brat. Look around." I gestured toward the street, to where the fancy houses stood winking at us in the sunlight. "This is a beautiful place. It's magical. All you see is ugliness. All you project is ugliness. Why not try to make life better for those around you instead?"

"You really are annoying, aren't you? I mean ... grow up. Life isn't puppies and ice cream."

"It's not venom and vitriol either. You have to let it go. You're the only one hanging onto this. You can't have a triangle when two sides aren't in the game."

"Oh, whatever."

Perhaps sensing trouble, Jack picked that moment to appear. His gaze was leery as it bounced between the two of us. "What's going on?"

"Don't worry," Laura snapped. "I was just making sure your precious girlfriend didn't wander away. She's perfectly fine."

"I wasn't worried." Jack shifted his eyes to me. "Come on. Chris wants to go inside the vaults. I didn't think you would want to miss that."

"Definitely not!" I smiled as I hurried to follow. "Did he find any zombies?"

"Nope, but he's nowhere near done looking."

EIGHTEEN

*J*ack was in a playful mood despite our location. He managed to slide me into a corner when no one was looking and give me a long kiss. I understood what Millie meant when she said we looked "shiny." I saw it in Jack.

"What was that for?" I asked, breathless when he pulled back.

"I'm still mad our morning got cut short," he admitted, grinning as he smoothed my hair. "I think I should be able to arrange for us to break off alone once we're done here."

I studied him for a long moment. "What about the zombies?"

His face fell. "I don't believe in zombies. We've been over this."

"I don't know if I believe in zombies either," I admitted. "But something is going on. Look at those vaults. They're empty.."

"I agree, and Chris is preparing to call Thibodeaux." Jack turned serious, his earlier smile essentially forgotten. "I would rather not be here when he arrives."

I could translate exactly what he meant. "You want me gone."

"I want you out of his line of fire."

"Isn't that the same thing?"

"I guess, but it doesn't matter." He was calm as he regarded me. "I think it's best if I take you out of here before Chris makes the call, just to be on the safe side."

I understood what he was saying. Worrying came naturally to Jack, and even though he was feeling invigorated and happy that didn't mean he had any intention of putting me at risk. I appreciated that about him. I had a more practical side, though.

"Hiding won't do me any good," I said. "Laura will make sure that he knows I was part of this excursion no matter what. Her nose is out of joint."

"Yeah. I saw you two talking. I don't suppose you want to tell me what she said?"

"The same stuff she normally says. That I shouldn't get comfortable because you'll get bored. That you're only with me to make her jealous. That I can't keep you over the long haul. Her repertoire never changes."

His eyes narrowed. "You know that's not true, right?"

"Which part? Are you saying I can keep you forever?"

The question obviously flummoxed him. "I'm saying that ... nothing I feel for you has anything to do with her," he said after a moment's contemplation. It was far too soon to promise forever. He got as close as he could, though, without crossing a line.

"I know." I rested my hand on his forearm. "She's going to tell Thibodeaux I was here, though. There's no sense slipping away."

"She can't tell him if we take her with us."

That sounded as if we were trading one form of hell for another. "Do you really want to do that?"

"No, but I really don't want you here when Thibodeaux arrives. You're right. She will tattle. That means we have to take her."

"Take her where?" That was the ultimate question. "Where are we going?"

"Leon. I haven't talked to him since before dinner yesterday. I want to see if he's found anything."

I knew what else he wanted to do with Leon. He wasn't nearly as slick as he thought. "You just want him to distract Laura and have him take her off our hands."

"Is that such a bad thing?"

"No, but ... she's only pretending to be interested in him."

"And he recognizes that and wants to see how far she's willing to go. He's not some fragile flower. He doesn't need to be protected."

"Okay, but I want lunch. That doughnut for breakfast wasn't enough."

"I'm sure I can arrange that. I was thinking someplace light today. Maybe we'll take a break from the local cuisine and you can have a hamburger or something simple so we can make sure your stomach is okay."

I had information he didn't – I knew what caused my stomach issues – so I was having none of it. "I can't be one of those people who totally ignore local cuisine." I meant it. "I want something regional."

"Fine." Jack held up his hands in defeat. "If you get sick again, I'm going to be really upset. I have plans for you."

That sounded intriguing. "Is this before or after we dump Laura on Leon?"

"After."

"Okay, but let's get a move on. It looks like Chris is getting ready to call Thibodeaux. I don't want to be here if I don't have to. I swear that guy hates me."

"I've got it. I won't let him go after you. I promise you that."

LEON PICKED A HUGE restaurant in the Garden District that was supposedly famous. Commander's Palace boasted cheap martinis, gregarious customers and some of the friendliest wait staff I'd ever met.

"They keep trying to make me drink a martini even though it's only noon," I told Jack as Leon got settled across from us. Laura's atti- tude had been nothing but evil since we'd left Lafayette Cemetery, but she perked up when she realized Leon was joining us.

"I'm so glad you're here," she announced, batting her eyelashes. "You've just made lunch a tolerable affair."

Jack rolled his eyes as Leon snickered.

"Well, I'm glad I made it, too." He gave her hand a pat before focusing on me. "And how are you, Little Miss? You look better than you did yesterday."

"Oh, she wasn't sick." Laura's expression momentarily darkened. "She made that up to get attention."

Jack's anger surged. "She did not. Not everything is about attention, Laura. You saw her. She was sick. You can't fake that."

"She seemed perfectly fine when you went back to the hotel early," Laura shot back. "We all know what you did then."

His interest piqued, Leon angled his head in our direction. "I don't know what you did."

"That's none of your business," Jack snapped. "Why must you keep digging into things that aren't your business?"

"I want to know what you did whether it's my business or not," Leon announced. "In fact ... ." He trailed off as his gaze bounced between us. "Oh, I know what you did. You dawg!" He grinned and wriggled his eyebrows, causing Laura's expression to darken as Jack's cheeks flushed with color. "It's about time. You guys were so sweet you were giving me a toothache."

Laura, who was caught between wanting to flirt with Leon because she thought it would make Jack jealous and annoyance, pinned him with a biting look. "They're not sweet. They're only doing this to get a rise out of me."

"I don't think so."

"I *know* so."

The conversation made me uncomfortable so I decided to change the subject. "What's good here? I want to try something new."

Leon, seemingly happy to escape from Laura's anger, offered me an indulgent smile. "They have gator bites on the menu. That's what I'm getting."

I frowned. "Gator bites? Is that like a special name for something?"

He nodded. "Yeah. It's what we call bites of alligator."

My stomach turned as I looked toward Jack. "Is he kidding?"

Jack chuckled. "No. I've seen him eat gator bites before."

"People really eat alligator?" Just the thought made me gag. "What's it taste like?"

"Chicken," Leon automatically answered.

"Does it really taste like chicken?" I wasn't convinced. "Wait. It doesn't matter." I vigorously shook my hand. "I can't eat alligator."

"What's the difference between eating alligator and chicken?" Leon asked. "I'm not trying to be a pain. I genuinely want to know."

"I ... don't ... know." That was the truth. In theory, he'd already won the argument. That didn't mean I could eat alligator. "It's just different."

"You mean it's not something you're used to," Leon countered. "Everything is new to someone at one point or another. I'm sure chicken was new to you when you first started eating solid foods. You still chose to eat it."

"Actually, I have no idea when I first ate chicken. I do know there was a notation in my state file that I absolutely hated liver. My adoptive mother tried to make me eat it because she loved it but I never grew to like it. I don't know that you can train someone to like something."

Jack's head snapped in my direction. "They made you eat foods you didn't like?"

His reaction made me laugh. "Um ... they asked me to try things even if I said I didn't want to. I didn't grow up in a restaurant family or anything. I never went hungry with them. I might've before they adopted me, but I don't remember much about that time."

"But ... ." Anger briefly pulsed over him and then he pulled it together. "I hate stories about how much you've suffered through the years," he grumbled. "You don't have to eat alligator. They have salads and soup. Try something else."

I didn't see it as suffering as much as he did but he had a very definite opinion.

"I don't understand," Leon countered. "Why are you so upset?"

"Charlie was abandoned by her parents," Laura explained. "Even they knew she was a loser and didn't want her. She grew up in the system ... and somehow we ended up adopting her. It's tragic ... for us."

Before Jack could jump all over her I grabbed his wrist and gave it a squeeze. "It's not worth it. Besides, I got adopted by wonderful people. I don't remember my life before them. If there were bad foster homes before that or something, I can't recall. It's okay."

I was determined to turn the conversation to something more pleasant. "I'll try the shrimp fritters. Just ... don't start yelling. I like this place. It's cool. I don't want you to start yelling and ruin things."

Jack glared at Laura for a long moment before turning to me and smiling. "Shrimp fritters sound good. What do you want me to get so you can try more than one thing? I'll eat anything."

"I suggest gator bites," Laura drawled.

Jack was so close to the line I thought he might lose it. Instead, he focused on the menu. "I'll get the turtle soup and a salad."

I was horrified. "You're going to eat a turtle?"

He burst out laughing at my expression. "I'll get the gumbo instead. How does that sound?"

"Better than eating a turtle."

"You'll have to make a list of things I can and can't eat."

"I'm more than willing to do that."

"Good." He rested his hand on top of mine. "That'll make dining so much easier for the foreseeable future."

WE DUMPED LAURA ON LEON. He planned to question several people who supposedly saw the late-night conga line walking around in the cemetery. Jack thought it best that we not go with them because we might risk running into Thibodeaux. Instead, we headed to the nearest library to conduct further research. He was fascinated with hoodoo and wanted more information. Because the library was air-conditioned — and we were away from Laura — I readily agreed.

"Where do you want to start?" I asked when we found the appropriate stacks. "There are a lot of books ... and they look interesting."

"Right here." Jack slid in front of me and dipped his head to give me a kiss. It was a soft moment, almost sexless, and it calmed me.

"What was that for?" I asked when he pulled back.

"I've been wanting to do that since we left the cemetery with Laura the Hun."

I pressed my lips together to keep from laughing too loud and drawing attention. "She's convinced herself she's in love with you. I don't think she means to be as difficult as she is."

"Oh, she knows exactly what she's doing. Don't kid yourself."

"Fine. Let me rephrase that: She knows that she's hurting me. She doesn't want to hurt you."

"Well, when you're hurt, I'm hurt. I'm pretty sure that's how this relationship thing goes."

"And that's why she wants you so badly. You're ... gallant."

"Gallant?"

"Like a knight."

"I guess I can live with that." He turned toward the shelf. "Let's grab some books and sit down. I want to hear more about this hoodoo stuff."

"Do you think hoodoo is behind what's happening?"

"I think that I'm intrigued by what you told me earlier," he clarified. "It makes sense that something is going on here. I think someone wants the public to believe the dead are rising."

"Why?" I wanted to hear his answer. "You saw the guy in the hallway. He was dead on the road, Jack. We both saw it. Then, suddenly, he was alive. He somehow found my room only to die again. How do you explain that?"

He worked his jaw. "I can't," he said finally. "I like that stuff Hannah was talking about. The drugs. Maybe someone injected him with drugs."

"And the missing bodies? Where do you think those are going? The ones taken last night weren't even fresh. I read the dates on the tomb plaques. They all died at least ten years ago. In some cases the bodies were fifty years old. What's the point of stealing bodies that old?"

"I don't have all the answers, Charlie."

"And here I thought you were Superman," I teased him ruefully.

"If I'm any superhero, it's Batman ... and not Ben Affleck's Batman either."

"Are you Christian Bale's Batman?"

"I was thinking more like Michael Keaton's Batman."

That was ... interesting. "He was before your time, wasn't he?"

"Sometimes I think I was born out of my time. I probably should've been born before I was."

"Yes, you have action hero written all over you," I said, enjoying the conversation. "You would've been great in *Top Gun* and *Commando*."

"Ha, ha." He tapped the end of my nose. "I'm just saying that sometimes I don't feel as if I fit in this world."

The admission caught me off guard. "Sometimes I feel that way, too. Maybe we were displaced together."

"Or maybe we didn't fit until we found each other." He looked momentarily wistful and then pointed toward the books. "I'm going to take these to the table. Why don't you get us coffee at that kiosk at the front of the building?" He dug in his pocket for money. "I'll have whatever you're having."

"What if I have something girly?"

"Then I guess I'm drinking girly coffee. I don't care." He briefly rested his forehead against mine before separating. "We have to focus on work. I find you distracting on a lot of levels today. However, I refuse to be the guy who ignores his job because there's a cute girl in the room."

"And I refuse to be the girl who goes gooey because you called me cute."

"So, we're agreed." He didn't pull away, instead giving me another kiss. "I just have to find the strength to be a grown-up. I don't know how it came to be that I would rather be a teenager."

"I think it's just a hormones thing. We'll get used to it."

"That would be nice." One more kiss and he released me. "I'm serious about the research. I think there's something here. We need caffeine to go through all this."

"I'm on it." I offered him a mock salute before moving toward the front of the building. I pulled up short when I caught sight of a familiar hoodie. The man from the cemetery hovered near the front row where the new releases rested. He was watching us, but he was too far away to make out his expression. "Son of a ... !"

I stormed in his direction, ready to make a scene if necessary. I didn't appreciate being followed. The library was surprisingly busy, though, and I had to duck around several people as I stalked toward him. I was ready to throw down when I rounded the corner, but the man in the hoodie was gone.

I was certain I'd seen him. There was no way I imagined it. He was so pale as to be distinctive, and I had a feeling that was somehow important.

I had a lot of questions.

Who was he?

Why was he following me?

Was he trying to isolate me from the rest of the group? Is that why he tried to draw me away?

On instinct, I turned to look over my shoulder. I could just make out Jack as he sat at a table. He was already engrossed in whatever he was reading.

I thought about calling to him. He would come running and insist on searching for the man. The problem was, I was starting to wonder if I was imagining things even though that seemed ridiculous. Still, I couldn't be sure Laura caught sight of him at the cemetery. She didn't acknowledge it. I was positive Jack didn't see our friend here. That meant I was the only one ... and I was terrified at the thought of Jack believing I was losing my mind. That seemed the wrong message to send given what I had to tell him when everything was settled again.

Instead of dwelling on it, I circled a few racks to make sure my new friend wasn't hiding and then made my way to the coffee kiosk. If he'd really been here, he was gone now. And if I was imagining him I had to figure out why. Perhaps he was a harbinger of sorts.

And that right there was chilling enough that I turned back to the matter at hand. Jack didn't want to believe in zombies but I wasn't sure I could believe in anything else. For once, I had no doubt that paranormal forces were at play. Figuring out which ones was the ultimate problem.

I couldn't give up. It was important. I believed that to my bones. The only thing left to do was sort out all the pieces of this particular puzzle. It felt like everything was there, waiting to be arranged into the right picture. Somehow I was missing something, and I really hated that.

It was time to dig deep.

NINETEEN

$\mathcal{W}$e spent hours digging through books. At a certain point, we kept reading the same information over and over. That's when Jack insisted that we head back to the hotel.

"We're not getting anywhere. We need to take a break."

"Okay." Arguing seemed unnecessary. "What kind of break were you thinking?"

He shrugged, noncommittal. "I don't know. I don't think a nap would be out of the realm of possibility."

I almost tripped over my feet as we crossed the threshold leaving the library. "Really? In the middle of the day when we're supposed to be working?"

He smirked. "I meant an actual nap. We didn't sleep all that much last night."

He had a point, but still ... . "I think you were talking about something else."

"You'll have to wait until we get to the hotel to find out."

"Okay, but if you're not careful you're going to get a reputation as a pervert."

"You say that like it's a bad thing."

. . .

THE REST OF OUR GROUP WAS gathered in the lobby when we arrived, and Jack's plans for a private nap flew directly out the window. He swore viciously under his breath, but pulled it together when Chris gestured for us to join them.

"How did your meeting with Thibodeaux go?" Jack asked as we sat.

"He wasn't happy." Chris looked more amused than worried by the encounter. "He demanded to know where Charlie was because he was convinced she had something to do with the discovery. We managed to hold him off, but he seems obsessed with her."

"Obsessed is a good word." Jack rubbed his chin, thoughtful. "I don't understand why he keeps fixating on her."

"I think it's because that guy's body was found outside my room," I offered. "He's convinced that the story I'm telling can't possibly be true — because if it is, then he's going to have to accept a wild potential horror movie as the truth — so he's basically decided that I'm lying. It's easier for him to believe that than the fact that zombies are running around."

"I don't believe in zombies and I still believe you," Jack argued.

"I believe in zombies and definitely believe you," Chris added. "Right now, he's not doing anything. I'm not sure things will stay that way. I suspect he will come sniffing around with questions, and I wouldn't be surprised if he tries to back Charlie into a corner."

"Then we need to make sure Charlie isn't alone." Jack was firm. "If his goal is to isolate her from us, we need to ensure that doesn't happen."

"I agree."

I thought about the man in the hoodie. Was that what he was trying to do? Isolate me so the cops could interrogate me without my colleagues there to back me up? That seemed unlikely, yet I couldn't rule it out.

"We've been doing some research on hoodoo," Jack explained. "There are parts of it that I find intriguing. For example, hoodoo practitioners believe they can influence things like luck, money and protection through spells. I also think that hoodoo is sometimes practiced by people who feel oppressed. What if that's what we're dealing with?"

"You mean you think someone is trying to build an army for a battle?" Chris was obviously intrigued by the theory as he leaned back in his chair and stretched out his legs in front of him. "To what end? I mean ... I agree that it's a possibility, especially since these zombies aren't biting people."

Jack exhaled heavily, his eyes flashing. "I don't believe in zombies."

"That doesn't mean they don't believe in you."

"Can we not argue about this?" Jack pinched the bridge of his nose. "You're not going to make me believe in something I don't believe in."

"And vice versa. You're not going to make me a non-believer."

"Which means we have to compromise." Jack adopted his most rational tone, which made me smile even as I tried to hide my mirth from both men. I didn't want them thinking I was taking sides. I had my own beliefs, and they tended to land somewhere in the middle. Sometimes I felt like a dog's chew toy when they got going.

"Then let's compromise," Chris suggested. "We need to talk to a hoodoo practitioner. This city must be bursting at the seams with them."

"I'm fine with that."

I glanced between their resolute faces for a moment before shaking my head. "I think you guys are the wrong ones to send." In typical fashion, I spoke before I gave much thought to what I was going to say. Once I opened my big mouth, though, I figured I should continue. "A hoodoo loa will see Chris coming a mile away. They'll feed into what he wants to hear ... for a price."

Jack's smile was victorious. "I agree. Charlie and I will visit a hoodoo store to see if we can get some information."

Again, I shook my head. "You can't go. A true believer will find your attitude off-putting and not share any information. I find you delightful, but I can see where you would grate on others. You can't go either."

Jack's smile disappeared so fast I couldn't be sure it was ever really there. "Well, you're not going alone. I can already guess what you're planning and there's no way I'm letting you wander around by yourself."

"What could possibly go wrong?" Chris challenged. "She's an adult."

"She is," Jack readily agreed. "She's also been targeted by these people. How else do you explain how a guy we saw mowed down by a car found her? I don't know why she's a target. I just know that she is and I want her safe."

"I understand that. Perhaps we can take her to the store and wait outside. Then we won't influence the outcome."

That sounded like an uncomfortable trip that I wanted no part of, which is why I picked that moment to focus on Millie. She sat at a table with Bernard, both of them laughing. She was a gregarious soul who managed to charm people even when she didn't believe in something. She had an open mind, which is exactly what I needed for this particular trip.

"No. You guys can't be around. Chris won't be able to stop himself from asking questions and Jack will start yelling because ... well ... he's Jack."

"I haven't yelled at you this entire trip," Jack pointed out. "I take umbrage with that statement."

I didn't bother to hide my smile. "You've been very good, even when I might've deserved a bit of yelling. I still think you guys both create different problems with this endeavor. I think it should be Millie and me."

Jack balked. "No way. You guys find trouble whenever you go out together."

"We didn't find trouble when we went to the voodoo store," I argued.

"You didn't come back with any actionable information either."

"That's because we were fishing blind. We know better what we're looking for now."

"I don't know." Jack looked pained with the suggestion. "How near are the hoodoo shops? I don't want you wandering all over town without me ... and not because I'm sexist. I really am worried that you've become something of a target for law enforcement and whoever is behind this. I'm not sure why, but it's becoming glaringly obvious that you've piqued someone's interest."

He wasn't wrong and I had no inclination to be a hero. "I'm sure we can find a place that's close. You can't protect me from everything, though, Jack. I'm still a person. I'm still a part of this team, and that means I need to carry my own weight."

"I know." He was morose. "Fine. You and Millie can track down a hoodoo loa. I want you to call me if something gets out of hand. I want your word on it."

I jutted out my hand for him to shake. "Deal."

He took it and shook his head. "Sometimes I think you'll be the death of me."

"What a way to go, huh?" I winked at him because I wanted to extend the moment of jocularity.

"Yeah. What a way to go."

MILLIE WASN'T NEARLY AS EXCITED about visiting what the map termed a "hoodoo museum" as I was. Once I found reference to it online, I couldn't seem to look away. Something inside told me that's where we should start looking, so that's where we ended up.

"How is this a museum?" she complained as she looked at the ramshackle building. "This looks like a slum more than anything else."

I glanced around, worried someone had overheard her. We looked to be alone. "Just ... let me do the talking." I reached for the front door. "I've got everything under control."

"Oh, so you're basically saying that Jack transferred his whopping ego to you during sex. That's a happy side effect. Oh, wait. It isn't."

"Just ... don't be you," I suggested as I slipped through the door. Inside, it took a moment for my eyes to adjust to the dim light. A woman sat behind a rectangular table in the foyer. She had a catalog open and a disinterested look on her face.

"It's ten dollars each for admittance," the woman muttered. "Leave your offerings in the basket."

I did as instructed, dropping a twenty in the basket and motioning for Millie to follow. She was busy giving the lazy woman a dark glare, but followed all the same.

"I hope you know what you're doing," she hissed as we walked into the first room. It was basically empty except for various masks mounted on the walls. "Is this like ... tiki masks? If they have fruity drinks with umbrellas here I'll take back everything I said to you."

I ignored her and moved to the nearest mask. It was long, African in nature, and I found it absolutely fascinating. "This is authentic. It's very cool."

"Everything here is authentic," a voice drawled from behind us, causing me to turn swiftly. The woman was tall — like, almost six feet tall — and statuesque in a way that models managed and I knew I could never pull off. Her bare shoulders were sculpted from hours of working out and a glittery turban covered her hair. Snakes protruded from one side, clearly part of a costume of sorts. The only thing I could hope was that the costume was the only thing that was fake.

"I didn't realize you were there." I smiled brightly at her, hoping she was the friendly sort. "This is a neat place you've got."

"Yes, I love it," Millie frowned. "Any building that makes me worry the ceiling might collapse is a great place to visit ... and an even greater place to disappear from."

The woman arched a perfectly-tended eyebrow. "The building is safe. I can promise you that." Her eyes never left mine. "You're a visitor to our city."

"I am." I extended my hand in her direction. "Charlie Rhodes."

"Interesting." She eyed my hand for a long beat and then took it, sucking in a breath when we made contact. "I am Tamara Abelard. You may call me Tam."

It was a friendly enough greeting, but I sensed trepidation behind her words. "We're here for information," I started.

"I know why you're here." She gripped my hand harder, refusing to release it. "You're looking for information on the dead who walk."

"We are." I knit my eyebrows, confused. "How did you know that?"

"How do you know things?"

I squirmed as she tightened her grip on my hand before I finally managed to wrench it free. "I read about them, learn about them. I listen when others are talking."

"You listen and learn," Tam agreed. "You learn in other ways, too. You're marked."

That was the first time I'd ever heard that term applied to me. "W-what do you mean?"

Millie, always looking for trouble, suddenly opted to serve as backup. She stepped forward and took the spot immediately to my right. It was a warning of sorts, and Tam had no trouble recognizing the potential threat.

"I'm not here to hurt you." Tam held up her hands. "You need not fear me. I, however, can't help but fear you."

"Why would you fear me?" I was clearly out of my element. I should've seen this coming, but it was too late to rectify. I had to persevere. "I haven't done anything. I don't plan to do anything."

"It's okay, Charlie." Millie rested her hand on my shoulder. "She's trying to agitate you. I've seen how people like her operate."

"People like me?" Tam was calm when she turned to Millie. "Please enlighten me about people like me."

"You're trying to frighten her," Millie replied without hesitation. "You're trying to upset her to the point she cowers and begs for a solution to some problem you tell her she has. Let me guess, she has an affliction, right? This mark you mentioned is going to be the end of her. We don't need to listen to this. We should go, Charlie."

I remained rooted. "What kind of mark?"

Tam's expression was almost pitying as her eyes locked with mine. "You're not of one world. You're of many worlds."

"I don't know what that means." I licked my lips. "I don't even know where I was born. I only know I was abandoned."

"Abandoned? I don't think that's the right word. You were ... sacrificed. Not in the way you think." Tam was intense as she stared me down. "People still look for you. They haven't given up. There is hope that you're alive and thriving. There is also fear that you're dead ... or somehow something worse."

"What's worse than death?" Millie challenged. "I'll bet you'll tell her for a fee, right?"

Tam ignored Millie and remained zeroed in on me. "There are several hearts out there that ache for you. There is desire for you ... and not everyone who searches has your best interests at heart. There is fear that something happened. There is also fear that somehow you were discovered and are completely lost to those who left you."

She was talking in circles and I found it frustrating. "I don't understand. Are you talking about my parents? Are they still out there?"

"She's messing with you, Charlie," Millie hissed. "She's trying to upset you, girl. If she can knock you off balance you'll be more susceptible to what she has to say."

"I am not trying to upset her," Tam countered. "I am trying to understand." She lifted her fingers and brushed them against my cheek. There was nothing threatening about the movement, but I cringed all the same. "Your time is still coming. It's not too far now in your future. You're going to be okay. No matter the fear that threatens to swallow you alive, you'll be fine. You have a new family to help ... and an old family to discover. It's ... muddied."

"Of course it's muddied." Millie was frustrated. "We need to leave this place, Charlie," she insisted. "We can't stay here. We never should've come. You especially shouldn't have come here."

Tam slowly tracked her eyes to Millie, understanding sparking in the dark depths of her eyes. "You want to protect her. That's noble. You think of her as the daughter you never had and want to make sure no harm befalls her. That is ... sweet. You can't protect her from everything, though."

"I can sure as heck protect her from you." Millie grabbed my hand and gave it a vicious tug. "We can't stay here, Charlie. It's not good for you. You can't see it, but I can. We have to get out of here."

I wasn't ready to leave. "What about the zombies?" I queried. "Do you know about the dead rising? What about the bodies disappearing from the cemeteries? Have you heard rumors? Do you think one of your people could be behind it?"

"My people?" Tam seemed amused at the question. "Whoever is

doing this is not one of my people." She followed as Millie relentlessly tugged me through the building toward the front door. "There are different types of magical folk, Charlie Rhodes. You of all people should know that. Not everyone is the same.

"You're different. I'm different. Your friend here is definitely different," she continued. "What is happening out there has little to do with what happens here." She tapped the spot above her heart. "I don't know what's waiting for you out there, but you must be vigilant. It won't be long until the answers are right in front of you. Even then you will have to make a choice. There will be several options. Only one of them will be the right one."

"Well, great," Millie groused as she tugged open the door. "That's not too much pressure to place on the girl or anything. You're a real peach. Has anyone ever told you that?"

Tam graced us with an odd, almost serene smile. "You'll make the right choice because it's inherent in you. That's good. Things come easy for you in some ways, but don't rest on your laurels."

"I don't even know what laurels are," I admitted. "I couldn't rest on them if I wanted to."

"Be careful," Tam called out as I turned. "Watch the shadows."

It was those words that were echoing in my head when I hit the front stoop. There, standing at the bottom of the steps, was the hoodie-clad man. His eyes widened as he realized I recognized him, and he broke into a run before I could form a single word. This time I was having none of it. I refused to lose him again.

"Wait!" I tore off, giving chase.

I left Millie behind. She sounded frightened when she called out to me. "Don't run after him, Charlie! What do you think you're doing? Oh, geez! Jack is going to kill me."

TWENTY

I wasn't familiar with the streets, but that didn't stop me from giving chase. Unfortunately for me, Mr. Hoodie knew exactly where he was going and managed to lose me after four turns. I was out of breath and annoyed when I slowed my pace.

I was also turned around.

I tried to backtrack, but it took me longer than it should have. When I found my way back to the hoodoo museum, Millie was gone. Tam, however, was standing on the stoop.

"Did you know I would come back?" I asked as I pressed my hand into my side to ward off a stitch. "Geez. I need to start working out."

She looked amused. "I knew you would come back."

"Do you know who that guy was? He's been following me."

"I didn't see his face. I'm sorry."

"Well, great." I dragged a hand through my tangled hair. "I guess I should head back to the hotel. That's where Millie went, right?"

"She was upset. She thinks of you as her child."

"That's kind of funny because I always wanted my parents to come back to life so there was someone out there – anyone really – who felt that way about me." The statement sounded more bitter than I'd intended, but I didn't feel bad about it. "Do you know why I can do the things I can do?"

"No, but I am curious about what you can do. Come in for some tea. We'll talk."

Under different circumstances I would've agreed. I didn't get a dangerous vibe from her no matter what Millie happened to believe. Things would be worse if I did that, though.

"I can't." I was rueful. "Millie will get the others in our group riled up. They'll come looking ... and one of them will kick down your door to find me. You don't want that."

"Yes. Jack."

I was taken aback. "How do you know his name?"

"It whispers throughout your mind."

"How really?"

This time her smile was amused. "Your friend said she was going to get Jack and acted as if that would be bad."

"Ah, well ... ." I exhaled heavily as my heartbeat returned to normal. "Are you sure you don't know anything about the zombies? I know that might not be the correct word to use, but it's the one I'm going with."

"I don't see why you can't use that word," Tam replied. "It's as apt as anything else. People are talking about the dead rising and the significance of it. They're missing the point. It's not that the dead are rising that should concern us. That has happened hundreds of times throughout history. People simply choose not to believe it."

"What should we be worried about?" I asked. "If it's not the dead rising, then what?"

"It's what they're wanted for. I don't think there's a good answer, especially now. You need to be careful."

"I'm always careful."

"No. You're brave ... and smart ... and loyal. You're outspoken and demanding when it comes to those around you doing the right thing. But you're not always careful. Before, you didn't need to be. You only had yourself to worry about. Now, you have a tribe."

"You mean Millie and Jack."

"And a few others. Even the one you think of as an enemy may be more important to your future than you realize."

"Laura?" The mere notion was hilarious ... and troubling. "I don't think so."

"Don't rule her out just yet. She might still have something to offer your tale. As for now, you should head back. I can feel the fear in your wake."

Jack. She was talking about Jack. The idea of him being afraid upset me on a level I wasn't aware I even had. "I might be back."

"I'll be here. I always am."

"Great. I have questions."

"Eventually you will get your answers."

JACK AND CHRIS WERE READYING to leave the hotel when I walked into the lobby. The look of relief on Jack's face was heartwarming. It was quickly replaced with rage.

"What were you thinking?" He strode toward me and placed his hands on my shoulders. I thought he was going to start shaking me, but he pulled me in for a hug instead. "I was afraid something happened to you."

"That wasn't smart, Charlie," Chris chided, adopting a more pragmatic tone. "Why would you chase someone on the street like that? You could've been hurt."

"That's the third time I've seen him today," I replied. "The first was at the cemetery. The second was at the library. There was no way I was going to let him get away a third time."

"Why didn't you tell me you were being followed?" Jack's eyes flared with accusation. "Didn't you trust me?"

Oh, geez. This was the last thing I needed. "Of course I trust you. It's just ... the first time I saw him I thought he might be a zombie. No, don't give me that look."

Jack turned away and planted his hands on his hips as he stared out the window.

"That's exactly why I didn't tell you," I supplied. "I thought you would think I was crazy and I hate it when you give me that look."

"What look?"

"You know the look. It's on your face right now, but you usually add a bit of a lip curl. You remind me of an angry Elvis when you unleash it."

Despite the serious conversation, he managed to choke out half a laugh. "You're definitely going to be the death of me."

"I didn't know if I really saw him or not," I admitted. "I thought my mind could be playing tricks on me. He looked young. There was every chance he was playing a trick on me because he was bored. Laura didn't act like she saw him, so I second-guessed myself."

"Fair enough." Jack lifted his hands in surrender. "Why didn't you tell me about seeing him in the library?"

"He disappeared really fast. He was there one second and gone the next. I didn't want you to think I was crazy or anything."

"Well, good job on that." His eyes flashed with annoyance. "Why would I think a woman taking off after a strange man in a city she doesn't know is crazy?"

"I just reacted." My temper started to ignite. "I'm not sure why I have to explain myself. I'm an adult. I wanted to know why he was following me."

"And did he tell you?"

"I lost him. He's obviously familiar with the city. But I know he was real. The hoodoo chick saw him, too. She was waiting when I returned. It was almost as if she was expecting me. She told me Millie went back to the hotel and planned to collect you. I hurried here as fast as I could. As you can see, I'm perfectly fine."

Jack shook his head. "I wonder how my death will come," he murmured. "Do you think it will be a heart attack? I'm leaning toward an aneurysm."

"Stop it." I decided to halt this freakout before he got up a full head of steam. "I'm fine. The guy managed to escape. As for Tam, she didn't tell us anything useful. She only said we should be trying to figure out who was behind this rather than how or why."

"I agree with that," Jack said. "That doesn't mean I'm not agitated."

"Yeah, well ... I'm fine. You can't be angry at me for following my instincts. I can't always think before I react."

"And that's why you're going to kill me."

WE HAD A BIT OF TIME TO burn before dinner. Chris and the others opted to spend it reading hoodoo books in the lobby. Jack, however, dragged me upstairs. I thought he was finally going to unleash the anger he'd been holding inside, but instead he pointed to the bed.

"Strip," he ordered.

I gaped. "That's really romantic, Jack. I guess the bloom is already off the rose."

"I've never really understood that saying, but that's not what I'm talking about." He dragged his shirt over his head and dropped his pants. "I need a nap."

"Oh, like a nap nap?"

"Like a nap nap," he agreed, his lips curving. "I can't trust you not to chase strangers and get in trouble, so I want you to take a nap with me."

Honestly, a nap sounded good. I didn't want to reward him for bad behavior, though. "You're kind of bossy."

"I'm your boss."

"Not on this matter." I folded my arms over my chest. "You need to ask nicely if you want a nap."

He stared at me for what felt like a long time, his jaw working. Finally, he exhaled and forced a smile. "Fine. Will you please take a nap with me so I don't freak out?"

"Yes." I stripped out of my clothes, leaving my bra and underwear in place because I didn't want him to think I was being too forward. His arms were already open when I rolled to meet him in the middle of the bed. "I'm sorry I didn't tell you about seeing him. It's just ... I don't ever want you to think that I'm stupid ... or even a little crazy. I also want to prove I should be a part of this team."

"Charlie." He sounded exasperated as he slid his arms around me. "We need to work on your self-esteem. I get that this is your first real job and you feel as if you lucked into it because it's something you only dreamed of being a part of, but you're valuable to me on several different levels.

"The first is obviously this level," he continued, burying his face in my neck and brushing his lips across my quivering skin in a manner that caused me to giggle. "This is only a small part of it. You're the most valuable member of this team in a lot of ways. You can't see it because you're new, but I see it."

I went warm all over. "Thanks."

"You're welcome." We lapsed into silence for a moment and I thought there was already a chance he'd fallen asleep. Then he spoke again. "You're still in trouble for running after that guy. I'm saying this as the chief of security, not your boyfriend. You could've been hurt."

"I'm sorry. I just ... reacted. I don't understand why he's following."

"I don't either, but I plan to find out. You have my word on that. I won't let anyone hurt you."

It was a sweet promise, one we both knew he couldn't keep. There were things in this world we didn't understand. He couldn't watch me every second of every day. Neither of us wanted that. Sure, we were in a new relationship and semi-addicted to one another. We would get over that eventually and settle into a more comfortable rhythm, though. I was looking forward to that.

"She said things to me," I whispered. "She knew about me being abandoned. She said ... she said that they were still out there looking for me. Do you think that's true?"

Jack tightened his hold on me. "I don't know. If you want to look, I'll help you. I already told you that. As for potential reasons for them leaving you, I can't say. I just know that I can't fathom how anyone could know you and leave you."

"Maybe I was a rotten kid or something."

"No, you have a good heart. That was the first thing I noticed about you. I don't think it was learned. It's inherent with you."

"That might be the nicest thing anyone has ever said to me."

He playfully swatted my rear end. "You're also a massive pain in the behind. Thankfully you seem to be worth it."

"Yeah, I'm a real catch."

He laughed against my ear. "Go to sleep. We both need the rest. If you're good, I might catch you again later."

"That sounds like a plan."

I WOKE BEFORE JACK. He was dead to the world and sleeping so deeply I didn't want to disturb him. I estimated we'd slept for about two hours. That was more than enough for me.

I carefully rolled out of bed and collected my clothes from the floor. I dressed in the bathroom and ran a brush through my hair so it didn't look as if I'd been walking around in a wind tunnel. I wrote a note on the hotel stationery and placed it on the pillow next to his head. The plan was to join everyone in the lobby and offer my help. It was empty when I reached it, though, which threw me.

I checked my phone to see if there was a group text. It was early enough in the afternoon that we still had an hour before we were expected to meet for dinner. It was possible everyone else was taking breaks — perhaps group naps were common with our merry band of monster hunters and I simply didn't know about it — but I decided to ask the concierge where the rest of our group had disappeared to before I started searching. Then a scream ripped through the air, and before I had time to think what it could mean I raced toward the front desk.

There, Emeline was screeching as she backed away from a man. He wore tattered clothing and growled as he tried to climb the desk to get to her.

"Go away," she howled, her voice clogged with tears. "I don't understand. I ... what are you doing here? Is this a nightmare?"

I stopped in the middle of the room, debating what to do. The only thing that could be used as a weapon was the lamp on the side table. I grabbed it without hesitation, ripping the cord from the outlet, and brandished it over my head as I hurried toward the man.

"Hey!"

He swiveled in my direction. The movement wasn't fast. Heck, it almost seemed as if he was moving in slow motion, and when he turned I realized half his face was missing. His eyes looked to be empty sockets. There was nothing in there to see from, yet I swear he looked right at me.

Spittle formed at the corners of his mouth and oozed through the gaps where several teeth were missing. I saw a tongue moving in there but it didn't look like anything that had ever belonged to a living, breathing human being.

"Holy ... !" I was aghast. "That's a zombie!"

"That's my husband," Emeline snapped. "He's dead. He's been dead for a year. I don't understand how this is happening."

I didn't understand either. I only knew I had to react. "Okay, well ... I've got this." I strode forward with more bravado than I actually felt and stopped two feet in front of the monster. "Hello, Barry. I wish I could've met you under different circumstances."

He lurched in my direction and was practically on top of me with a single step. "Uh-huh." I swung out with the lamp, catching him square on the side of the head. He listed to the side, making a hiss that sent chills running down my spine. My inclination was to put distance between him and me, so that's what I did. In my haste to get away, though, I barreled into the table and it knocked me sideways.

"Ow." I stumbled, but managed to remain upright. When I turned, Barry was still giving chase. He looked deranged ... and hungry. "I thought these things weren't supposed to want to eat people," I complained.

"This is just a dream," Emeline chanted over and over, making the sign of the cross. She was in her own little world and apparently wasn't keen on offering help. "Lord, protect me from this unholy thing."

"You could've included me in the prayer," I groused as I stared at the thing that had once been a man. It was as if I was trapped in a bad horror movie. I couldn't allow this to continue. Innocent and unknowing guests could wander into the lobby at any time. I had to do something.

I had to use my magic. It was a reflex when he closed the distance again. This time I lashed out with my powers, sending a strong wave of magic into him. It hit with such force he was lifted from his feet and slammed into the wall.

He had to be down, I reasoned as I rubbed my shaking hands against my jeans. Nothing could survive that blow.

Barry was still moving. He reached out with his hands and grunted as he failed to find traction enough to climb to his feet. I heard people on the other side of the door. The lobby was about to be invaded.

With no other ideas and actual lives about to be put on the line, I gathered my strength and lashed out again. This time I used the magic to gather the furniture — the couch, two chairs and three tables grouped in front of me — and sent them careening toward the man on the ground.

They hit with a sickening thud, the sound of bones breaking and wood smashing against flesh echoing in my ears. Barry stopped moving and fell silent. Emeline sobbed harder. I dropped to a knee to collect myself.

The front door opened and two women entered. They were having a good time, laughing and cavorting. Then they saw the body and the chuckles turned to screams.

It was at that point I wished I'd stayed in bed with Jack.

TWENTY-ONE

$\mathcal{I}$ was still kneeling on the ground recovering my strength when I felt a hand on my shoulder. I swiveled quickly, expecting another attack, but it was only Millie. Her eyes swam with worry as she hunkered over and met my gaze on an even level.

"You need to get up."

That sounded ridiculous in my head. "I am up."

"You're not."

"But … ."

"Get up, Charlie." She was firm. "Chris is coming, and if he sees you on your knees it will be hard to explain."

In the back of my head I understood she was trying to help. I sucked in a breath and stood, earning an energetic head nod from Millie before she dragged me away from the front desk and directed me toward a couch.

"Sit here."

The order baffled me. "I thought I was supposed to stand."

"No, you were just supposed to get off the floor," Millie shot back. "You need to get it together, Charlie. I understand something went down here, but … well, actually I have no idea what went on. There's a dead guy at the end of the room who looks as if he's been dead for a very long time."

"Barry," I volunteered dully. "He was Emeline's husband. He died a year ago ... and came back."

Millie's eyebrows hopped. "Seriously?"

"He was dead." I ran the information through my head and tried to make sense of what I'd seen. "He was dead and yet he was on his feet. He was growling ... and snapping his teeth." I focused on her for the first time. "I thought these zombies weren't supposed to want to eat people."

"Yeah. That's the word on the street." Millie kept her hand on my shoulder as Chris and Hannah rushed into the room.

My stomach did a small somersault as my boss scanned for familiar faces and finally landed on us. "What happened?" he asked breathlessly.

"I'm not sure," Millie replied. "There was a lot of screaming and hoopla. There's a dead guy at the end of the room. Be careful. People say he might be a zombie. Don't let him bite you."

Chris appeared almost giddy. He looked right past me and searched the area behind me for clues. There were none, so he turned his attention to the other side of the room, to where Barry rested under a pile of furniture. "Do we know who that is?"

"Emeline's husband," I replied dully.

"Seriously?" Chris's eyes widened. "Hasn't he been dead, like, a year?"

"That's the word on the street." I laughed, although it was totally mirthless. "Millie says 'word on the street' all the time."

Millie shot me a look but remained silent.

"Awesome." Chris kicked his heels together and took off in the direction of the body, Hannah scurrying behind. That left Millie and me alone.

"We need to come up with a convincing lie ... and fast," she announced, glancing around. "I ... have ... no ... idea." She looked lost. "How are we going to explain this?"

I didn't get a chance to answer because Jack joined the party. He glanced around, stunned disbelief washing over his features when he saw the body. He initially stepped in its direction and then froze, as if sensing me staring, and turned to find me. He completely forgot about the zombie and raced to me.

"Charlie?" He brushed my hair from my face and stared into my eyes. "What's wrong? What ... happened?"

Those were two excellent questions. "I don't know." I shifted on my seat, uncomfortable. "I ... ."

"Things happened really fast," Millie announced, taking control of the situation. "Emeline was screaming and Charlie rushed to help. That thing was in here and attacking. I don't even know what happened because things happened so fast."

"I don't understand." Jack stroked his hand over my hair in a soothing fashion. "I'm not sure I follow what you're saying."

"I'm not sure I follow it either," Millie admitted. "Like I said, it all happened too fast. I think ... I think maybe that hoodoo queen did something. That's the only thing that makes sense."

It was Millie trying to blame someone else for my deeds that finally brought me completely back to reality. "No." I vehemently shook my head. "She wasn't here. Don't blame her."

Jack looked relieved when I became more animated. Millie, on the other hand, was obviously annoyed. She didn't want me screwing up her lies. I understood, but I couldn't let an innocent woman take the blame for something I did.

"Okay." Jack forced a smile that didn't touch his eyes. "What did you see?"

That was the question, wasn't it? "I heard Emeline screaming. When I first walked into the lobby, I wasn't sure what was happening. I just saw him from the back. I knew right away something was wrong, though. His clothes were all tattered ... and there was a smell."

"What smell?"

"Embalming fluid. I recognized it because I had to take a class in school in which we worked with cadavers. It was faint but obvious."

"You knew he'd been embalmed." Jack looked to where Chris and Hannah stood, their heads bent together as they excitedly talked about something. It was clear they were practically overflowing with delight thanks to what they'd found at the other end of the room. "You think it was a zombie, don't you?"

I wrapped my fingers around his wrist to make him look at me. "It was a monster, Jack." There was no way I could lie about that. "He was dead. It was Emeline's husband. He's been dead for a year. I'm not making it up. I swear it."

"I know you're not making it up." He leaned forward and pressed a kiss to my forehead. "It's okay. I believe you. Don't freak out over nothing. Save the meltdown for something that's real ... like the dead guy in the corner. I'm on your side."

Millie beamed at him. "Of course you are. That's who you are."

Jack momentarily furrowed his brow and then shook his head. "I believe Charlie. She's obviously shaken, and there's a dead guy who smells pretty bad on that side of the room." He straightened and glanced around. "What I don't get is how the furniture ended up on top of him."

My stomach twisted. "I ... ."

"How is she supposed to know that?" Millie challenged. "Whatever went down was weird from the start. She didn't have anything to do with it."

It was then that I realized how Millie intended to play things. Straight-up ignorance and denial. It wasn't a bad plan. We were dealing with a zombie, after all. I was still uncomfortable lying to Jack. It made me feel guilty. Of course, it wasn't as if I could tell him the truth ... especially in front of an audience. He wouldn't understand.

"Things just started moving?" Jack asked, looking around for confirmation. His gaze finally landed on Emeline, who stood on shaky legs behind the desk, her hands resting on the counter to help her balance. "What did you see? They say the furniture just started moving. Is that what you saw?"

Technically there was no "they" in that statement. Millie made the announcement and I just sat in my spot like an idiot. Jack assumed I saw the same thing, so he glossed right over my part in it. I was lucky on that front.

"I don't know what I saw." Emeline's eyes filled with fright. "All I know is that Barry was in here and he wanted to kill me. I couldn't believe it when I first saw him. It was like something out of a dream ... and then I realized it was a nightmare because bits of his face were missing. It was ... horrible. He was foaming at the mouth and snapping as he tried to get to me."

"What did you do?" Jack asked.

"I screamed. I didn't know what else to do. That's when the girl came in. She jumped right into action and hit him with a lamp."

Jack slid his eyes to me. "You hit the zombie with a lamp?"

I shrugged. "What else was I supposed to do? I didn't have a machete."

"Uh-huh." This time he mustered a real smile as his hand went to the back of my neck and rubbed at the tension there. "What happened then, Ms. Landry?"

"I'm not sure." Emeline looked bewildered. "The girl didn't back down. She was afraid, but she kept fighting. The next thing I knew, Barry flew across the room and half the furniture went with him. It all crashed down there." Slowly her eyes tracked to me. "I think she did it."

Panic raced through me like a high-speed passenger train. "What?"

"Don't be ridiculous," Jack said, his hand a soothing presence on my back. "She was trying to save you. There's no way she could make the furniture fly across the room like that."

"Maybe she's evil, like the police said," Emeline argued. "That detective was here. He said she was behind all of this. Maybe he was right."

"And how did she pull that off?" Jack challenged. "She was up taking a nap with me for two hours. You have cameras on every floor. It will prove that we went into her room and didn't leave for a long stretch. When she finally did leave, I'm betting she didn't go anywhere but down here."

"I was looking for the others," I offered glumly. "I thought ... well, I thought I could help. I didn't want to wake you."

"I know." He was a wall of protection that refused to budge as he stared down the shaken hotel owner. "I'm guessing that whoever caused your husband to return from the grave took him down. Maybe ... maybe he got out of hand or something. I don't know. There's no way Charlie did this."

"But she was right there," Emeline protested.

"That doesn't mean she did this." Jack refused to back down. "She was trying to help you. Don't attack her for it."

Millie winked at me. She looked much more relaxed than I felt now that things had gone her way with Jack. "Charlie is an innocent victim who risked herself to help you. Don't make her regret her decision."

THIBODEAUX WAS A RAGING MESS when he arrived. Jack, who had been sitting next to me and whispering in low tones, immediately hopped to his feet and placed himself between me and the furious detective.

"Don't even think about it," Jack warned when Thibodeaux attempted to push him aside in an effort to get to me. "She's been through enough."

"She's been through enough?" Thibodeaux's eyebrows looked as if they were going to take on a life of their own and crawl off his forehead. "She doing this."

"She is not. I don't understand why you're so fixated on her."

"Because she's turning my city into a laughingstock," Thibodeaux exploded. "She's the only common denominator in all of this. She supposedly opened her door to a zombie. She found an empty crypt at St. Louis Cemetery. You can deny it all you want, but I know she was there for the theft at Lafayette Cemetery. It's her and I'm taking her in."

I felt sick to my stomach at the outburst. "You're going to arrest me?"

"No, he's not." Jack's expression told me he was readying himself to start throwing punches. I appreciated the gesture, but all that would accomplish would be a night in jail for both of us.

"Jack, don't." I got to my feet and shook my head. "You can't stop this. If he's going to take me into custody he'll do it no matter what you say. Don't risk your job over me. It's not worth it." I lifted my wrists to the seething detective. "I'll go with you. Just ... don't arrest Jack. He's upset."

Thibodeaux stared at me for a long beat and I could tell he was debating what to do. He hadn't expected me to volunteer myself for incarceration.

"Don't take her," Jack snapped. "She didn't do anything. How can you possibly blame her for this? She was nowhere near the city when it started. She's been with me the whole time. She didn't do this." His voice cracked at the end and I thought he might cry. I didn't see tears, but he appeared on the verge.

Thankfully, Chris picked that moment to interrupt us. "There is a body on the floor over there that has obviously been dead for some time," he noted. "My understanding is that it's Mrs. Landry's husband, who died a year ago. How is it that you think Charlie somehow managed to find his body and get it here when she was taking a nap? Check the hallway security camera footage. She and Jack went upstairs together hours ago."

"She's the common denominator," Thibodeaux insisted. "She's the one thing that ties this all together."

"Except she doesn't," Hannah argued. "If you want to make the argument that Charlie is at the center of this then you have to say that we all are. We came to this town together. We've stuck mostly together. Why is it you're so interested in Charlie alone?"

"Because ... because ... ." He either couldn't – or wouldn't – answer. I found that curious.

"I swear I didn't raise the zombie," I offered. "I wouldn't even know how to start. We've been trying to solve this. If you need to take someone in, though, make it me. Don't take Jack. He's a hero."

"Don't take either of them," Chris argued. "You know it won't end well if you do. You're familiar with my uncle. The first call I place will be to him. He'll have lawyers descending on your precinct so fast you'll barely get Charlie processed. You can't hold her and we both know it. If you do, you'll end up tarnishing your own image."

Thibodeaux looked away from Chris and focused on Jack. There seemed to be a silent challenge flowing between them.

"I won't let you just take her." Jack was firm. "She didn't do anything but try to help. Why are you so hell-bent on punishing her for nothing?"

Thibodeaux heaved out a sigh. "Whatever," he said finally. "There's no reason to be so dramatic. I'm not taking her in. But I am watching her."

"How great for you," Jack muttered, moving closer to me. "You won't find anything. She's not responsible for this." He ran his hand over my hair as I waited for my pulse to return to normal. "Focus on the dead people, not the people trying to solve this. You're looking in the wrong direction."

"I'm not, but I obviously need more proof. I'm going to get it."

"No, you're not. She's not guilty."

"I guess we'll have to wait to see who's right."

"I guess so."

JACK LEFT THE HOTEL LONG enough to pick up dinner before dragging me upstairs. He refused to eat with the others, even though Laura made a series of pouty passive-aggressive remarks aimed at trying to force his hand. He didn't engage, and by the time we reached my room with burgers and fries, exhaustion had etched its way across his handsome features.

"I'm sorry for all this," I offered as I changed into a comfortable pair of shorts and a T-shirt. "I didn't mean to do this to you."

His expression didn't change. "What did you do to me?"

"I ... put you in a bad position. You almost got yourself arrested."

"Charlie, I would get myself arrested ten times over to protect you. That's my job."

"It's not your job to get arrested. That's going above and beyond in the boyfriend department."

The chuckle he let loose was weak and dry. "I would have myself arrested for you because I'm your boyfriend. I can't deny it. But that's not what I was doing tonight. I was acting as chief of security."

I hadn't even considered that, and I felt like an idiot. "I bet it wouldn't look good to the shareholders if I was arrested."

"Chris has been arrested three times. Millie has been arrested six. There will come a time when you probably get arrested because that's the nature of this group. I will not, however, sit back and let that guy terrorize you for no good reason. I can't. I won't."

I blew out a sigh. "I still don't know what happened." That wasn't a lie. Everything that occurred in the lobby was a blur. "I don't know how any of it came to be. I just ... it was freaky."

"I know." He pulled me in for a hug, pressing a kiss against my neck as he swayed back and forth. "You had to be terrified.

"Chris is trying to figure out a way to get Hannah into the autopsy," he continued. "There's nothing else we can do tonight. The door is locked and we're safe in here. We even have greasy comfort food. How about we turn on something completely innocuous on the television and try to relax?"

That was an intriguing offer. "Can we watch *Friends*?"

He lifted an eyebrow. "Why do you want to watch *Friends*?"

"It's like comfort food, completely mindless."

"*Friends* it is." He grabbed the bag of food and directed me toward the bed. "Get comfortable. We're not leaving again until tomorrow morning. We have hours of food, *Friends* and ... frolicking ... in front of us." He grinned at his own alliteration. "That was pretty good, huh?"

It was easier to return the smile than I anticipated. "Very good."

We settled on the bed together, the covers wrapped around us and our legs touching as I found the channel I sought. "I don't understand how he could've possibly been raised from the grave," I admitted, my voice low. "He wasn't like the others. He was half rotted away."

"I don't understand either. I definitely don't understand how the furniture ended up on top of him."

I swallowed the ball of guilt lodged in my throat. "Are you willing to admit it's zombies?"

Instead of being angry, he laughed. "That's what you're really worried about?"

"I just want us to be on the same side."

"I'm on your side, Charlie." He pressed his kiss to my cheek. "I still hate the word, but I can't see any other way to explain things. We're definitely dealing with zombies."

I perked up. "Finally we have something we agree on."

He grinned. "That's something to celebrate, huh?"

"Definitely."

TWENTY-TWO

Things turned romantic. It was inevitable. I was glad for the distraction. Jack seemingly was, too. We were both so exhausted we passed out before midnight.

I hoped my sleep would be easy. I was not that lucky.

I woke in an odd dreamscape, one I didn't recognize. I was in a house. It looked a lot like the hoodoo museum, at least what that house probably looked like fifty years before. Tam sat in a chair by the fire in a room I didn't recognize. I didn't get a chance to search the entire museum before Millie had insisted we leave, so I figured I was probably projecting.

Of course, there was always the possibility that I wasn't ... and that was even more terrifying than zombies.

"What am I doing here?" I asked the quiet woman as she flipped through a magazine. The cover read "Loas for Dummies" and she seemed disinterested in my presence.

"I don't know. What do you think you're doing here?"

"I think my mind is a twisted place to visit right now," I replied without hesitation. "Are the zombies here? I don't know if I want to spend the entire night running from them."

"The zombies can't get you here." She closed the magazine and slowly got to her feet. "Come with me."

I wasn't sure I wanted to do that either, but I didn't see where I had much choice. She led me through the house, to the room with the masks that I'd visited earlier in the day. It looked markedly different. There was furniture, old and in poor shape, spread about. Candles burned in every corner, giving the room a homey feel despite the pervading chill air.

"What are you showing me?"

"Look." Tam gestured toward the window. I hesitantly joined her, frowning when I realized what she wanted me to see. There, on the front lawn of the house, a hundred zombies weaved back and forth. They were waiting for ... something. I had no idea what, but my inner warning alarm told me they were waiting for me.

"Are there really that many zombies on the loose?" I asked when I'd found my voice. "That doesn't seem right."

"It doesn't," she agreed. "They're growing in number every day. Why do you think that is?"

"I don't know." That was the truth. "I thought that was why my mind conjured you in this dream. I'm looking for answers, right? I must think you have them."

"*You* have them," she countered. "You simply have to open yourself to the possibility of learning. If you do that, you'll figure things out."

"That sounds easier said than done."

She let the drape she'd pulled back drop into place. "You have a visitor."

The change in her demeanor threw me. For the first time since I'd met her the previous day, she looked frightened. The shift came out of nowhere. "I don't understand."

"He's here." Her voice was barely a whisper.

"Who is here?"

"I believe she's talking about me," a folksy voice said from behind us, causing me to jolt.

Even though inherently I knew it was a dream — really, what else could it be? — I was ready to do battle with whatever enemy awaited.

Instead, sitting on the couch, I found the man in the hoodie. He looked different, his skin tone more robust, but his eyes were filled with keen interest.

"Who are you?" My frustration bubbled up. "I don't understand why you're here. I don't understand any of this."

"You will, my child." He patted the open spot on the couch next to him. "Sit. We have some things to discuss."

That sounded unlikely. "I can't sit next to you. You've been following me all day. You tried to separate me from my group."

"I did," he agreed readily, his grin only widening. "I wanted to talk to you earlier. That wasn't possible when you were surrounded by your friends. I kept trying, but you refused to move too far away. Even when you gave chase you thought better of it and returned to the hotel. It was as if you understood that you shouldn't be separated even as you yearned to follow. I find you ... interesting."

"I'm glad for you." I made a face. "Who are you?"

"I go by many names."

"Which one would I know you by?"

"Perhaps the name Papa Legba rings a bell."

I thought I might fall over. "No way!"

"Yes, way." His eyes twinkled. "Please sit, Charlie. We're not yet pressed for time, but there's a lot to go over."

For some reason the idea that I was sitting with a famous loa — perhaps the most well-regarded and famous loa ever — eased some of my fear. I sat next to him, making sure not to touch him, and waved off the tea he offered.

"No offense, but I'm not drinking anything you offer me."

"That's probably smart." He sipped his own tea. "What do you know about me?"

"You're a crossroads demon," I answered automatically. "You're the counterpart to a couple of saints and famous religious figures, including Lazarus. You're supposed to be kindly, and if someone grows too pompous you teach them a lesson."

"That's a good start." He smiled. "It's probably good that 'pompous' is the one word that can never be used to describe you."

205

"No, but Laura is in our group and she's all kinds of pompous. Can't you teach her a lesson and get her off my back for a bit?"

"Who do you think convinced Jack and Millie to report her to Human Resources?"

My mouth dropped open. "No way!"

"I've been watching you for a long time, Charlie," he offered. "You're of great interest to me. The power you wield, the goodness of your heart, it all makes for an interesting convergence."

"Do you know what I am?" The question escaped before I could think better of it. It was self-serving, but I couldn't stop myself.

"You're more than one thing, my dear. As am I. I understand your confusion and your yearning for answers. Those answers are coming. You need to focus on the here and now."

Something occurred to me. "Did you send Harley to visit?"

"The coin called to Harley. I told her to let you keep it. Most people who possess the coin want to make a trade. You're too smart to make a trade, yet you're still important to us. That's why you should keep the coin. If you ever need us when this is over, the coin will allow us to always find you."

That sounded far too easy. "So, what? Are you saying you're my magical loa godfather?"

He barked out a laugh, his amusement obvious. "That's an interesting way of looking at things. I think I like it."

"Well ... I'm not sure how I feel about it."

"You have a lot going on." Papa Legba sipped his tea again. "In the interests of saving time, I'm going to expand your knowledge base regarding me. I am a gatekeeper of sorts. St. Peter is the gatekeeper to Heaven. I am the gatekeeper to ... other places."

"Some people believe you're the same as St. Peter," I noted. "Although ... I've always heard you looked like a kindly old man."

"I can look however I wish," he explained. "Right now, when activity is high in the French Quarter, I need to be able to fade into the background. This disguise allows me to do that."

"You're pale enough that you look like a zombie."

"I thought that would entice you."

"You thought I would chase a zombie?" I snickered. "That doesn't make me sound very smart, does it?"

"You're sharper than you give yourself credit for. Harley told me of meeting with you. She seems to like you a great deal. I've handed your case over to her."

"I'm not going to make a deal for my soul." The declaration came out shriller than I intended. "I won't do that."

"I don't intend for you to do it. We don't want your soul. You're going to need it for a long time."

"I ... well ... that's good." I worked my jaw and narrowed my eyes. "Why would you seek me out this way?"

"You're important for a great many reasons," Papa Legba replied. "You're important to what's happening now and you're important to events that won't happen for years. You, Charlie, are very special."

He said it in such a matter-of-fact way that there could be no arguing with the sentiment. I kind of wanted to push him on it, though. I recognized now wasn't the time. The zombies were more important.

"What's happening out there?" I gestured toward the window Tam had showed me several minutes before. "Who would want to raise the dead this way?"

"That is the question, isn't it?" He set his tea on the table and held out his hand. "We need to take a walk. There are some things I need to show you."

I eyed his extended hand with trepidation. "I'm not sure that's a good idea."

"I won't hurt you, Charlie." He sounded sincere. "Search your heart. What does it tell you?"

"That I should trust you."

"So, trust me. It's important that I show you how this world looks from the other side."

I had no idea what that meant, but I'd already decided to give in. "Okay, but if you try to steal my soul Jack will cross three worlds to get it back."

Papa Legba chuckled as he wrapped his fingers around mine. "Oh,

Jack. We've been watching him, too. For different reasons, of course. He also has a magical soul. He's your protector in this world. I'm almost convinced he will be your protector in the next."

That was reassuring. Er, well, kind of. "Where are we going?"

"Not far." He blinked and the museum dissolved, Tam with it. We found ourselves in a fogbound cemetery. I recognized it as St. Louis Cemetery No. 1 because of Marie Laveau's tomb.

"I've been here," I murmured.

"You have," he agreed. I noticed a cigar and bottle of rum had magically appeared in his hands. He happily puffed away as I looked around the dark tombs. "What do you know about brujas, Charlie?"

I wasn't expecting the question and yet I still had an answer ready. "They're witches. Powerful witches at that."

"You've met witches before."

"The Winchesters," I confirmed, thinking about the outrageous family of witches I'd met in Michigan months before. "The first job I went on when I joined the Legacy Foundation was in Hemlock Cove. They're not evil."

Legba chuckled. "No. They're not evil, although I've considered holding open a special spot for Tillie when her time comes. She'll probably tell me to stuff it when I tell her what I have in mind for her. The asking will be entertaining regardless. That's not important right now.

"Brujas is the term used more often in the South, especially here," he continued. "Witch is the more common term in the north. Essentially, they're the same. Witches, much like people, are not one thing. They can be good or evil. They can be both ... and at the same time. Just ask Tillie Winchester."

I smiled despite myself and then sobered. "So ... basically you're saying that we're dealing with an evil witch," I mused.

"That's a bit simplistic, but essentially, yes. It's unfortunate, but that's where we're at."

"Do you know who it is?"

"No. This bruja has clouded itself. I don't even know if it's a man or woman."

"I thought most witches were female."

"They are, but men join the craft just as readily as women. Come with me again." He grabbed my hand without waiting this time, and when we arrived at our next destination I realized we were back in my hotel room.

Jack, his chest bare, slept soundly in the bed. I was next to him, our fingers joined. It felt weird to look at myself that way, yet I understood I was having an out-of-body experience rather than a dream. Somehow — it made no sense, but somehow — I was fine knowing that my consciousness was taking a trip while leaving my body behind.

"He is of this world, both feet firmly planted," Legba explained. "I thought he was a lost cause to bring to our side because he refuses to believe in the impossible. Then he met you. He thought it was impossible to have feelings even though they threatened to overwhelm him."

"He's a good man." I felt the urge to stand up for Jack even though it wasn't necessary. "He always does what he believes is right. You can't have his soul either."

"Ugh. You need to let go of the soul thing." Legba made a face. "Soul deals are rare. We make them, it's true, but we're not interested in your soul. We're not interested in Jack's soul either. You two are far too intertwined now to be separated."

That was reassuring ... sort of. "Then why are you so interested in him?"

"He's an important example of people being willing to change even when you think their belief system is set in stone. Jack didn't believe in anything but being a stand-up guy until you came along. Now he is more than he was. His adoration for you will make him stronger. Your feelings for him will make you a warrior."

I was back to being confused. "What does that have to do with the zombies?"

"I cannot see the bruja," Papa Legba explained. "Why do you think that is?"

"Because ... because he or she doesn't want you to see. They're hiding."

"It takes powerful magic to hide from me. The Quarter is full of powerful magic. It was birthed on the sort of magic that sustains for generations. That magic will continue for a very long time. There are hundreds of people in the Quarter with a little magic, which makes for a powerful experience for those in the know. There are very few individuals with a lot of power, though."

Realization dawned. "That's why you want me. You think I have a lot of power."

"I know you do," he corrected. "You have more power than most of the pretenders to the throne. You have more power than those who really play the game for altruistic purposes. You are unique. The person we're looking for is unique. You're like different sides of the same coin."

He said it with pride, but I was hardly happy to hear it. "What am I supposed to do?" I felt helpless. "How am I supposed to fight evil when I'm hiding who I am? I can't drag Jack to a magic fight, but there's no way he's going to sit back and let me go on my own."

"Jack has a few struggles ahead of him. They're not nearly as bad as you think. He'll be fine. You said it yourself. He's a good man and that won't change. I am not worried about Jack."

"What are you worried about?"

"You're a target, Charlie. Whoever is doing this knows you're here. He or she recognizes you for what you are. You're a threat to their ultimate plan and they want to take you out."

"But ... how could they know I'm here?"

"Think about it."

"I ... ." It didn't take long for things to slip into place. "I've met whoever it is, haven't I?"

"I don't know about 'met,'" he cautioned. "This individual has seen you, whether it be through your travels in the Quarter, your visits to various stores and restaurants, or even your presence in the cemeteries. You leave a ripple when you pass, Charlie. It's a ripple not everyone can see."

"So ... what do I do?"

"Keep your eyes open. Listen to your heart. There will come a time when you hear a warning. It will be little more than a whisper on the wind. Don't ignore it. Not only does your life hang in the balance, but Jack's as well.

"He won't leave you," he continued. "You know that deep down. Your fear clouds your judgment, but he will not leave you no matter the circumstances. He's already bonded himself to you even though he doesn't realize it. He did it from the start.

"He told himself that he wanted to protect you because you were young and he saw you as vulnerable," he said. "That wasn't the reason. He was drawn to you on a spiritual level. He continues to be drawn to you on that level. I don't believe it's something that will ever wane, but that's still to play out.

"Your enemy grows close, but I still can't see through the mist." He pointed toward the window, to the growing fog. "Whoever it is grows desperate. I don't think you have much time. You need to be careful. Open your mind. Trust your senses."

"And then what?" I was rapidly getting fed up with this dream. "What happens when I find who it is? Will I have to kill him or her?"

"Yes."

"But ... I don't want to kill people."

"Because you have a pure heart." His expression was almost piteous. "You can't change who you are, Charlie. You can't change what you are either. You're a champion. Champions fight. You won't have a say in the matter."

I watched the figures on the bed. The other me looked almost distressed in sleep. And, even though he was dead to the world, Jack sensed it. "Charlie," he murmured, wrapping his arms around the other me. "It's okay."

I swallowed the lump in my throat. "I don't want to risk him. It's not fair."

"Let him decide what's fair," Papa Legba instructed. "Don't fight the battles that are unimportant. Focus on those that are necessary."

"How much time do I have?"

"Not long. Be ready."

"Will you be there in the end?"

"I am everywhere, Charlie. You need not worry. Much like Jack, I will never abandon you. It is written in the stars. Trust your heart. Trust me. Trust Jack. You cannot be led astray if you do those things."

"And what about the other stuff? What about my parents?"

"All in good time. Fight this battle first. We'll tackle the war after that."

And just like that, he was gone and I was back in my body, Jack wrapped around me. I was warm and safe. But how long would that last?

TWENTY-THREE

I woke with Jack still wrapped around me. His breathing told me he was awake, so I rolled to face him. His smile was the first thing I saw and it eased some of the tension building inside of me.

Did I dream everything last night? I didn't think so.

"Good morning," he murmured, leaning forward to give me a kiss. "Are you okay?"

"Why wouldn't I be?"

"Thibodeaux was a jerk last night."

"Oh, that." I shook my head. "I'm okay. I don't understand why he seems so fixated on me, but I'm okay."

"Yeah. You're tough." He kept his eyes on me. "You were restless for a bit last night, but you settled down. You said something weird."

"I said something?" I furrowed my brow as I tried to remember. "What did I say?"

"You said you don't want to kill people."

I vaguely remembered that from my conversation with Papa Legba. "I had a dream." That was the truth. It *was* a dream. Sure, the odds of the conversation being real were high, but it was still a dream. "Do you know who Papa Legba is?"

"Am I supposed to?"

"He's famous in hoodoo circles. He's been referenced in all the books we've been reading."

"Now that you mention it, I do remember that name. Did you dream about him?"

"Yeah. He said I was going to have to fight a bruja."

"What's a bruja?"

"An evil witch."

"Ah." His lips curved. "Maybe he was talking about Laura."

"Wouldn't you like that?" I snuggled closer, our shared body warmth rapidly diminishing. "I'm afraid that there's a fight coming."

"You don't have to fight. I'll keep you safe."

"That's a nice offer and I appreciate it. I'm all about feminist power, though. I'd like to be able to protect myself."

"Meaning?"

I shrugged. "I don't know. Maybe when we get back you can teach me some self-defense moves. You probably know a ton of them."

"I could do that."

"It will be another bonding exercise."

"Yes, a sweaty one at that."

I laughed when his lips moved to my neck. "I see you're much more interested in the prospect now that you've worked out it's going to be sweaty."

"I'm a guy. Sue me."

"What time is it?"

"We have an hour until breakfast."

"I bet I know how you want to fill that hour."

"I bet you do."

WE MADE IT TO THE TABLE in the restaurant with two minutes to spare. Everyone was already seated and conversation was flowing. Only Laura looked annoyed at our appearance.

"It's nice to see you guys could tear yourselves away from each other," she sneered.

"Shut up, Laura." Jack's mood was markedly brighter than it had been the previous evening. That didn't mean he was willing to put up with her crap. He grabbed two menus from the center of the table, handed me one, and then focused on Chris. "What's the deal today?"

"We have a plan," Chris announced. "Hannah has managed to wrangle an invitation to the autopsy of Mr. Landry. I don't want her there alone. In fact, I prefer no one is alone from here on out."

"Send Laura with her," Jack suggested.

"Ugh. Thank you for that." Laura made a face. "I don't want to see an autopsy. Besides, I'm going with you and Chris. You need my expertise."

She looked smug, which set my teeth on edge. "And where are you going?" I asked.

"We're doing a forensic survey of St. Louis Cemetery," Chris replied. "We've already talked to your friend Leon, and he's agreed to get us in. Only three of us can go, and we need Laura's expertise on this particular subject. She's the only one who has conducted multiple surveys of cemeteries."

Yup. Laura was definitely feeling full of herself. The way she puffed out her chest was a dead giveaway.

"And where is Charlie going?" Jack demanded.

"I thought she could go with Hannah to the medical examiner's office. Nothing will happen there."

Jack didn't look convinced that was true. "I don't know." His thoughts were right on the surface. He wanted to say "I want her with me," but he knew better. That would constitute a security snafu. He was supposed to be present for surveys, something he'd mentioned not long after I joined the team, and Chris was technically the boss. "Maybe Charlie should stay here at the hotel," he said after a beat. "Millie can go to the medical examiner's office and Charlie can stay here with Bernard."

I hated that idea with a fiery passion. "No way."

He shot me a quelling look. "I'm just saying that if you stay here the odds of Thibodeaux being able to jump all over you are slim."

"I know you're worried." Chris adopted a pragmatic tone. "I'm worried, too. Nothing will stop Thibodeaux from taking her into custody if he gets a bug up his butt. Besides, yesterday's attack happened on these grounds. It might be better for her to be away from the hotel. What are the odds an attack will happen at the medical examiner's office?"

That seemed a fair question. Jack still wasn't happy.

"I just don't like it." Jack growled and shifted his eyes to me. "What do you think?"

I wasn't expecting the question. I thought he would dictate terms. Instead, he was asking my opinion. "I don't want to stay here," I answered truthfully. "I'm not all that keen on the medical examiner's office, but I don't want to be cut out of the loop."

He turned his eyes to Millie. "What are you doing today?"

"Myron knows a hoodoo historian at Loyola University," she replied. "Bernard and I are heading over there. I thought Charlie might be good on that assignment, but we'll be out in the open and if someone really is zeroing in on her ... ." She left the statement hanging.

"Then she would be easier to access at the university," Jack finished. "I get it. I just don't like this. I cannot for the life of me fathom why someone has decided to make Charlie a target."

"I can think of a few reasons," Laura muttered.

"Shut up, Laura," Chris snapped. He rarely lost his cool, but he was obviously on edge today. "I'm with Jack. The focus on Charlie is troubling. All I can figure is that she makes an appealing target to someone who has been watching us. They know we'll be crippled if something happens to her."

"Which is why I don't want to be separated from her," Jack admitted.

"I understand, but we need three bodies for the survey." Chris didn't back down. "I think the safest place for her is the medical examiner's office. There will be police officers and authorized personnel there. She's less likely to be attacked in that location. Plus, if she's at the medical examiner's office, they have cameras. She can't be accused of anything if she's on camera."

"I get what you're saying." Jack was resigned as he glanced at me. "Try to be good when you're out and about, huh? No wandering away."

"I don't wander," I said primly as I looked at the menu. "I'll be fine. You worry about doing your job and I'll worry about doing mine."

"Your safety falls under my purview," Jack reminded me.

"Don't worry," Laura offered. "I'm sure I'll be able to distract you from worry over your pet bunny."

"Shut up, Laura," Hannah growled. It was rare for her to lose her temper, but she was testy. "If you weren't such a pain we could work as a seamless unit. I don't understand why you always have to be the difficult one."

"I guess I was just born that way," Laura drawled.

"Well, maybe it's time for some behavior modification," Hannah suggested. "I hear they've made great strides with electroshock therapy. Perhaps you should look into that."

I had no idea if Hannah was joking, but I couldn't stop from laughing. Within seconds, everyone at the table — other than Laura, of course — had joined in. It served to ease the tension.

"It's going to be fine," I promised Jack, squeezing his knee under the table. "You don't have to worry. I'll be perfectly fine."

"That would be a nice change of pace."

THE NEW ORLEANS CORONER'S Office was located outside the French Quarter, near the Mercedes-Benz Superdome. I wasn't someone who cared about sports teams all that much, but the building was impressive.

"That's neat, huh?"

Hannah barely spared a glance. "It's fine. If you like that sort of thing, I mean."

Hannah wasn't always talkative, but she seemed even more distracted than usual this morning. Our driver dropped us in front of the office with instructions to text when we were ready to leave. Hannah was engrossed in a report she was reading on her phone.

"What is that?"

"The preliminary report on Mr. Landry," Hannah replied, glancing around to make sure nobody was eavesdropping before we entered the building. "There's no scientific explanation that can explain how he was on his feet. None."

"So ... you're basically saying he was really a zombie."

"Scientifically, zombies are nonsense," she countered. "The elements would kill them in both humidity and cold climates. When part of the human body goes awry, we don't move. We become inert. The human central nervous system controls movement and that goes out the window when you're dead.

"White blood cells would attack any zombie virus to the point we'd be overloaded," she continued, deadly serious. "We eat food to convert to energy, but there's no such thing as a metabolism if you're dead. Animals would attack the dead before we were even aware of them.

"Without all five senses we can't survive, and if you're dead you don't have any of them," she said. "Living tissue heals. Dead tissue rots and falls away from the bone. There's no waste system if you're dead, which means there's no process to eliminate waste from the body."

"You're basically saying that zombies would explode because of poop," I smirked.

She ignored the statement. "And, finally, zombies can't wear dentures and their teeth would fall out right away. That makes zombies impractical."

"I see you've given this a lot of thought," I said.

"I have," she agreed. "Zombies can't be real."

"Then what do you think is going on?"

"I don't know." She looked helpless as she reached for the door. "It's just ... do you believe in magic, Charlie?"

I didn't expect the question, especially from her. "I do."

"Well, I never have. I believe that there are miracles in nature that seem like magic, but there's always a scientific reason. If I'm wrong, then what place do I have in this group? If that's really a zombie in there, what do I have to offer?"

Suddenly it dawned on me that even people as self-assured as Hannah had moments of self-doubt. It steadied me. "Hannah, you're the smartest person I've ever met." That was the truth. "Just because something defies logic doesn't mean you're unnecessary. You offer more to this group than you can possibly realize."

"I don't think I can believe in zombies no matter what this autopsy shows."

"Well ... then cling to science." It sounded like the sort of advice she needed. "I'll handle the magic part."

"Oh, yeah?" She cracked a smile. "How?"

"Let's just play it by ear."

THEY ALLOWED US INTO THE ROOM where they were conducting the autopsy after a basic check of our credentials. Given what Hannah had told me about the first autopsy she'd participated in, I thought they would set up a quarantine zone around the body and make us stay behind a line. I was wrong.

Lawrence Carlin, the coroner in charge, handed Hannah a scalpel within minutes of our arrival. He offered one to me, too, but I politely declined.

"I'll just watch from over here," I offered, positioning myself close to a wall. I could see the action but I wasn't within touching distance. I'd already been close to Barry when he attacked his wife in the hotel. I didn't need to be near him again.

"You'll be fine," Hannah reassured me as she slipped on a surgical mask and gloves. "I'll call out anything interesting. You can write it down in a notebook."

"That sounds like a plan."

I thought the autopsy would be interesting. I was wrong. At first, Hannah and Carlin noted a variety of things they found worthy of note, but I couldn't make heads or tails of what they said. I eventually gave up even listening and started wandering.

The autopsy room was sterile and largely empty. That's why I eventually exited into a dark hallway. It was empty, nobody around that I could see or hear, and it allowed me to peek into the different rooms along the way. Almost all of them looked exactly the same as the room Hannah and Carlin toiled in.

That changed when I reached the last room. "Wow," I said to myself as I shuffled inside, my mouth dropping open. "Is this ... ?"

"The freezer room?" a voice asked from my left, causing me to jolt. I'd assumed I was alone.

"I'm so sorry." I felt like an idiot as I gaped at the young man in a lab coat. He held a clipboard and appeared to be in the middle of a task. "I didn't mean to interrupt."

"That's okay." He offered me a lopsided smile. "I'm Mike Gentry. I work here."

"Charlie Rhodes." I didn't extend my hand in greeting. I really didn't want to make contact with his surgical gloves anyway. "I'm here for the autopsy on Barry Landry. I got bored and started to wander. If I'm not supposed to be here I can head back."

"No, it's okay." Gentry didn't seem bothered by my sudden appearance. "I heard an important autopsy was going on today. Only a few people have been allowed into the building. Do you know anything about it?"

That was a tricky question. "Well ... ." I trailed off when I heard an odd buzzing. "What's that?"

Gentry looked around blankly. "What's what?"

"That noise? Don't you hear that?" I stuck my finger in my ear and jiggled it. "It's a buzzing sound."

"I don't hear anything." Gentry's expression was blank. "Maybe you're getting sick or something. One of the first things to go when an illness is coming on is inner-ear balance. Do you feel as if you're going to fall over?"

"Not last time I checked," I replied dryly, jiggling my ear again. The buzzing wouldn't stop. "I don't know if I'm supposed to talk about the autopsy. What have they told you?"

"Just that the guy who attacked people at the Royal Dauphine yesterday had been dead for a year." Gentry's expression reflected enthusiasm. "Everyone is dying to get a look at the body, but they're holding us off so far. Apparently some woman has been invited to the autopsy. She has special knowledge. I guess that's you."

"Not me." I vehemently shook my head. The buzzing was growing in magnitude. "It's my co-worker Hannah. She's in there right now. I'm kind of her sidekick."

"Oh, well, there are worse jobs."

"Yeah. What's this room for? I mean ... I get what's on the other side. There's, like, fifteen bodies over there. What's this specific room for?"

"The room on the other side of the glass is refrigerated," he explained. "This is an observation room where we can warm up between notes and stuff."

"That's nice. I ... son of a ... !" The buzzing grew so loud I thought it might drop me to my knees. "Why won't that stop?"

"Maybe I should call for help." Gentry looked concerned. "In fact ... ." Whatever he was about to say died on his lips. His eyes made a quick trek to the room on the other side of the glass before landing on a phone on the wall, but he jerked his head to stare in the direction of the glass a second time. "Oh, my ... ." He went slack-jawed and pale.

"What's wrong?" I forced my attention to the refrigerated room and almost fell over from the shock. The bodies, which had been resting quietly under sheets just moments ago, were all sitting upright and staring.

Old men, young women and even children — fifteen of them in total — stared directly at me. None of them moved, but they all were fixated on the spot where I stood.

"What are they doing?" I asked, breathless.

Gentry didn't immediately answer, so I risked a glance in his direction and found he'd fled, the door standing wide open. The only proof that he'd ever been there was the clipboard he'd been carrying. He'd abandoned it on the floor in his haste to get away.

"Well, great," I muttered, turning back to the refrigerated room. All the bodies had raised an arm and were pointing at me. They made no sound as they stared.

The buzzing grew in magnitude so that I had to cover my ears.

The bodies didn't move, but I was quickly being swamped with feelings I couldn't put a name to all the same.

"Papa Legba," I gasped, hoping he could help. "I ... you ... ."

I couldn't take the buzzing another second. It dropped me to my knees as I let loose a guttural cry for help. It was already too late. My face started careening toward the floor and the last thing I remembered was the linoleum flying toward me as I lost consciousness.

There, in the darkness, I thought I heard laughing. It was gone before I could wrap my head around it. I floated into an empty abyss. I had no idea how long I drifted in the inky blackness.

TWENTY-FOUR

*H*annah's was the first face I saw when my eyes opened. I was on the floor, on my back, and she leaned over to stare directly into my face.

"How many fingers am I holding up?" she asked as she wagged three in my face.

"I'm not blind." I shoved her hand out of the way and frowned. "My back hurts." I tried to shift, and groaned.

"I should think so," she readily agreed. "You fell ... hard. Should I call an ambulance?"

"I really rather you didn't." It was then that I remembered why I fell and made an effort to scramble to my knees to look through the windows into the refrigerated room. The bodies looked to be back on their gurneys – unmoving — though it was obvious something had occurred. "What happened?" I asked even though I knew the answer.

"I was just going to ask you that." Hannah hunkered down and drew my gaze to her. "Follow the light please." She clicked what I thought was an ink pen and I automatically did as she asked when a small pen light switched on. "I'm going to touch the back of your head looking for a bump," she announced. "Don't pull away."

That's exactly what I wanted to do, but I managed to maintain a modicum of calm. "I'm fine, Hannah. I just ... fell over. Kind of."

"According to the man who was screaming in the hallway when he exited this area of the building, that's not the case." Hannah, ever placid, placed gentle fingers on the back of my head. "He said that all the bodies sat up and pointed at you."

Mike Gentry. I'd almost forgotten about him. I guess that answered the question of where he took off to right before I passed out.

"I don't know exactly what I remember," I hedged. Honestly, I wasn't certain how much I should say. "It's all a blur."

"Well, I can't find a bump." Hannah flashed a bright smile. "I don't think you have a concussion. That's good."

"Yes, that's lovely," I agreed. "Does that mean I can get off the floor?"

"Sure." She helped me to a standing position, and the first thing I did was scan the refrigerated room a second time. It was still, quiet, but all the sheets had been disturbed. They weren't flat as they should've been, as they were before Gentry ran and I lost my head. "What do you think happened?" I asked in a low voice.

"I don't know." Hannah was the sort who liked to chew on problems and puzzle them through from beginning to end. The look she shot the bodies now was troubling. "Tell me what you saw, Charlie. I need to know."

I felt caught. I couldn't lie to her. Things were starting to spiral and I didn't want them to get out of control. I didn't want to be the person who swept an uncomfortable truth under the rug because I was afraid to own it.

"I heard a buzzing in my head." I thought back to the moment right before the bodies sat up. "It was too much. It hurt. Gentry — he's the guy who was in here with the clipboard — didn't act as if he heard it. I should've run.

"The buzzing got worse and all the bodies sat up," I continued, my stomach threatening to revolt as I returned to the moment. "They pointed at me. That's when the buzzing got so bad I passed out."

Hannah was calm. "Did they say anything?"

"No."

"Did they get up from the gurneys?"

"No."

"Did you feel as if your life was in danger?"

"I ... don't know."

"Okay." She ordered my hair and flashed a smile that was more a grimace. "Jack is going to melt down."

"Yeah. He really is.."

"We need to go back to the hotel," she explained. "I finished the autopsy and I have some interesting information."

I perked up. "What? Did you prove he's a zombie?"

"I only want to go over the information once. We need to get out of here. I'm starting to think this was the worst possible place to bring you given everything that's happening. I'll call for the car."

"Wait." I wrapped my fingers around her wrist. "Did you find anything good?"

"Let's just say I found a lot of interesting things and leave it at that. Come on. The moment Jack finds out what happened he's going to throw himself on top of you like a live grenade is about to go off. I'm kind of curious to see it go down."

That made one of us.

JACK, AS EXPECTED, WAS apoplectic when he stormed into the lobby and found Hannah and me sitting together on one of the couches.

"Are you okay?" He headed straight for me. Instead of giving me a hug or expressing how glad he was that I was okay, he grabbed my chin and tilted my face up to stare into my eyes. "How many fingers am I holding up?" He flashed four.

"I'm fine." I pulled away from him, annoyed. "You don't need to treat me like I'm a child."

"Maybe that's how he feels about you," Laura suggested as she strolled into the room. Her expression was hard to read, but I sensed mayhem. "I couldn't figure out why he would possibly be interested in you, but I think you just nailed it. He wants someone to boss around and treat like a child. That's why he gravitates toward you."

"Stuff it, Laura," Jack snapped. "That is not true, and I'm sick of your mouth."

He wasn't the only one. But I couldn't help wondering if she was right. He'd spent all his time since we arrived in New Orleans worrying about me. Perhaps he wanted something to protect, a wilting flower. That was never going to be me.

"I'm fine." I pushed his hand away with force. "I'm not a little kid."

Jack's annoyance was obvious. "Did I say you were a little kid?"

"No, but ... I'm fine."

He didn't look convinced. "Great. I'm glad you're okay." He shifted his eyes to Hannah. "What happened? Your text to Chris was rather cursory."

"I'm not sure what happened," Hannah replied. "I was in the middle of the autopsy when she wandered off."

"You wandered off?" Jack's expression was pained as he rubbed his forehead. "Why would you do that?"

"I was bored," I shot back, my frustration growing with every snide question. "I didn't understand what was going on with the autopsy. I couldn't help. I decided to take a look around. I didn't think it would be a big deal."

"You never do," he groused.

"I went into this ... observation room of sorts. It was basically a half circle surrounded by glass. On the other side was the refrigeration room where they keep the bodies. There was a guy in there. He was young. He was asking about the autopsy. I kept hearing this ... sound."

Chris leaned forward, intrigued. "What sound?"

"I don't know how to explain it. There was a ... buzzing. It was really loud and overpowering."

Chris shifted his eyes to Hannah. "Did you hear the buzzing?"

She shook her head. "No. Only Charlie did as far as I can tell."

"Maybe she's on a different wavelength," Chris noted as he stroked his chin. "Maybe she can sense things we can't."

That was definitely true. I didn't want him leaning in that direction, though.

"Or perhaps she imagined it and is just looking for attention," Laura smirked.

I hated to admit it, but it would be better if they believed that ... even though I found it insulting. With nothing better to do, I heaved out a sigh and rubbed my forehead. Jack caught my hand as he sat next to me, his eyes somber.

"Are you okay?" The question was quiet but heartfelt.

"I didn't hit my head or anything going down. It happened really fast."

"I still don't know what went down," Chris admitted. "Hannah didn't tell me anything in the message she sent."

"Which meant Chris couldn't tell me anything," Jack added.

"Which meant that I had to listen to both of them whine for the entire ride back," Laura supplied. "Jack was obviously worried about his little girl." Her tone was mocking and it took everything I had not to launch myself at her and start squeezing her neck. She really was a master when it came to agitating people. "Maybe you should buy her a doll, Jack. That might calm her."

"Shut up, Laura." Jack's eyes flashed with a level of anger I'd only seen once or twice before. It was obvious he was working hard to rein himself in.

"Don't let her get to you," I admonished. "She likes messing with you. If you keep reacting this way, she wins. That's not what you want."

He turned back to me and frowned. "I'm worried, Charlie." He was seemingly incapable of keeping his feelings to himself. "You're being targeted here from multiple angles. I'm starting to think ... ."

"You're starting to think what?" I prodded.

"I'm starting to think that we should send you home." He held firm when I immediately started shaking my head. "Someone here wants to hurt you. I don't know who. I don't know why. Do you have any idea how frustrating that is?"

"I'm fine." My voice came out squeakier than I'd intended. "You can't send me home. That just reinforces the idea that I'm different from the rest of you."

"Charlie." Jack sounded exasperated. "I don't want you feeling different, but ... I'm not sure you're safe here. I don't know why, but someone is zeroing in on you. How else do you explain what happened in the medical examiner's office? I mean ... you passed out."

"I think she passed out because her senses were overloaded," Hannah offered helpfully. "I think it was a multitude of events colliding. The buzzing she couldn't seem to shake is the overwhelming factor, but when all the bodies in the refrigerated room sat up and pointed, that had to be terrifying. You can't hold that against her."

Jack's mouth dropped open as excitement bubbled over Chris's handsome features.

"What?" Chris was breathless. "All the bodies in the morgue sat up and pointed at you?"

Oh, well, great. He was going to go off on a tangent. "That's what I remember, but I wasn't on my feet for very long after it happened. It could've been a dream."

"Oh, it was a dream." Laura mock clutched at her heart and looked to the sky. "Poor Charlie is being haunted by dreams."

"I will physically pick you up and throw you in the dumpster out back if you're not careful," Jack warned. "I'm not kidding."

"Oh, you're all talk and we both know it," Laura shot back, rolling her eyes. "Tell us about the zombies sitting up and pointing, Charlie. That sounds like a scene right out of a horror movie. Twenty bucks says she's making it up."

"Except Charlie isn't the one who told me about it," Hannah argued. "There was another worker in there. He was talking to Charlie when the buzzing started. The only reason I knew to check on her is because he ran from the room screaming. He was going on and on about the zombie apocalypse when he ran."

Chris was so excited I thought he was going to burst. "Did the zombies get up from the gurneys? Did they walk out of the coroner's office?"

Hannah shook her head. "No. They were all back in place by the time I got there."

"There you have it," Laura sputtered. "Charlie and this attendant worked together to perpetuate a hoax."

"I very much doubt that," Hannah shot back. "Charlie was on the floor when I entered and she was confused. Her pulse was racing. You can't fake a reaction like that. Besides, the sheets on all the bodies were disturbed. They were meant to be drawn over the heads, nice and neat. Some fell on the floor and others were askew. There's no way Charlie could've managed that in the short amount of time she was gone."

Jack shot Hannah a grateful smile. "You have a very organized mind."

"I do," she agreed. "Besides, I have some rather unusual results from the autopsy. Barry Landry had definitely been embalmed. He was decaying at a relatively normal rate. That's to say that there is no such thing as a normal rate when embalming is involved because a number of factors play into the results.

"I don't know if oxygen got into his coffin ... or water ... or something else," she continued. "Embalming is meant to be a temporary preservation. For example, if there are several weeks between a person's death and the funeral, something will have to be done to that body every day to make sure it keeps looking fresh."

I made a face at her choice of words. "Nice."

"Mr. Landry was suffering from the normal wear and tear you'd find a year after being interred," Hannah said. "In fact, I'm starting to think that he was better preserved than he should've been ... especially if he had a sealed casket. Most bodies liquify in those."

My stomach threatened to flop. "That is lovely."

Jack moved his hand over the back of my head but remained focused on Hannah. "So, basically you're saying that we're dealing with zombies."

I wanted to laugh at his expression. If it wasn't such a serious moment, that's exactly what I would've done. He looked depressed, though, and it lightened my mood. "I never thought I would see the day when you would say something like that," I murmured.

He slid his eyes to me. "What else should I say? I saw the guy on the floor. There's no explaining what happened to him other than calling him a zombie. I'm not ready to admit that there's a virus or anything about to take down the world yet. I won't go that far."

On impulse, I grabbed his hand and squeezed. "Thank you."

He cocked his head, surprised. "For what? I didn't say I agreed with you. In fact, I'm still trying to get you shipped out of here because I don't believe you're safe. I thought you would be fighting me, not thanking me."

I grinned because it was the only thing I could do. "You're not going to send me away. You might think it's a good idea, but when it comes to it you'll change your mind at the last minute because you're afraid whoever has targeted me here will follow me and I'll be alone once I'm separated from the group."

Jack scowled. "Oh, geez. I hadn't even thought about that. But now that you bring it up ... ."

I was amused. "You're not going to send me away."

"I'm not." Jack agreed after a beat, leaning forward so our foreheads almost touched. We weren't the only ones in the room, but he obviously didn't care that we had an audience. "You have to be really careful, Charlie. Something weird is happening here."

Something was definitely happening. I needed to find out what ... and I had an idea how I was going to do that. Unfortunately, he couldn't come along for the ride. There was no way I could explain what I had in mind. He would be angry and upset.

"I'll be careful. I can't back away from this. You have to realize that."

He blew out a long-suffering sigh. "I realize you're not going to back down. It's hard for me to admit that, but ... I get it. You can't turn away from this. You're at the center of it."

"Even if I wasn't at the center I wouldn't be able to turn away," I admitted. "This is the biggest thing I've ever been a part of. We're so close to proving zombies exist. I mean ... I could put my name on that report and it will be out there forever. No one would ever forget me."

"Is that what you're worried about?" Jack was flustered. "Charlie, no one who meets you would ever be able to forget you."

"I will," Laura countered. "As soon as she's kicked out of this group I'm going to throw a party and then immediately forget her. Just you wait."

Jack ignored her. "You'll always be remembered. I know you can't see that, but you will. Zombies don't need to be a part of that."

"What if I want them to be a part of it?"

He exhaled heavily. "Then that's up to you. My biggest concern is your safety. Why do you think you've been targeted?"

That was a good question. I didn't have an acceptable answer. "I don't know. I've been thinking about that. I think I had to have crossed someone's path in the early days. I probably didn't even realize what was happening."

"Who did you talk to?"

"I don't know. It could be someone staying in the hotel or someone who works here. I mean ... we haven't exactly been quiet about our plans. People are aware of why we're here."

"But focused on you, Charlie, above the rest of us?" Hannah pressed. "I know that someone could've overheard us. Wouldn't Chris make the most sense to fixate on?"

"Unless they're looking for a woman," Jack countered. "Chris is the biggest believer in the group, but he's a man. There's a lot of matriarchal power in the history of voodoo and hoodoo culture. Charlie is the biggest believer with ovaries."

I made a face. "That's a really weird way to phrase it."

Jack's grin was back. "Sorry. But you know what I mean."

"So, we need to move forward on the assumption that Charlie being a woman is somehow important," Chris said. "How do we do that?"

TWENTY-FIVE

*M*illie and Bernard joined us about twenty minutes later. We moved to Chris's suite so we could talk without the risk of people eavesdropping. We bounced a lot of ideas about, but no one had a firm plan.

I moved out to his balcony and sat in one of the chairs. I was interested in hearing what the others were talking about, but I wanted to work out my own plan in privacy. Jack was getting increasingly annoyed with some of Chris's ideas — like using me as bait and shoving me in the middle of a cemetery alone to see if the zombies would come calling — but I knew that would never come to fruition.

Millie found me on the balcony and sat down next to me, quietly sliding the door closed – at least as much as possible without drawing attention to us. "You're going to do something, aren't you?"

The question caught me by surprise. "What makes you say that?"

"I know you," she replied. "You've got a certain look about you when you're planning something. What are you going to do?"

"I'm going back to see Madame Brenna," I replied.

Millie balked. "Why? She didn't offer any help the first time."

"Didn't she?" I wasn't so sure. "She pegged me as different the moment we walked through the door."

"That's what grifters do. They read people."

"You sound like Jack."

"That's not always a bad thing. What do you hope to accomplish by going back there?"

"I want to have a seance."

Millie's mouth dropped open. "You can't be serious. Why? It's not as if she's able to communicate with the zombies."

"You assume that because you struggle with believing," I countered. "I don't labor under that particular problem. I think there's a chance that the zombies will know who raised them if we manage to make contact. The human soul goes on. I'm certain of that. While I don't believe the creatures who are being raised have souls, I still think the soul is partially tethered to the body. They have to know who is doing this to them or at least be able to give me a description."

"And why do you think Madame Brenna can help?"

"I sensed a glimmer of power while I was there." It was the simplest answer I could come up with. "Whether she's completely the real deal or not, I can't say. I do believe she's my best shot, though."

"What about the hoodoo chick?" Millie almost looked desperate as she licked her lips. "She seemed to know what she was talking about."

"She did," I agreed. "I don't think she's capable of conducting the form of seance I need. I don't understand why you're getting so worked up about this. It probably won't work. But if it does, we'll have a place to start investigating."

"Yeah, but ... you're going to have to do this alone," she pointed out. "We both know you're going to use your magic while you're there. That means Jack can't go with you." She looked thoughtful. "I can. I know, so I can be with you."

"You can't be with me." I was firm. "That won't work. You need to stay here and distract Jack so I can get away."

If Millie was annoyed when she first heard my plan she was downright livid now. "No way! You could be hurt if I let you go by yourself."

"Now you definitely sound like Jack." I refused to back down. "That place is only two blocks away. I can get there, do what needs to be done and get back before anyone knows I'm missing."

"And how do you intend to do that? Jack will notice if you try to sneak out."

"Who said anything about sneaking?" I slowly got to my feet and brushed off the seat of my pants. "I think I need a nap."

"Of course you do." Millie looked disgusted. "What happens if he offers to take a nap with you?"

"He might want to. He won't, though. He's too busy working things out with Chris. Testing all the possibilities in a plan is part of his job description. He won't shirk his duties. That's not who he is."

"No, but ... ." Millie trailed off and then regrouped. "You've already worked this all out in your head, haven't you?"

"Yes."

"There's no talking you out of it."

"Nope. Once I go back to my room you can help. Keep Jack here for at least two hours. I should be done by then."

"And what if he checks on you and you're gone? What then? He'll melt down if he thinks you purposely walked into danger."

"I'm going to leave him a note explaining things."

"But leaving out the truth."

"For now," I agreed. "I've been thinking about this nonstop for days. He needs to know. It's not fair to keep him in the dark. The closer we get to one another, the harder it will be for both of us if he decides this relationship isn't something he can deal with for the long haul. It's best for me to tell him as soon as we're clear of this. It might already be too late."

"I think you're wrong on that front," she countered. "But I get it. It's the right thing to do. He'll stand by you. I have no doubt about that. I agree that now isn't the time to tell him. He's already struggling with the fact that you're a target and he can't figure out why."

"You can figure it out, though, can't you?" I kept my voice soft. "You've figured out why whoever is doing this has zeroed in on me."

"I have. Whoever it is — man or woman — has marked you as an equal. Your magic is powerful enough to stop what's coming. That's why the hoodoo chick was all over you. She recognized how powerful you are.

"Just from a bystander's point-of-view, Charlie, when scary things are afraid of you it throws people off," she continued. "I recognize your heart. I know you're a good person. I'll stand with you no matter what. You have good instincts even if I believe your current course of action is madness."

"Does that mean you'll help me?"

"I will, but I hope this doesn't backfire in your pretty face."

"I don't know what else to do." I felt helpless. "We need divine intervention, and this is the only way I can think to get it." I thought about relating the dream I'd had, my conversation with Papa Legba. There was every chance that would send her careening toward the ledge, so I couldn't risk it. "This is the only thing I can think to do."

"Then do it." She was blasé as she leaned back in her chair. "I'll do what I can. If I sense Jack is getting restless and wants to check on you I'll text. That's all I can do."

"I don't expect you to do more. If this blows up, I'll leave you out of it and face the music on my own."

"Well, let's not get maudlin." Millie mustered a smirk. "Even if Jack finds out, he'll only rant and rave for five minutes until he gives in. You two are in that heady beginning part of your relationship. He won't be able to hold onto his anger because of that."

I hoped that was true, but it very likely wasn't the reality I faced. "I'll see what I can find out. This might be our only shot."

"Good luck."

"Thanks. I'm going to need it."

IF JACK WAS SUSPICIOUS WHEN I told him I was going to take a nap, he didn't show it. He looked relieved. He walked me to the room, helped me get comfortable in bed, and then left to return to his argument with Chris. He was unhappy that every scenario our boss came up with to get our hands on tangible proof included using me as bait. He didn't come right out and say it, but it was obvious he felt that way.

I waited five minutes, until I was sure he was gone, and then hopped up and dressed. I pulled my hair back in a loose ponytail and used the back stairs to slip out of the building. I checked over my shoulder multiple times to make sure nobody followed me and then stared straight ahead when I hit the street.

The faster I could get through this, the better.

Madame Brenna was alone in her shop when I entered. She didn't appear surprised to see me. Instead, she looked as if she'd been proved right on some debate she'd been holding with herself.

"I knew you would be back," she said.

"Really? That's interesting. I didn't know it." I moved toward the table where she sat drinking her tea. "I have a proposition for you and I don't have much time."

"Well, now I'm doubly intrigued."

I swallowed hard as I sat. The woman really was striking. She was in her sixties but could pass for being in her forties if she put a little effort into it. She obviously didn't care what others thought. Her persona was based on the image she wanted to project, and I decided that was exactly how I wanted to be when I got older.

"Can you help me with a seance?" I blurted out the question without giving it much thought. We really didn't have much time.

"You want to conduct a seance?" She knit her eyebrows. "Why? I thought you were looking for zombies."

"I am," I assured her hurriedly. "The thing is, I have a hunch." I told her what I'd told Millie. When I finished, she was more open to the possibility than my friend.

"I understand," she said after a beat. "You think there will be trace magic left behind that will lead you to the guilty party."

"That's my hope," I agreed. "I think that if we focus on one of the dead souls — maybe the neighbor you mentioned — we might be able to figure out who's doing this."

"Have you considered the individual behind this has a bigger plan? I mean ... is anyone really getting hurt by those that are rising? The dead are already gone before the bodies are being co-opted."

"I get that, and up until yesterday I probably would've agreed with you. The thing is, Barry Landry came back yesterday. Did you hear about that?"

She shook her head. "I'm not sure I recognize the name. I feel as if I should, but ... I don't."

"His wife, Emeline, runs the Royal Dauphine Hotel."

"Ah." Madame Brenna bobbed her head, realization dawning. "I'm familiar with who you're talking about. I never spent much time with Barry. Emeline does most of the work. She always has. We've been to several business meetings together. Are you saying that Barry is one of the risen?"

"He attacked his wife in the lobby yesterday. I intervened and he went after me, too."

"What happened?"

"He's not a threat any longer," I replied simply. "I'm not sure exactly how he was taken out, but they did an autopsy on him this morning. He's ... gone again. At least for now."

"That is terrifying." She made a tsking sound with her tongue. "I can try to help. I can reach out to my neighbor. I'm sure he would be willing to share information if we can find him. You'll have to help. I usually call out to whoever is willing to talk. This time we'll be looking for a specific soul. It will take more power than I have at my disposal."

"I can help, but I've never done this before." I got comfortable in the chair beside her. "You'll have to direct me."

IT TOOK MADAME BRENNA TWENTY minutes to arrange things to her liking. She locked the store door, turned the sign to "closed" and then focused on me as we sat in the middle of the floor.

"You must concentrate," she ordered as she extended her hands. "You strike me as the sort who has a mind that wanders. That cannot happen today. You must follow my lead."

"I'll do my best." I meant it. "Just tell me what you want me to do."

"I'm going to create a dark room," she explained. "I want you to stand in the center of the room with me. We will call to my neighbor."

"What's his name?"

"I don't know his name. I only know his essence."

"Won't that make things more difficult?"

"Yes, but I don't see where we have another option. I will recognize his soul. Unless you have specific knowledge of one of the other bodies that have risen, he's our only shot."

She had a point. "Let's do it." I worried my hands were sweaty as I pressed my palms to hers and closed my eyes. "Lead away."

"Keep your mind open," she ordered. "Here we go."

She began chanting. The words sounded French, which made sense. She was a Creole woman, and that meant the magic she knew had been passed down from various ancestors. The further back she went, the more French she got.

I opened my mind as she instructed, allowing the words to flow over me. I didn't understand them, but somehow I got the gist. Before I even realized what was happening, I was floating in darkness. The only thing I heard was her voice; she was yelling at me to listen.

"You must anchor yourself to the room," she snapped.

Slowly, I opened my eyes and looked around the black cube she called a room. There was no light fixture attached to the ceiling, yet I saw her clearly.

"What is this place?" I was intrigued as I glanced around. "It's ... weird."

"It's a meeting room of sorts between the two sides," she replied. "My grandmother taught me how to access it. Think of it as a thought museum."

"That's ... kind of cool." I turned to study the darkness that surrounded us. There seemed to be no limit to the space. "How did you know you could access this place when you first started practicing? Did your grandmother teach you?"

"No. She was long gone before I came into my powers. That didn't happen until I was in my twenties. I was something of a late bloomer."

"Well, at least you realized it before it was too late."

"True. You, however, were an early bloomer. I feel the power radiating off you. It is ... like being in a warm bath of light that makes me feel stronger with every breath."

She sounded covetous. "What?"

If Madame Brenna realized she'd made a mistake, she didn't show it. Instead, she let her excitement take over. "We could join together. Do you have any idea the things we could do if we linked your powers with mine?"

The idea made me distinctly uncomfortable. "I'd rather not do that. Thanks for the offer, though."

"Why not?" She sounded petulant. "You have a power those in the Quarter would love to harness. People are whispering about you. They can't identify what you are, but they know what you're not."

I swallowed the lump that had formed in my throat. "And what am I not?"

"A fluke. You're not someone who will generate magic and then lose it. Your magic is in your blood. You were born with it. Most of the bokors and priestesses here were made. That makes you the greatest power most of them have ever seen."

"I don't want to be the greatest power. I'm happy just being a woman."

"No one is happy just being a woman. Don't kid yourself. Power is craved for a reason. If you share yours we can teach those who would hold us down a very powerful lesson. Isn't that what you want?"

That was the last thing I wanted. "You sound like you want to be an overlord."

"And what is wrong with that?"

I could think of so many answers to that question, but I didn't want to anger her. I wasn't sure I could find a way out of the box without her. "I don't want to be an overlord. I prefer being normal, if that's even really a thing. I've never understood my powers."

"I can help you."

"From the sound of it, you don't know what I am. I don't know what I am either. You can't control what you don't understand."

"I don't want to control you. I want to join with you. Together we can control others."

Wait … what? "And why would I want that?"

"Why not?"

It seemed a simple question, but there was no easy answer. "This was a mistake." I could see that now, but I feared it was too late to break away. "I'll come up with another method to talk with the displaced souls. I'm sorry to have bothered you." I moved to step away, but there was no place to go.

"I can't just let you leave."

"No?"

"No. I need you. You don't realize it yet, but you need me, too. We must join."

"That sounds kind of perverted," I countered, buying for time. "Again, I have to say thanks but no thanks. This isn't what I want."

"Perhaps I don't care what you want." Her voice turned chilling. "What will you do if I don't allow you to leave?"

She was backing me into a corner and I had no other choice. "I'll have to make my own exit."

"And how will you do that?"

"You really don't want to know."

"But … I do."

"Then I'll have to show you."

TWENTY-SIX

*W*hen it came to fighting strategy, I wasn't one to think about the correct method or course before doing it. I was impulsive, and that's how I operated now.

I lifted my hands, sparks emanating from my fingertips and causing me to widen my eyes. That rarely happened, which made me think the room somehow amplified powers. If I was surprised, though, Madame Brenna was stunned.

"What is that?" She was awed by the show.

"Just let me out," I pressed. I wasn't sure what would happen if I started unleashing magic in the mind room she'd built. There was every chance she might be able to absorb it, which would be bad.

"All you have to do is agree to join with me." Her voice was calm, smooth. "You're a woman of your word. I'll believe you."

"I *am* a woman of my word," I agreed. "That's why I can't do that. I don't want to see whatever endgame you're trying to leverage. It was a mistake to come here."

I knew that deep down. That begged the question of why I felt the need to see her in the first place. The urge was strong at the hotel. I kept hearing Papa Legba's voice in the back of my head. He wanted me to listen to my heart, which is how I ended up chasing a woman with an obviously dark soul. How could I have gotten so turned around?

"Show me more," Madame Brenna insisted. "Show me all of it."

"You couldn't handle all of it," I shot back. Of course, I couldn't handle all of it either. I often felt shaky unleashing my magic, as if I was about to lose control of who I was and become something else. That was the greatest fear I harbored. What if the magic made me into something I didn't want to be?

"I want to see." Her eyes shifted in the light, momentarily looking reptilian and causing my blood to run cold. "Show me." She was insistent, brutally cold.

I had no choice but to give her what she wanted. The longer I stayed, the greater the chance I would become lost. If I gave her power over me, let her feel my fear, I'd lose control. "Fine."

I shook my hands, several sparks flying loose.

"Yes. That's what I want to see." Madame Brenna was greedy as she shifted closer. "Do it again."

"You want to see it again?" I had an idea. When she nodded, I leveled an evil smile at her. "Fine. Here you go." Quick as lightning — or as fast as I could move because even I can't match lightning — I shifted my hands to the sides of her head and poured as much magic as I could muster inside. "Show me," I ordered.

Madame Brenna was confused. Her instinct was to pull away — and that was the right move — but I gripped her so tightly that she didn't have the strength. "What are you doing?"

"Show me," I ordered, peering inside her mind. "I want to see what you are."

"I ... you ... ." She went slack-jawed as I took control. "This isn't right." She sounded bitter about the turn of events. For some reason, that made me happy.

"Show me." I burrowed deep, forcing myself past her defenses. As far as shields go, she had an impressive arsenal. I was stronger. She probably should've taken that into account.

"No! What are you doing?" She threw everything she had into breaking away from me. I refused to allow it.

"Be still." I was in deep enough that she had no choice but to acquiesce. Her eyes went blank and she stopped struggling as I looked for hints of what she was really after. It wasn't hard to find information. Unfortunately, I couldn't absorb the information very well.

Memories flashed through her head like a movie as I tried to pick the most important ones. I was on a limited timetable.

I saw a young girl who looked remarkably like Madame Brenna. She was in her early teens, wild hair standing on end, and she looked to be fighting with several other girls. The typical pre-teen insults flew and then the image dissolved.

Madame Brenna again. She was older now, probably early twenties. She was in a park and a handsome man made eyes at her. He was dressed in simple khakis and a shirt, but the smile he sent her was knee-weakening. My knees went weak at the same time hers did.

Another flash. Madame Brenna in a house, standing next to a stove, a toddler wailing at her feet. She didn't even remotely resemble the self-assured woman in front of me now. Instead, she looked wrecked, as if life had taken a swerve she hadn't expected. She didn't lean over to help the child. Instead she glared at him, as if he were the worst thing that had happened to her.

Another flash. The child was older, walking, quiet, a set of dark eyes that promised he would not be ignored forever. He sat in a window seat, his eyes fixed out the glass, as two people screamed in the adjacent room. I recognized Madame Brenna's voice. The male voice was an enigma, but he bellowed about a dirty house and a child falling behind in school. He called her a bad mother. Her only response was to laugh.

She was still laughing in the final flash. The child was older still. He didn't look happy or unhappy. He simply stood next to the door as his mother carried a suitcase toward it. She promised she would be back for him someday. She explained that his father wouldn't let him go and she didn't have the strength to take him. She swore she would eventually find the strength to return. The child didn't appear to be affected by the announcement. He merely nodded.

Other visions lurked at the outskirts of her mind. All I had to do was reach for them and I could've gained more insight. Something told me, however, that I'd already seen the necessary memories. I simply had to figure out the bigger picture and escape from the mind room.

I expanded my magic, pushed hard, and was gratified to see her mind barriers crumble like dry cookies. She was nowhere near as strong as me. Whether that was because she didn't realize what she was up against and was caught unawares or she was simply weaker, I couldn't say.

I forced a hole in her mind and stepped through it. The second I was free, I gasped in a breath. The real me, not the image trapped in her brain, remained sitting on the floor, cross-legged. She was across from me and looked dazed. She listed to her side, leaning on her elbow as she meekly crawled away from me.

"You shouldn't have done that," she hissed. Her eyes were back to normal and yet I couldn't shake the memory of the reptilian slits in her head. "I'll make you pay for that. You have no idea what I'm going to do to you."

I was the one in control — at least by appearances — so I climbed to my feet and clenched my hands at my sides as I stared down at her. "Don't come after me again. You won't like what happens if you do. That was a simple taste of the power that I wield."

"You don't deserve that power." She was back to bitter. "You don't even understand what you have."

"It doesn't matter. It's not your power. You need to let it go."

"I won't."

"Then you'll fall. I'm not here to deal with you. I thought you could help. Obviously you had other ideas."

"Obviously." She rasped out the single word, glaring as she propped her back against the wall. "We're not done."

"Oh, we're done. I don't have time for you." I headed toward the front door. I hoped to make a smooth exit, but I couldn't quite manage it because I wasn't familiar with the lock.

"You can't solve this without me," she warned. "You'll have to join me whether you like it or not."

"I don't believe that."

"That doesn't mean it's not true. You will be back."

"I promise you I won't." I pushed open the door, sucking in a breath of fresh air, and pulled up short when I found Laura standing five feet away. Her arms were crossed, her eyes suspicious, and I knew she'd seen some of what happened inside the store. The question was, how much? "What are you doing here?" I blurted out, frustrated. "Why are you following me?"

"I knew you were up to something," she replied, matter-of-fact. "There's no way you would willingly pull away from the rest of the group to take a nap. Do you think I'm stupid?"

I very much doubted that was a rhetorical question. "What did you hope to accomplish?"

"Well, I figured you were lying and all I had to do was follow you to figure out what you were really up to. You're not very stealthy, by the way. I'd say you need to practice those skills, but you won't be with the group long enough for it to matter."

My heart skipped a beat. "What do you mean?"

"Jack won't be happy that you lied to him." She looked thrilled at the prospect. "He'll finally see you for what you really are. I was convinced he'd grow tired of that naive schoolgirl thing you've got going eventually. This is so much better. There's nothing Jack values more than honesty. You, my dear, have officially burned your bridges."

I merely stared. She was right. I'd lied and Jack wasn't going to be happy. Worse than that, he would be hurt.

"Aren't you going to beg me not to tell him?" Laura chortled. "Aren't you going to appeal to my fellowship as a woman to help you?"

"No." There was no reason to lie. Laura wasn't a friend. She was an enemy. "You'll do what you feel is necessary."

"I will. Jack will be crushed." She rubbed her hands together. "I bet that means he'll be looking for someone to help him pick up the pieces."

I wasn't especially worried. "That will never be you."

"You don't know. It could be me."

"No, it couldn't." I shook my head. "Jack is a man of substance.

You're an empty vessel. You'll never be able to give him what he needs."

"And you think you will?"

"I don't know."

"Well, I know. I'm off to tell him the truth. I wonder if he'll cry. I know you will. I guess I'll see you back at the hotel." She skipped off, gleeful, leaving me nothing to do but follow at a much slower pace.

I scuffed my feet against the sidewalk as I trudged to what I was certain would be imminent doom. It appeared I was never going to get the chance to tell Jack the truth after all. Maybe that was for the best. I would never have to see the look on his face when I crushed his belief system. He might be better off.

What about me, though? An inner voice kept whispering the question. Would I be better off? I knew without a doubt that the answer was no.

JACK WAS IN THE LOBBY, and Laura was with him. She gestured wildly as she talked, her lips moving at a speed I'd never witnessed. He didn't react, but his eyes slowly tracked to me when I crossed the threshold. I saw betrayal lurking there, and it pained me.

"Charlie." His voice was deceptively mild. "I think we should talk."

"He thinks you should talk," Laura repeated. She was clearly having a great time. "I wonder what he wants to talk about."

"Sure," I offered, resigned. "We can talk. Where do you want to do it?"

"Upstairs." He pointed toward the elevator. "Come on." He didn't reach for my hand. He didn't brush his fingertips over my cheek or smooth my hair. He kept at least a foot between us at all times, even in the elevator.

We made the ride to our floor in silence. I wasn't sure if he wanted to argue in my room or his, so I hung back and watched as he headed toward my room. I followed him inside, resigned that I was about to lose everything important.

He kicked off his shoes and left them on the door rug before throwing himself into one of the chairs in the small sitting area. He looked like a man on the edge of a precipice. I wanted to soothe him, but there were few words I could offer to make things better.

"Laura said you were out with Madame Brenna," he started. "What were you talking about?"

"I thought she could help me conduct a seance," I replied dully. "I thought maybe if we could track down one of the spirits of the stolen bodies that he or she could answer some questions."

"That sounds ludicrous."

"I know."

"You did it anyway."

"I did. I just ... I don't like being painted as someone who needs constant protection. It's frustrating. I'm a grown-up, but I'm constantly treated as a child. That's not an excuse, mind you. I deserve whatever you're about to unload on me. I lied and snuck out."

"You did," he agreed, tapping his fingers on the arm of the chair. He looked antsy, frustrated to the extreme. "Why didn't you tell me what you had planned?"

"You know why. You're a non-believer. I can't make you believe like I do. I knew you would fight me. I wanted to give it a try."

"You left the hotel alone."

"I did."

"You could've been hurt, Charlie!" He practically exploded as he glared at me. "What would've happened if that woman had done something to you? What if she was involved? What if she overpowered you? She could've taken you anywhere and there's nothing I could've done to help."

I understood he was talking from a place of strength. In his mind, he was head of security. That made him the strongest individual in our group. That wasn't reality, though.

"I wanted to try," I shot back. "I don't like being treated like everyone's little sister. There are times I can be helpful. I thought that's what I was doing today. I hoped I could come up with a name and help point you guys in the right direction.

"Believe it or not, I wasn't trying to be a hero or purposely stupid," I continued. "I only wanted to help."

"And you don't feel as if I allow you to contribute?"

The question caught me off guard. "I feel as if you want to protect me. It's not a bad instinct, but it's smothering sometimes. Since we started dating, you've been worse. I want to be a fully-functioning member of the team. I want to matter."

"You matter to me."

"I know. You matter to me, too. I didn't mean to hurt you. I just ... wanted to help."

"I know." He pinched the bridge of his nose and closed his eyes. "This is hard for me, Charlie. I've never been in this position. I never thought I would be the sort of person who dated a co-worker. That always seemed a distraction I didn't need."

I swallowed hard. "Is this when you dump me?"

His eyes flashed with something I couldn't quite identify. "Do you want me to dump you?"

"No! I care about you so much it makes my head spin sometimes. I don't want to lose you. Even more than that, I don't want to lose myself. I can't be something other than what I am."

"What you are is inquisitive and enthusiastic," he said. "I knew that when we got involved. Those are two of the qualities that attracted me to you from the start. The thing is, Charlie, we have to come to a meeting of the minds here.

"You are a full member of this group whether you believe it or not," he continued. "You are smart and you can figure things out faster than most of us combined. That doesn't mean you're infallible.

"We're in this relationship and I don't see that changing," he said. "I want to be with you. I want to protect you. You want some level of independence. You say you want to be with me."

"I do want to be with you," I said hurriedly. "The last few weeks have been the best of my life. I didn't know it was possible to be this happy."

"Oh, geez." He dropped his head in his hands. "You're so earnest it's painful at times. God help me, I like that about you, too. We need to compromise. I have to find a way to let you follow your instincts and you have to find a way to allow me to be part of the fight. You're not alone any longer. We're in this together."

I was stunned. "Does that mean you're not dumping me?"

He almost looked amused when he raised his head. "No. I'm not dumping you. It would take so much more than that to get rid of me."

"Seriously?"

"Yeah."

I hopped to my feet and crossed to him, sliding into the chair with him. He grabbed my legs and turned me so I was crosswise on top of him. He smiled when I leaned close.

"I'm sorry. I just ... wanted to help."

"I know." He kissed the tip of my nose and wrapped his arms around me. "Charlie, I want this to work. I feel in the depths of my soul that it's going to work. But you have to meet me halfway. That means you can't run off half-cocked."

"What if there's no other choice?"

"Then ... text me to tell me what you're going to do. That has to be the minimum compromise here. I want to keep you safe. It's not just because we're dating. We're members of the same group."

"I get it." I did. We both would have to step up our efforts if we expected to meet in the middle. "I'm sorry."

"I know." He tipped up my chin and gave me a soft kiss. "I'm going to spank you later for this. I hope you know that."

I cocked an eyebrow. "Is it going to be in a dirty way?"

"Yes."

"Fine. I'll take my punishment with a smile and a giggle."

He cracked a legitimate grin. "All right. Come here a second." He sighed as he embraced me. "Laura is going to be really upset that we're not breaking up."

"Yeah, well, Laura is a jerk. I can't wait to rub it in."

"That makes two of us. But I want five minutes of quiet first."

"I can live with that."

"Good. Once we're done, we'll head to the lobby. Everyone is meeting there before dinner. We still have no idea what we're going to do."

I was officially right there with them. We were at a crossroads and there was no sign telling us which way to turn. Something was coming – I could feel it – but we weren't yet prepared to deal with it.

I was afraid … and I had no idea what to do about it.

TWENTY-SEVEN

*J*ack seemed okay on the surface when we made our way down to the lobby. Everyone agreed to set up shop there for an hour before breaking to eat. I could tell he was troubled, though.

During the past few weeks I'd gotten used to a series of small touches on his part. He put his hand to my back, stroked my hair or even brushed his fingertips against mine if we were on a job and couldn't draw attention to ourselves. He did none of those things now.

"I want to buy you dinner tonight," I announced when we settled in chairs away from everybody. We were close to the front desk — and Emeline was behind it working, although she looked nervous — so I figured now was the time to spring my news on him. "I think we should eat alone."

He cast me a sidelong look that was hard to read. "I think Chris wants everyone to eat together," he said finally. "Maybe when we're done with this."

Maybe. He was already pulling away. "Jack ... ."

He stopped me by holding up a hand. "I don't think this is the time to talk about this."

"You're still angry."

"I can't simply forget that you lied to me, Charlie. It's going to take time. I'm not angry as much as ... disappointed. I'm sorry."

He tagged that last bit on to make me feel bad. *I'm sorry.* It was to let me know that he wasn't sorry and he shouldn't have to be. He was right. I was the one who wandered off because instinct told me it was the thing to do. I couldn't exactly explain that to him, so ... here we were.

"Right." I rubbed my forehead and sank deeper into my chair. "I guess I'll just sit here and stare at the wall."

"That would be great," Jack said with faux brightness.

Laura sat on one of the couches in the middle of the room and scowled. "Why are you guys still sitting together?"

"We're working," Jack replied. "Mind your own business, Laura."

I pinned her with a hateful look because it was one of the only things I could do. "Yes, mind your own business," I grumbled. "If you would just mind your own business we'd all be better off."

"Oh, what are you complaining about?" Laura snapped. "He obviously didn't break up with you. He might be upset, but you haven't been kicked to the curb. I don't understand that."

"You can't understand anything," I complained. "You're completely and totally ... useless."

"It takes one to know one," Laura said in a sing-song voice.

"Knock it off," Jack ordered, his eyes landing on me. "I mean it."

I was in the doghouse and desperately wanted out, so I had no choice but to comply. He was entitled to his anger. I lied to him, made him feel vulnerable. I should've realized a five-minute argument wasn't going to cut it. He was waiting until we were back home to have a serious discussion.

That left me with a ball of dread in the pit of my stomach. With nothing better to do, I focused on Emeline. "Do you know Madame Brenna? She owns a voodoo store about two blocks from here. She's a little ... weird."

Emeline stared blankly at me for a long beat, so long that I thought she was going to ignore me before she perked up. "I know who you're talking about. She has quite the reputation in the Quarter."

"What can you tell me about her?" I rubbed my damp palms on the knees of my jeans. "I mean ... what sort of rumors have you heard?"

Jack knit his eyebrows but didn't ask the obvious question. He clearly wanted to know why I was so interested in Madame Brenna.

"She has a terrible reputation," Emeline replied. She was busy organizing files so she didn't look up. I was fine with that. It made what I had to do easier. "People say she's crazy."

"Crazy how?" Jack asked, avoiding the curious look I shot him.

"She really believes she's magical."

"You don't believe in magic?" I asked. "Even after what happened?"

"I ... ." Emeline broke off and chewed her bottom lip. "I guess that's a fair question. I'm still not sure what happened. The coroner's office called and said I don't have to pay to inter Barry a second time. They're going to do it for me.

"They acted as if I should be thankful for that," she continued with a hollow laugh. "Like that's supposed to make me feel better. What happens if he gets up and goes wandering again? Will he come here? Will he go after me?"

She was afraid. I didn't blame her. "I don't know. We need to find the source of this. That's why I'm asking you about Madame Brenna."

Emeline's eyes went wide. "You think she's behind this? Why?"

"I don't know that I believe she's behind it," I hedged. "It's just ... there's something about her." I muttered the second part more for my benefit and frowned. "Tell me what sort of stories you've heard about her."

"Oh, well, nothing that really sticks out," Emeline replied after a beat. "You hear stories about the voodoo folk often when you work in the city. Most of the tourists are excited to visit the shops. Madame Brenna, however, has a certain reputation. I never recommend people go to her if they ask."

That sounded about right. "Does she take money from the tourists?"

"Well, they all take money from the tourists," Emeline hedged. "I mean ... they're running a business. I don't have a problem with some of the things they do. It's the others ... ."

"Tell me some of the 'others.'" I was deadly serious. I couldn't get Madame Brenna's reaction out of my mind. She was clearly powerful enough to have caused real trouble. "I want to know what she's done to the tourists."

"Charlie, why does it matter?" Jack asked in a low voice.

"Because there's something wrong with her," I replied. "She's sick ... or maybe deranged."

"Did she do something to you? Laura said it looked as if you'd done something to her. I didn't believe that part of the story, but ... did you fight with her?"

"In a manner of speaking." I focused on Emeline. "What does she do to the tourists?"

"A variety of things," she replied after a moment. "A lot of the guests who stayed here visited her shop. They said that Madame Brenna told them they were cursed and would have to pay her to remove the curse."

"That's a standard ploy here," Jack argued. "I've had beggars tell me the same thing on street corners."

"It is a standard ploy," Emeline agreed. "It's just ... the guests said they felt sick right before she told them about the curse, as if they were going to throw up and maybe pass out. At the time they paid the money, they didn't think they had a choice. And, of course, after she got the money there was no getting it back."

"Right." I tapped my toe on the floor and pursed my lips as I considered the situation. Did I think Madame Brenna was the person we were seeking? Not at first. For some reason, though, she was all I could think about now that I was safely away from her store. Something was definitely wrong. "Tell me what you know about the woman. I get that she's a user and abuser. What do you know specifically about her? Does she have any family?"

"Not that I know of," Emeline replied after a moment's contemplation. "I've never really thought about it. I can't ever remember seeing her with family. Heck, she runs that store by herself most of the time, with a few trusted workers. She's something of a loner."

"That makes sense," I muttered, rolling my neck. I was getting antsy.

"What makes sense?" Jack reached over and grabbed my leg to keep it from bopping around. "What are you thinking?"

"Madame Brenna was acting odd." I couldn't tell him everything and yet I couldn't get her out of my mind. "She's looking for power. She wants to be in control."

"Yeah, but ... what does that have to do with the zombies?"

"I don't know. I'm glad you're finally using that word." I flashed a smile for his benefit. He returned it, but didn't put much effort into it.

"There isn't much I can tell you about Madame Brenna," Emeline offered. "All I know is that she's been in that spot for about ten years. No one knows what she was doing before then. She was going under a different name before she joined the ranks here, but I'm not sure what it was."

"Are you saying she's not local?" Jack asked, suddenly interested in the conversation.

"Oh, no." Emeline vehemently shook her head. "She's definitely local. I mean ... I'm pretty sure she grew up in New Orleans. Whatever name she was going under before, people recognized it. I remember hearing a story that someone called her by that name and she completely melted down."

Now we were finally getting somewhere. I shifted closer to the edge of my chair. "Do you remember what name she supposedly went under before becoming Madame Brenna?"

Emeline shrugged. "I'm sorry.."

I shifted my eyes to Jack, conflicted. "Do you think that's information Leon could track down for us?"

"I don't see why not," Jack responded. "Are you going to tell me why you think it's so important?"

"It's a feeling I have." I pointed at my stomach. "I can't explain it. I can't stop thinking about her. I know that's not what you want to hear. You like definitive answers. I just ... can't shake the feeling that answers are right there and we simply have to reach out and take them."

He held my gaze before finally digging in his pocket for his phone. "I'll call to see if he can hop on this for us. After that I'm taking you up on your dinner offer. I think we should head out alone."

A brief bout of fear rippled through me. "Why?"

He sighed. "Stop always thinking the worst," he admonished. "Fighting is not the same as breaking up. I get that you're afraid, but I really wish you would have faith in me for once. I have no intention of breaking your heart."

That's when I realized the truth. I was letting fear rule me when I should've been letting faith take my heart by the reins. Jack wasn't a bad guy. He was the best guy. That wasn't going to change just because I told him the truth.

"I'm sorry." I impulsively reached out and grabbed his hand. "I've never had anything I was afraid to lose once my parents were gone. I'd already lost everything and didn't think I wanted to risk caring enough to lose someone else. Then came you."

He blinked several times and then growled. "I wish you wouldn't say things like that. It makes it impossible for me to stay angry. I get that you're trying really hard. It's a difficult balancing act for you. You want to be the perfect employee and the perfect girlfriend."

He had me dead to rights there. "And you don't think I can do both," I mused.

"I don't think anyone can be perfect one-hundred percent of the time," he countered quickly. "You are perfect the way you are, Charlie. That includes flaws. If your enthusiasm causes you to make a mistake on the job ... or even with me ... that's okay. No one but you expects perfection.

"You live in fear because your parents left you," he continued. "I understand that. I don't know how I would feel in your position. I'm guessing it would be similar. But I am not your parents. I have no intention of leaving you."

"You have got to be kidding me," Laura muttered from her spot several feet away. She was clearly dumbfounded by the speech. "What does she have that you find so magical?"

Jack ignored her and focused on me. "I don't want you being constantly afraid. That's no way to live. I am occasionally allowed to get angry with you without fear of crushing your spirit. That compromise we talked about earlier is important. I told you upstairs that we're okay and I meant it. I'm still a little angry, but it will pass. We'll work on our communication skills tonight."

"You're still going to have Leon check on Madame Brenna, right?"

"I am." Jack squeezed my hand and then turned his attention to his phone. "Sometimes I feel as if we're two idiots stumbling through a dark tunnel. I wish I was smoother when it came to relationships."

That's when I realized he wasn't lying when he said he felt as awkward as I did. We both had work to do on the relationship front, and not because we were willingly hurting one another. We were simply inexperienced.

"We'll start at dinner," I suggested. "I'm paying."

"You're not paying."

"I have to. I was in the wrong and need to offer the olive branch. That seems only fair."

He let loose a world-weary sigh that emanated from the depths of his toes. "Fine. You can pay. But I'm buying dessert."

"Fair enough."

"I'm also having a drink." He locked gazes with me. "You make me want to drink, Charlie. What do you think about that?"

"Maybe I'll have a drink with you. I need to loosen up. I feel tense."

"I'll buy the drinks, too."

"See, we're already compromising." I sent him a blinding smile. "This is good."

"This is ... something. We're a work in progress."

This time the smile Jack mustered was small but heartfelt. "We'll get through this."

I had faith he was right.

· · ·

THE RESTAURANT I'D PICKED WAS quiet and romantic. By the end of the meal we were both feeling better. I did my best to explain why I needed to see Madame Brenna — without mentioning the magic, of course — and he listened without judgment. When I finished, I could tell he was still confused as to my motivations, but he was over being angry.

He held my hand as we crossed the street, our earlier strife seemingly forgotten. I knew it wasn't completely behind us — it couldn't be until I told him the truth and we muddled through that mess — but things were better. We understood one another on a different level. It was something of a relief.

We slowed our pace when his phone rang. He sent me an apologetic smile and released my hand before he started digging in his pocket. I took a moment to survey our surroundings. We were on a side street, and we were mostly alone. In a city the size of New Orleans that was rare ... and it immediately made me leery.

"Maybe we should head that way," I suggested, pointing toward Bourbon Street. I could hear it several blocks over but I couldn't yet see the bustling traffic.

"Just a second," Jack admonished as he pressed his phone to his ear. "Hey, Leon. That was fast. Did you track down the woman I asked about?"

I kept one ear on the conversation and studied the alley to our left. It was dark and grimy. The ambient noise that accompanies any city had disappeared, replaced by an eerie quiet. I didn't like it and sensed trouble.

"Uh-huh." Jack obviously wasn't paying attention to our surroundings because he was too busy listening to Leon. He turned his back to me and stared across the road, leaving me to watch the alley.

It was warm and muggy and the occasional bolt of heat lightning split the sky. It happened every night, although sometimes the heat lightning turned to regular lightning. The downpours that followed took the edge off the heat, so they were almost welcome. I had no doubt a storm was brewing tonight.

I wished for the heat lightning because the oppressive atmosphere hanging over the French Quarter was starting to get to me. In my mind's eye, I saw zombies shuffling along the alley as they tried to make their way to us. There was no reason for me to believe that was a possibility ... and yet something inside told me that we were dealing with just that scenario.

"Well, that can't be a coincidence," Jack said. I couldn't hear Leon's side of the conversation, but I knew Jack would tell me once he ended the call. I wasn't worried about whatever information Leon provided. I was worried about the alley.

"We need to move, Jack," I said after a beat. "We can't stay here." I felt that deep inside. Something very bad was about to happen.

The sky flashed again, lightning illuminating the area. Movement caused me to stare down the alley, to where at least thirty bodies headed in our direction.

"Oh, my ... !" My mouth dropped open and I gave Jack another shove, this one more vicious.

"What is your deal?" Jack asked, annoyed. "Give me a second. Leon got some very good information. We owe him."

"Leon is a prince among men," I shot back, shoving Jack as hard as possible. I heard growls rolling up the alley and knew we were almost out of time. "We have to run now."

"What do you mean?"

I gestured toward the alley as the first hand appeared on the brick exterior wall of some business I had zero interest in. The light wasn't bright, but Jack could still see the problem. Worse, he could hear it. The zombies were growling and gearing up.

"We have to run right now," I insisted.

Jack gripped my hand and pulled me with him as he started moving across the road. "How is this happening?"

"Madame Brenna," I replied. "It has to be her. It's the only thing that makes sense."

"Come on, Charlie." Jack increased his pace. "We need to get out of here right now."

"I believe that's what I was telling you."

"So, we're both right."

"Fine. I was right first, though."

"Yeah, yeah, yeah."

TWENTY-EIGHT

*J*ack didn't move fast enough for my liking. It almost felt as if we were trapped in solidifying amber. The dumbfounded expression on his face as the first zombie spilled through the alley opening was straight out of a bad SyFy movie.

"Move." I shoved him hard to push him away to the sidewalk across the way.

"Charlie!" He grabbed my wrist before I could move too far and dragged me with him. "What are you doing?"

That was a good question. "We can't move that way." I gestured vaguely toward the opposite side of the street. "That leads to Madame Brenna's voodoo store. That's where they're coming from."

He worked his jaw. Finally, he asked the obvious question. "How do you know that?"

I pointed toward the nearest zombie. He had a symbol on his wrist — either drawn or tattooed — and I recognized it from a book. The thing is, I saw it flash in my head moments before the zombie reached from the alley. The image was clear ... and I'd seen it multiple times since arriving, including on a certain coin. "That's Papa Legba's symbol," I explained. "But it's not a complete design. I think that's because she doesn't want him to see what she's doing."

Jack was flabbergasted. "I don't understand."

"It's been her the entire time." I pushed him again. "We have to move."

"Oh, we're moving." He made sure he had a firm hold on my wrist and tugged me after him. "We're also talking. Tell me what you're trying to say."

I felt lost as I increased my pace. "Do you really think this is the time?"

"I really think that ... whoa!" Jack changed course fast. The second we hit the side street the lights went out. Before that happened, though, I caught a glimpse of more reanimated bodies moving in our direction. There was a second group and it was closing in.

"What do we do?" I asked, my heart rate picking up a notch.

"We keep moving." Jack was firm as he dragged me away from the zombies. "Can you run?"

I nodded. "Where to?"

"Away from here."

"She won't stop sending them after us," I argued. "If we keep heading toward Bourbon Street we'll put other people in danger."

"But ... ." Jack sputtered as his eyes went wide. "What do you suggest we do?"

"We can't lead them out in the open." That was true for a variety of reasons. "If zombies spill over onto Bourbon Street, what do you think is going to happen?"

"Panic," he answered without hesitation. "People are going to panic and things will be worse."

"Exactly."

"But you'll be safe. I can lock you in your room and then figure this out."

"You can't do this without me." I was resigned to that fact. "We've got to find Madame Brenna and take her down."

"And how do you plan to do that?"

"I have no idea at this point. We have to keep the zombies away from the tourist areas. I don't know if they're trained to attack anyone but us, but we can't take that risk. There are children over there.

There are elderly people. Even if the zombies don't attack there will be casualties. You know that."

"What I know is that you're suddenly talking weird." He gripped my hand tighter. "What is going on?"

I opened my mouth to answer, the truth on the tip of my tongue and ready to spill forth. That's when another party joined the fray.

"He asked you a question, Charlie." Madame Brenna's voice was cold as she emerged from the shadows to our left. I heard the zombies shuffling behind her. They were close, and probably all she needed when it came down to it. She obviously wanted to participate in this particular takedown. "Don't you want to tell him what's going on here?"

I narrowed my eyes and frowned. "What do you hope to accomplish by this? I mean ... what's your endgame?"

"What makes you think I want the game to end?"

She sounded annoyed. "I've been waiting for this moment for a long time. I'm not going to let you steal it from me ... no matter how powerful you are."

I could feel Jack's gaze slide to me, but I didn't risk turning from Madame Brenna. I could almost hear the gears in his mind working.

"Powerful," he muttered.

Madame Brenna let loose a deranged laugh. "He doesn't know, does he? He has no idea what you are."

"I don't even know what I am," I reminded her. "How can he know?"

"Charlie?" Jack's voice rasped. "What is she talking about?"

"I'll explain later," I said quietly.

"She'll explain later," Madame Brenna mimicked. "Oh, that is priceless. She'll explain later why you're being chased by zombies. She'll explain later why she's been lying to you."

I hated that word. *Lying.* But it fit. I had been lying to him. I had been keeping the biggest part of myself hidden. That would all change now. I had no choice. Magic would be necessary to get us out of this.

Jack would see.

He would know.

The carefully constructed house of cards I'd built in my mind would tumble. There was no longer any way around that.

I drew a deep breath and risked a glance at Jack. He was watching me with unreadable eyes. I could feel the sense of betrayal emanating off him and it was strong enough to crush my spirit.

"It's not like that, Jack," I said hurriedly. "I didn't lie to lie. I was afraid."

"Afraid of what?"

"Yes, Charlie," Madame Brenna mocked. "What were you afraid of? Poor Jack, here, is a stalwart guy. He's done nothing but stand up for you even when you were off running around with crossroads demons and secretly meeting with me."

I couldn't hide my surprise and shifted my gaze back to her. "How do you know about the crossroads demons? That happened in a dream."

"I recognized Harley. I saw in your head today at the same moment you saw into mine. I had trouble understanding what I was seeing, but Harley is impossible to forget. She's an old ... well, friend isn't the word. She's an enemy I've been hiding from. I know you've been working together."

Something clicked inside my head. "Papa Legba didn't tell me the whole truth," I muttered, shaking my head. "He said he was looking for the person behind this but couldn't see far enough. He didn't mention he'd somehow lost you."

I gnawed on my bottom lip as I worked through what I knew. "You made an agreement with Harley. You bartered your soul for something in return. I'm guessing it's the magic you wield, which isn't all that powerful."

Madame Brenna's eyes filled with fire. "It was powerful enough to raise the dead." She lifted her arms into the air, causing the zombies to groan in unison. "I did that! Me!" She thumped her chest for emphasis. "I'm more powerful than you can imagine."

I flicked my eyes back to the zombies. They were in a holding pattern, waiting for orders. The symbols on their wrists were clearly visible under the nearby streetlight, and I took a moment to really understand what I was seeing.

"That's Papa Legba's symbol," I said finally. "You modified it with two missing bars. That's to insulate yourself. You've made him blind to you so he won't come calling on your deal."

She snickered, a brow arching in amusement. "You're smarter than you look."

"I don't understand," Jack interjected. "What's going on between the two of you? Why are you attacking Charlie?" The question was directed at Madame Brenna, but his eyes briefly locked with mine.

"Charlie has something I need," she replied. "I wasn't born with magic, but I was meant to have it. Born magic is so much greater than taken magic. You have no idea. Charlie was born with magic. She's the single most powerful being I've come across. I need that magic and she won't give it to me. I tried to take it this afternoon, but she fought me off. I won't give her a second chance to do that."

The explanation clearly wasn't enough for Jack. "Charlie?"

I felt sorry for him. This wasn't how I saw my secret being revealed. "I wanted to tell you." Tears pricked the back of my eyes. "For some reason, from the moment we met, I wanted to tell you what I was. But you couldn't take it. You don't believe. Even now you're trying to rationalize a way to explain all this."

"You still should've told me."

"I should have. I shouldn't have let this go on as long as it has without giving you the option to walk away."

This time I was certain I recognized the emotion flitting across his face. It was annoyance.

"How many times do I have to tell you that I'm not going to run?" he gritted out. "You're not going to scare me away. For crying out loud, suck it up and be an adult. Tell me what's going on in that head of yours and we'll work it out together. Don't hide things from me!"

He was enraged. I didn't blame him. Because I had underestimated Madame Brenna we were in a deadly situation that was going to take both our brains and my power to get us out of. It was hardly an ideal place to find ourselves as our relationship blew up.

"That's so cute," Madame Brenna sneered. "Even now he clings to you. He wants to protect you. He doesn't realize you're ten times stronger than he is. When he adjusts to that new reality, his ego won't be able to withstand it. He'll walk away."

Something about the way she said the words caused me to remember the scenes I'd seen in her head. "Is that why you left your husband and abandoned your child?"

She balked. "Who said I abandoned my child?"

"I saw it. When you were getting a look at the dream I had about Papa Legba and the conversation I shared with Harley, I saw you as a child. I saw the other kids bullying you. I saw your husband. I saw how unhappy you were as a mother. I also saw you abandon your son."

"That is not what happened," she seethed, fury lighting her features. "I didn't abandon my son. I had to leave him for a bit because his father wouldn't let me take him and I didn't have the standing to win a custody battle. I never left my son's life."

"Not even when he became a cop, right?" Jack challenged, taking a more proactive stance in the conversation.

I jerked my head in Jack's direction, confused. "What do you mean?"

"That's what Leon called to tell me. He found out Madame Brenna's real name. It was Brenda Thibodeaux."

And that's when the final pieces of the puzzle slipped into place for me. "Oh, geez." I shifted from one foot to the other, antsy. "I should've recognized him in the memory. He still looks the same in a lot of respects."

"He got more genes from me than his father," Madame Brenna agreed. "He was always a beautiful boy."

"A beautiful boy you abandoned as a child."

She narrowed her eyes. "I didn't abandon him. I couldn't raise him the way I wanted because of his father. That wasn't my fault."

"What do you know?" Jack whispered. He'd moved closer to me now. It wasn't exactly a protective stance, but he wasn't recoiling at the idea of being near me either.

"Just small things. I was in a hurry to get out of her head. She tried to trap me earlier. I should've realized then that she was behind this. I thought she could help. She knew Myron, after all. I figured that was an indication that she was on our side."

"You were shaken up when I first saw you," he mused. "I thought it was because you were afraid Laura was going to convince me to break up with you. I'm guessing I was wrong on that."

"I was shaken," I agreed. "But I didn't think Laura would force you to break up with me. I was afraid you would be angry about the lying."

He practically exploded. "I am angry about the lying!"

"And you have a right to your anger." I meant it. "I didn't mean to fall for you. I just wanted to learn some information from the group when I signed up, maybe dig and find a way to track down my parents. I thought hiding in plain sight was smart. I don't want to end up on a gurney being dissected because people are curious. You don't even believe in supernatural beings. I didn't know how to tell you."

The look on his face was pained. "I want to shake you."

"That'll have to wait. We need to deal with this first."

He straightened his shoulders. "Fine. We have a lot to talk about."

"Yeah." Sadness threatened to overwhelm me before I snapped back to reality. If he was going to leave there was nothing I could do to stop him. I was better off knowing now than when I'd completely given my heart to him. I might not recover from that blow.

"You're going to deal with me?" Madame Brenna laughed. "Do you think I'm going to allow that to happen?"

"I don't see where you have a choice," I replied, calm despite the overwhelming emotions battering my heart. "I can't let them continue wandering around. You're controlling them, so ... I've got to shut you down."

"And you think I'll just let that happen?"

"I think it's already over and you simply don't see it." I took advantage of the fact that she tilted her head back and laughed like a cartoon villain — I was expecting it, after all — and shoved Jack as hard as I could toward the alley across from where we stood.

Momentary confusion split his face, But he let me lead.

We raced into the alley. I knew it wouldn't be long before Madame Brenna gave chase. I picked the alley for a reason. It was narrow and surrounded by businesses. Two of the buildings were undergoing construction, which meant they were empty. Nobody lived in the edifices as far as I could tell, and that was important for what I had to do.

"There." I pointed toward a dumpster behind a small Creole restaurant.

Jack made a face. "You want me to hide in the dumpster? No way."

"I want you to get behind the dumpster," I corrected, refusing to back down. "You don't have a choice. Things are about to get hot."

"How so?"

I almost felt sorry for him. "They just are. Move over there. Please. I want you to be safe. That's the only thing I care about right now."

"I want you safe, too. I'm not leaving you."

I heaved out a sigh. "Fine. I ... ." I trailed off when I saw a hint of movement at the far end of the alley. I heard Madame Brenna and her zombies closing behind us. The face at the other side of the alley should've been surprising, but it oddly made sense.

"Detective Thibodeaux," I forced out, shaking my head. "I guess it was too much to hope you weren't involved."

He didn't look upset about being called out. "I told you to stay away from this."

"I guess now we know why you were so hell-bent on framing Charlie for the zombies," Jack groused. "You knew your mother was behind it."

"You should've just stayed out of it," Thibodeaux snapped. "Why couldn't you mind your own business?"

I pressed my hand to Jack's chest, resting my fingers above his heart. The steady beat calmed me as I readied myself. "You should leave now, detective. You should run."

"I'm not going to run." He was incredulous. "My mother is going to help me get everything I ever wanted, including my father's spot as chief of police."

"That's what you want? You need to surpass your father because she's convinced you that it's necessary."

"My father was a terrible man who kept me from my mother because he had power and enjoyed wielding it over her."

"I saw what happened," I countered. "Your mother was bristling under the expectations of your father. She didn't have to stay. She could've left and fought for you. She willingly walked away from both of you. She could've stayed in your life, but she chose not to."

"That's not true!" Thibodeaux's face reddened with rage. "You weren't there. You don't know."

He was too far gone to help. The sound of Madame Brenna's breathing told me I was almost out of time. If I expected to help myself – and Jack – I couldn't be distracted.

"You killed your ex-husband, didn't you?" I pinned her with an expectant look. "I know how this works. You earned power from the murder and passed it on to your son. That's how he saved those kids and became famous."

Madame Brenna smirked. "You really are smarter than you look. You're right. I needed to bolster my power. The jolt Harley gave me wasn't even close to what I expected. I was supposed to be something extraordinary. Harley screwed me, yet she still searches for my soul as payment for an unfulfilled deal."

"You're wrong about that," a voice called from a nearby rooftop. I'd sensed her a split-second before I heard her, so I wasn't all that surprised to find out we weren't alone. It was Harley. I could barely see her because of the darkness, but I recognized her. "I don't need to search for you. I realized right away that Charlie had been in contact with you. I just had to wait for the right moment to make my move."

The fear that worked across Madame Brenna's face was legitimate and profound. "What do you intend to do?" Her voice turned squeaky. "You can't take me. You missed your deadline."

"I can take you whenever I want." Harley looked smug. "If I take you now, though, Charlie will still have to take out the zombies and your son. It's probably best we do it together at the same time."

I realized what she was suggesting. "How?"

"You know how." Harley snapped her fingers and conjured an odd lantern out of thin air. It was octagonal and didn't look as if there was any way for it to sit flat on a table. "The world will end in fire."

I recognized the words and frowned. "The barker."

Her smile was kind. "Papa Legba likes playing dress-up."

I swallowed hard as a multitude of images collided in my mind. He always knew exactly how this would end. He didn't want my soul, but what was to come would leave a mark on it.

"Is there no other way?" I asked finally.

"I'm sorry." Harley appeared sincere. "I'm not even supposed to get this involved, but I want to help you. This is a problem partially of our making. We can finish it together. Right now."

I heaved out a sigh, uncertain. Then I felt warmth rush over the fingers resting against Jack's chest. He placed his hand over mine and caught my gaze.

"I don't know what you're going to do but I have faith in you," he said quietly. "Do what you have to do. We'll get through it."

He sounded so certain. "I ... ."

"It's okay." He tightened his grip on my fingers. "Look at me. Keep your eyes on me. I'll tell you to do it when it's time ... even though I have no idea what you're going to do."

"How can you tell me if you don't know?"

"I have faith."

A lone tear slid down my cheek as I gulped.

"It's time," Harley announced.

I wasn't watching, but I knew the moment she released the strange lantern. Jack moved closer and rested his forehead against mine. "Now," he said on a sigh as I let loose my magic.

It rushed out of me, causing me to press my body against his. Automatically, he wrapped his arms around me as the lantern exploded and the flame ignited.

We were safe in our small alcove, the dumpster serving as a barrier of sorts, but the wall of flames spread along the alleyway faster than I could've imagined. The zombies didn't scream. They didn't run or flee in panic. They just stood there as the flames absorbed them ... and then they were gone. Madame Brenna and Thibodeaux were different stories.

I was certain I would have nightmares about their screams for weeks to come.

Jack kept his arms around me, his forehead against mine, and neither of us watched the mayhem. It was time to look forward.

We still had a mountain to climb, and I wasn't ready to stop until I reached the peak.

TWENTY-NINE

*J*ack and I were filthy messes when we got back to the
hotel. The aftermath of the fireball that swept through
the alley drew emergency personnel in the form of paramedics, firefighters and numerous police officers. That was on top of
the looky-loos who gathered to watch from a distance.

We lied. We said we'd been walking down the street and had no
idea what occurred. We said we'd heard voices, a man and a woman –
which would explain Madame Brenna's body found twenty feet from
that of her son. We didn't mention recognizing Thibodeaux. We
played dumb. Jack said that was the smartest move and I was too tired
to argue.

I heard the emergency responders talking. They marveled at the
number of bodies found, assuming the loss of life was profound. We
knew better. Only two lives were lost – evil lives at that – but we
couldn't share information.

The coroner's office would be busy the next few days. When it
came time to identify the bodies, they would find that the deceased
had been gone for days … weeks … and months. Heck, given how
some of the bodies looked in the glimpse I got before bringing down

the fire, there was every possibility some of them had been gone for years.

"They'll assume it was some sort of hoax," Jack explained on the elevator. We hadn't spoken since leaving the scene. It took twice as long to trudge to the hotel as it would've under normal circumstances. Our bodies simply wouldn't let us move faster. "They won't accept the possibility that it really was zombies."

"They don't want to believe, so they won't believe," I said dully. "I get it."

"Charlie ... ." He said my name with a mixture of frustration and exhaustion.

"I'm sorry." I held up my hands, frowning at the grime I found there. "I'm so sorry." I broke on the second apology and started crying. Emotion simply overwhelmed me. I'd never put my magic on display like I had this evening, never expended that much power. The fact that I took two human beings out in the process made things worse.

"Oh, Charlie." He pulled me to him, allowing me to bury my face in his neck as he led me off the elevator. He pulled up short, causing me to prepare myself for another fight. Instead of an enemy, I found Leon and Laura standing outside her door. She was in a T-shirt and nothing else, her bottom barely covered. His hair was a mess and he had a goofy smile on his face. It was obvious what they'd been up to.

"Let me handle this," Jack whispered into my ear as he gripped me tighter.

I was only too happy to comply. I couldn't find words anyway.

"What happened?" Leon asked, his smile slipping as he took a step in our direction. "What's wrong?"

"There was a fire," Jack replied. "It was a few blocks over. I'm not sure what happened. We were close."

"Are you okay?"

"We're dirty but fine. We're heading to bed."

"But ... ." Leon was obviously perplexed. "Do you want me to head out to see if I can get some information?"

"That would be great." Jack stroked his hand over the back of my head. "They're not saying anything yet. There were a lot of ... bodies ... in the alley. I'm not sure how many people died."

"Do you think it has something to do with what we're working on?"

"I don't know." Jack sounded strong even though I knew he felt anything but. His weariness tangled with mine. "I don't know what to think. I only know the paramedics said there were a lot of bodies in the alley."

"How did the fire start?"

"I don't know that either. Someone mentioned a possible gas leak, but none of the buildings went up. I just ... don't know."

"Well ... you guys should get cleaned up." Leon was decisive. "Sleep. I'll head over there and see what I can sniff out."

"That would be great." Jack steered me toward my room, making sure to keep his arm around me as he sheltered my face. "We're going to put up the 'Do not disturb' sign. Charlie needs sleep."

"I don't think she's the only one."

"No."

Laura, who had been silent until now, tilted her head to the side. "Do you want me to wake Chris?"

"Why?" Jack challenged. "We don't know anything yet. Leon will be better at getting information than Chris. There's nothing to do tonight."

"I could ... help you," she offered after a beat. "You can drop Charlie off and I'll help with whatever you need."

It was a ballsy move given how she was dressed. Despite the worry plaguing me over the imminent discussion Jack and I had in front of us, I knew he wouldn't take her up on the offer.

"Charlie and I are going to take care of each other." Jack waved the extra keycard in front of the reader on my door and used his foot to open it. "We'll come down in the morning when we're up. Don't bother us."

Laura narrowed her eyes. "Whatever. I was just trying to help."

"I know what you were trying to do. Just ... knock it off." Jack was gentle as he prodded me into the room and allowed the door to swing shut.

Silence greeted us. Part of me wondered if Harley would make another appearance, but the room felt empty.

"I need a shower," I murmured.

"We both do." Jack pointed me toward the bathroom. "Strip out of your clothes. We should probably just dump them. They'll never be the same again."

"Okay." I followed his instructions. At a different time I probably would've been embarrassed to be naked in front of him like this. Sure, we'd seen each other several times at this point, but this somehow made me feel more vulnerable. I didn't even bat an eyelash, though.

Jack gathered our clothes, dropped them in a garbage can and slipped it outside the room. He pulled the safety bar into place and double-checked the locks and then strode into the bathroom to start the shower.

We cleaned up together. There was nothing romantic about it, not as much as a flirty glance. We soaped ourselves, washed our hair and then exited the bathroom bundled in robes.

"It's going to be okay, Charlie," he said as he lifted the covers. "You need some sleep. We'll talk about everything in the morning."

He sounded remote, something that pierced my heart. "I would rather talk about it now."

"Really?" He seemed surprised. "Don't you want to sleep?"

"I won't sleep until I know … ." I left the statement hanging.

"Until you know what?"

"What you're going to do?"

His hair was damp. The room was almost completely dark, but his eyes flashed with surprise. "What are you asking?"

"Are you done here?"

He let loose a low groan, frustration taking over. Oddly enough, it made me feel better. He wasn't so defeated that he was done fighting. "Done with you?"

"I guess that's what I'm asking."

He rubbed his hand over his chin. He hadn't shaved in the shower, so he had a bit of stubble going. It only made him more attractive. "I'm not done, Charlie. I told you that as it was going down, but I understand why you're worried. For the record, you can't chase me away that easily. We're just getting started."

My heart soared ... and then settled. "Aren't you angry?"

"Angry? Not really. I'm sad. I'm sad that you didn't trust me enough to tell me the truth from the start."

I opened my mouth to argue, but he silenced me with a raised hand.

"No, baby." He shook his head, firm. "I have a right to my feelings."

Because that was true, I waited for him to continue. "I know why you didn't tell me. I get it. I also get what you were trying to do here. Hiding in plain sight makes a lot of sense. Why would Chris ever look at you when you're supposed to be hunting with him?"

"I don't like the term 'hunting,'" I argued. "If you think I'm pretending to be curious about paranormal beings, that's not true. I want to know."

"Because you don't know about yourself," he surmised. "I can't imagine how horrible this has been for you. I want to know all of it. I want to know how young you were when you figured it out. I want to hear your feelings. I want to know what you can do.

"I'm not leaving you over this, Charlie, because I get it," he continued. "I saw the terror on your face when things started tumbling out. Not all of that was about the zombies. And, yes, I recognize what they really were. You've changed my entire outlook in the course of one night."

"Is that a good or bad thing?"

"You're the best thing in my life right now." He was earnest as he held my gaze. "That hasn't changed. I understand that there's a learning curve ahead of me. We don't have to do it all tonight.

"You're magical." He said the words with a hint of humor. "You're special. I knew that from the moment we met. I sensed something about you. I have a lot of questions. I suspect you don't have all the answers. That's okay. We'll figure it out together."

I wanted to cry again, this time for an entirely different reason. "Okay. I just … there's something I need to say to you."

"All right."

"I wanted to tell you," I started, my voice cracking. "I've wanted to tell you since … well, since we started getting closer. I was so afraid. Part of me thought that you would leave me because of it. You're not a believer."

"I am now."

"Yeah, but … I thought you would think I was a freak."

"No. I can't think that about you."

"I thought you would be disgusted enough to walk away. Even as I was thinking that, I knew you wouldn't. Millie kept telling me you wouldn't. I was still afraid because … you're the one thing in my life I don't want to lose.

"You make a lot of noise about me not having anything because I don't have a lot of money," I continued. "As far as I'm concerned, I have everything because I have you. I didn't mean to hurt you. I didn't mean to lie. I try really hard not to lie. I was just … terrified."

"I know." He moved around the end of the bed and pulled me into his arms, his lips automatically going to my forehead. "You don't have to be afraid. I don't ever want you to be afraid. I also don't want you lying to me."

"I won't."

"Okay." He tipped up my chin and brushed his lips against mine before sighing. He looked lighter. I felt lighter, so we made a pair. "We need sleep. Tomorrow will bring a whole new set of problems. But we'll be working together to keep your secret. It's going to be okay."

"I hope so."

He was gentle as he helped me out of the robe, discarding his own before joining me under the covers. He slipped his arm around my waist and pulled to him, my head resting on his shoulder.

"It's going to be okay," he whispered, his lips against my ear. "I won't let anyone hurt you, Charlie. We're a team … and that's not going to change. Get some rest."

Even though it had been a horrible night, even though there had been a moment I thought I would lose everything, including my soul, I felt surprisingly happy. Jack knew. Things weren't perfect, but he wanted to move forward together. I had another ally in this world.

For tonight, that was more than enough. The rest could wait until after sleep. We would come up with a new plan and go from there.

A new adventure was on the horizon, and I couldn't wait to see where it would lead.

Made in United States
Cleveland, OH
20 March 2025

15335102R00163